The Mean Streets of Chicago

Trevor Hughes

What they said about *The Mean Streets of Chicago*

'*The prose really crackles.*' David Shelley, Little Brown

'*In parts it reads like a Raymond Chandler novel,*' Wayne Brookes, Harper Collins

'*One of the most entertaining novels I have read this year,*' Jon Wood: Orion Publishing Group

Trevor Hughes was born in Wigan, now part of Greater Manchester, but has spent most of his adult life overseas in Bangladesh, India, Thailand, Singapore and Hong Kong where he now lives and works.

He has won various short prizes for short fiction and is currently working on a non-fiction book: *The Poppy and the Pen*, an examination of the effects of opium on the works of the Romantic authors, poets and artists.

The Mean Streets of Chicago is the first in a series of novels featuring Manchester private eye, Tom Collins.

See: trevor hughes-writer.com

For Karl

One of the good guys.

Chapter One

Chicago, July 1957

*J*ake Fist stood in the darkness of the alleyway. He'd been careless. *Careless and stupid. And in his business careless and stupid was generally followed by dead.*

It was the kind of night when the stars lose interest in trying to pierce the layer of smog lying like a blanket on the thick, still air. The cheap crooks and hoods and the husbands cheating their wives sweltered and sweated in the alleys and the backstreets and the low-down dives; the women lying in dingy motel rooms next to guys they weren't supposed to be with told their guilty consciences that a girl has to look somewhere for a little affection; the drunks told themselves it was one last drink, the junkies swore it was one last fix, the working girls promised themselves it was one final trick, and over it all not a breath of wind blew through the mean streets of the Windy City.

It had been just a couple of hours ago that he'd pulled his Chevy over to the sidewalk, flicked away his cigarette butt and leaned on the doorbell of his great-aunt Pauline.

"This is Suzie," he said, "and I need you to look after her for a few days. And no-one, repeat no-one knows she's here."

"Yes, Jake, of course," she replied. "She's a lot prettier than the

1

last one, Jake, dear," and Suzie had given him that woman's look: the one you get when they think you've been foolin' with one of their girlfriends. It was then Jake had looked at Suzie, and he'd felt something he thought had gone away a long time ago. Which was maybe why he'd decided to drop into Joe's.

Now he was stuck in a stinking back alley with Bruno Scarletti standing in front of him.

"How many times we gotta tell you, Fist? How many times before you start to listen?"

Jake shrugged his shoulders. "Maybe I don't hear too good these days."

"Always the same, always the wise guy. Jake, Jake, how many wisecracks you gonna make when you're dead? You think dyin's gonna make you into a comedian?"

Scarletti shook his head sadly. "You could have been a good boy, Jake. What made you think you could go up against me? I'm sorry about Tanya, but that's the way it goes. And ever since then you been livin' in a bottle."

The feeble street lamp at the end of the alley was throwing just enough light so that Jake could make out the kicked-over trash-cans and the broken bottles and the rats and the guns in the hands of Scarletti's hoods

"You shouldn't have killed Willie, Jake."

"The Weasel? Yeah, I'm sorry about that. Sorry I wasted three slugs on him. I should've put my foot on him and stomped him out."

"There you go again, Jake, bein' the wise guy. I'm sorry, I can't help you this time."

Scarletti's eyes showed no trace of emotion in the darkness.

"OK, boys," he said. "Let's get it done."

*

Manchester, September 2005

That's the thing about clichés. They're called clichés because everyone uses them all the time, and everyone uses them all the time because they're mostly true. Like: it always rains in Manchester.

The rain was falling in opaque sheets as I parked the car in the open-air car-park and walked, cold wet and miserable to my office through the sodden streets. I waved to the four naked models in the window, unlocked the door and walked up the stairs. I unlocked the office door, hung up my raincoat and wondered how the hell I was supposed to get through the day.

I filled the electric kettle, switched it on and went back down the stairs to check my mailbox: nothing. Then I hit the button on the answering machine and listened hopefully for phone messages: none. Finally I booted up the computer and checked for e-mails. There weren't any.

I put coffee and powdered milk into a mug, sat at my desk and stared gloomily at the faded gold lettering on the rain-streaked window of my office. I had bought the stick-on letters myself, and spent half a day applying them carefully to the glass in a half-crescent exactly like those on Sam Spade's office window in *The Maltese Falcon*.

The letters spelt:

TOM COLLINS

PRIVATE DETECTIVE

I don't think my parents realized they'd named me after a cocktail. Maybe that's why I'm probably the only private eye in the history of the world who doesn't really drink.

And as for being a private detective, well I wondered if they could prosecute me under the Trades Descriptions Act.

I picked up the file on my desk and read through the case notes.

Name: Arthur Golightly.
Age: 41.
Address: 17 Brickford Terrace, Worsley.
Problem: Wife keeps winning at bingo.

I don't have much in the way of office furniture. Frankly I don't have much in the way of an office, but I do have a small round table where I can sit and talk to my clients. Not that I have many of them, either. That's where, on the previous Friday I had interviewed Arthur Golightly.

"It's not right, you see," he said. "Well, it stands to reason, doesn't it? I mean, once in a while, you'd expect that, me being a fair-minded sort of bloke and all - but every time? It just doesn't make sense."

It appeared that every Monday and Thursday Arthur's wife, Agnes went off to bingo with her mother. And won.

4

Every single time. Sometimes just twenty or thirty quid, others fifty or sixty and on one special occasion, a hundred and twenty pounds. "She must have hit the jackpot," said Arthur, gloomily. "Not that she's mean or anything; she always slips me a fiver. But every single bleedin' time? It's not normal, is it?"

Now I don't play bingo but I had to agree it did sound unusual. It also seemed unusual that she'd a) tell him about it, and b) shell out part of the proceeds, but we detectives are a tactful lot so I kept that to myself.

Arthur had given me a photograph of Agnes. Blood-red lipstick. Bottle blonde. Not bad-looking if you liked them as tough as a dinosaur steak. Or did I detect a sense of humour hidden somewhere behind those dark-mascaraed eyes?

I looked at my watch. Two hours before I could even go for lunch. I picked up the cold, unappealing remains of my coffee and wondered again how on earth I had ever allowed myself to be talked into becoming a detective

In Chicago, private eyes are called in by the cops in the morning and asked to help solve six baffling murders. They then have four Martinis for lunch before being dragged off to bed by a Dangerous Dame and probably her sister as well. They roar around the mean streets in a cherry-red Chevy convertible with a gun in one hand and a bottle of bourbon in the other; shoot a couple of bad guys; discover it's the Dangerous Dame and her sister committing all the murders then wander down to Joe's for half a dozen nightcaps.

Unfortunately that's not how it works in Manchester. My professional life generally involves taking surreptitious snaps of half-dressed women in the back seats of large cars their owners can't afford or wandering the mean streets in search of a missing poodle attempting to discover whether in Cheetham Hill they've stolen it, or in Chinatown they've eaten it.

I gazed through the window at the dark, heavy storm-clouds. Why, I pondered gloomily, couldn't it happen for real just once in the miserable existence of a Manchester private eye?

The minute she walked in he knew it was trouble. Trouble from the top of her pretty little hat to the painted tips of her dainty toenails.

"You always greet your guests that way?" she asked, her scarlet lips drawing in smoke through her cigarette holder. Reluctantly Jake Fist put down his gun.

"It's my doctor," he said. "Said I should take better care of myself."

She looked around the office: the peeling wallpaper, the old threadbare carpet; the Chicago Gazette *lying on the desk; the half-empty glass of whisky.*

"You busy?" she asked.

Jake took his feet off the desk, stubbed his Lucky Strike into the ashtray.

"Not so you'd notice," he drawled like he didn't know exactly who she was, this babe posing in front of him like something out of a Hollywood movie.

"Take a seat," he said.

It was hot and airless in the room, the traffic noises sounding faintly from four floors below, the air conditioning wheezing and groaning like a terminal asthmatic. There were two beat-up old chairs facing Jake. She pulled out one of them, perched on it, blowing smoke, pretending she was tough and unconcerned, like she was the one in control.

Those eyes stared at him. Eyes as hard as diamonds, tough as tensioned steel. Eyes that could kill you at ten paces he thought, or soften and melt you till you were pliable as a pussycat, make you drool like a fool. But there was something else in those eyes. It wasn't like he hadn't seen it before. This lady was scared: scared as hell.

He took out a new cigarette, tapped it on the box. "Something I can help you with, Mrs Scarletti?" he said.

She dropped her ash lazily onto his desk. "It's my husband. I think he's trying to kill me."

Just once: was it too much to ask?

So tonight, on this dismal wet Monday instead of beating up bad guys, solving impossible crimes and fighting off hordes of Dangerous Dames, what I had to look forward to was using all my sharply honed detective skills to follow Agnes Golightly and her old mum through the back streets of Worsley in the pouring rain.

I looked again through the window. There didn't seem any hope of golf in this weather. Not that I have the faintest interest in golf but I had sent my sometime associate Wally Holden to check out a keen golfer called Mrs Masterson whose ever-loving husband suspected she was loving someone else as well as him. I just hoped Wally would keep his head down. I didn't want him beaten to death with a seven iron

I put my feet up on the desk and waited hopefully for a mysterious message on the computer, a husky female voice on the phone or some beautiful distressed woman to walk through my door.

It was a long wait.

Chapter Two

*I*t was nights like this you could take a knife to it, thought Jake. Take big slices out of the Chicago night and eat it like a slab of cheesecake. He grinned at Scarletti.

"I kinda thought the usual courtesies ran to the dyin' man getting one last request."

Scarletti shrugged. "Sure. Go ahead. Make it," he said.

"Could you ask Suzie to put flowers on my grave?"

Scarletti's eyes narrowed. He held up a hand adorned with a diamond ring the size of a Brazil nut and grabbed Jake by the front of his coat.

"What the hell are you talking about?" he snarled.

"Did you check the bedroom and the kitchen before you came out tonight, Scarletti? Make sure your pretty little lady wife was there?"

Scarletti stepped back, his face dark with anger. "What d'ya mean Fist?"

Jake straightened his coat. "Bet you don't know where she is now, Bruno. Bet you I do. When I see her I'll tell her you sent your best."

He pulled out a pack of Luckies and struck a match. "Now if you don't mind there's an old friend I gotta see. Name of Jack Daniels."

Scarletti glared at him. "I was making it easy for you, Fist. It won't be so easy next time."

8

"Dyin's never easy, Scarletti," said Jake.

He walked down the alley towards the street. The eyes of Scarletti's hoods stared at him in the darkness, mean and malevolent, like rats.

"See y'around, boys," Jake said.

Then he walked away in the darkness.

*

The rain had stopped so I decided to treat myself to a gourmet lunch. I locked the office door, negotiated the narrow staircase and walked through the back streets, past the Oxfam shop, the Ukrainian supermarket, the bookies, the grilled and boarded off-licence, to where my car glistened wet in the tiny open-air car park. It's a super-charged cherry red '75 Chevy convertible with whitewall tyres on wire wheels. Well actually, it isn't. That's what I wish it was. In fact it's a ten-year-old Ford Escort with the aerial long ripped out and more scratches than a male stripper at a hen night. I drove the mile or so to the nearest Marks and Sparks where I purchased a tuna fish sandwich, a pork pie and a can of ginger beer. These I consumed sitting on a bench by the road-side. There are days when I do get concerned about my decadent life-style.

I spent as long as I could chewing the sandwich and sipping the ginger beer but eventually there was nothing left on which to waste my time so I drove reluctantly back to the office. I still had four hours to kill before I was due to embark on the inestimable pleasure of trailing Agnes Golightly through the mean streets of Manchester.

At three o'clock the phone rang.

"Well Mr Collins, they played three holes then the rain

started again."

"And?"

"Well they sat around the golf club having a bit of lunch."

"Get on with it, Wally."

"And then they all went back to her place."

"Any problems getting in?"

"None at all Mr Collins. Piece of cake."

"Pictures?"

"Lots of 'em. Very interesting game it is this golf, Mr Collins. I'm thinking of taking it up meself."

I grinned. "Bring them in tomorrow, Wally."

I put the phone down, musing over just how safe it was to keep using Wally Holden. Wally was forty-something years old and had moved to Manchester when he got too well known in his native London. He still had a broad Cockney accent, though when it suited him he could speak in authentic, impenetrable Mancunian. Wally was a thief. He could open any lock ever invented, climb drainpipes and balconies like a chimpanzee and get through window spaces that thirteen-year-old Russian Olympic gymnasts would have sworn were impassable. His trademark was to steal anything small, portable and valuable and, if there was a lady in the house, to help himself to a pair of her knickers as he left. It was the only love life he had.

However Wally's greatest skill was that he was invisible. He would case his prospects in broad daylight using a delivery van or a street-sweeper's brush, or simply pinch a few traffic cones and sit there on the pavement poking around with a pick-axe and a shovel and no one noticed him. He had got away with it several times after being picked up because in the line-up they simply didn't recognize the thin-faced, apologetic little man with the flat cap and the sad, droopy smile.

I'd picked him up once when I was a copper and after he'd completed his stretch inside he'd come to see me. Now there aren't a great number of career opportunities for a habitual ex-con with a knicker fetish but he'd sworn to me that he was going straight: that his thieving days were over. Still every time I gave him a job another old cliché went through my head. Something about leopards changing their spots.

The last case in which I'd used Wally I'd been hired to track down a dachshund called Frank (short for Frankfurter). His owner, a little girl of about eight who'd weighed about the same as me, had been playing with him in the park when some kid had walked over and dragged him off by the lead.

A few days later the family had received a ransom demand asking for fifty quid and stating that if they went to the police then the sausage dog would be turned into real sausages. In any case, the police are rather more preoccupied with people getting mugged and burgled and stabbed and shot than people running off with dogs, especially dogs named after sausages, so the little girl's mum had come to me. She'd been approximately the size of a barrage balloon, and any dognapper in his right mind would have been a damn sight more terrified of her than of me, but with my usual tact I didn't mention this and took the case.

Wally Holden showed up in the park with the ransom money and when the kid appeared with the dachshund on a lead we collared him. We dragged him, yelling and screaming round to his council house where we discovered thirteen assorted dogs ranging from six inches high to the size of a small horse, and a regular little racket being run by a twelve-year-old.

I asked his mother whether she'd been curious about where her little treasure (also called Frank) had got all the dogs from. She lit up another cigarette, poured herself a large neat gin and told us in pure unadulterated authentic Mancunian that for some strange reason she'd taken an instant dislike to us and that it would be a really terrific idea if we went away, quite quickly.

I told little Frank that next time he tried to pull this stunt I'd get him taken away and put in a home, which come to think of it would probably have done him a lot of good. Then I took away the dogs and had a highly successful couple of days returning them to their rightful owners and collecting the reward money, such as it was. I also got bitten by two of the dogs.

And that, you see, is the fascinating, cutting-edge perilous life of a Manchester private eye.

I sat at my desk reading about Jake Fist and Bruno Scarletti and Suzie, Bruno's stunning wife who was holed up with Jake's great-aunt Pauline. Meantime I watched the office door waiting for a breathless blonde ready to offer me her gorgeous body in return for murdering her gangster boyfriend.

She didn't show up.

Chapter Three

Jake parked his Chevy, took out his gun and looked carefully around the car park. He saw nothing hiding in the shadows. He lit up a cigarette, walked carefully into the street and spent a few minutes watching the door of his apartment block.

He figured he should be safe for a couple of days. Until Scarletti knew where Suzie was hiding he couldn't order Jake a terminal car accident or a midnight swim in a concrete suit.

Jake opened up the main door and climbed the stairs. He checked the hair he'd stuck over the frame of his apartment door; checked the lock for scratch marks; checked the kitchen and the hall closet and the bathroom, all the time cursing himself that he hadn't taught the routine to Tanya. Locking the stable door, he called it. After the horse has been shot.

When he was satisfied he poured himself a nightcap and sat staring out over the Chicago skyline. It was quiet now, just the odd few late-night sounds: a car door slamming; some dame yelling at her old man for being late and drunk; a police siren a few blocks south.

Jake picked up the bottle. There was a half-inch still left in it. What the hell, *he thought.* There was no one to see, nowhere to go, no one waiting for him. After a while he climbed into bed and settled down to sleep, his hand holding tightly on to Betsy.

Betsy was his gun.

*

At six-thirty I left the office and walked back to my car. I climbed in and drove through the rain to Brickford Terrace. It was a dark, dismal row of dilapidated red-brick houses, the kind of place where the rats stay home at nights with the doors locked. I switched off the engine and lights and sat staring at the doorway of Number 17. The rainwater ran down the gutters, carrying old newspapers and Coke cans and cigarette ends. The terraced houses looked as if they had huddled together for protection against some malevolent external force. Like the Manchester weather.

Eventually the door opened and Agnes Golightly appeared under an umbrella, accompanied by a nondescript woman in her fifties dressed in a long coat and sensible shoes. I waited until they were barely distinguishable in the rain. Then I picked up my umbrella and followed.

Along the dark streets they walked, past grimy, neglected houses with windows boarded up or covered with wire mesh and walls splashed with graffiti. I hoped the neighbourhood hard-cases were staying at home until the rain stopped. It would be just my luck to get mugged by a couple of fourteen-year-olds.

After a while we came to a dark, dismal old pub. According to the peeling sign creaking in the wind the pub was called The Kings Ar s. I watched the ladies enter and waited for a few minutes before I walked into the bar. The regulars all sat there nursing their pints and staring malevolently at me as if I were the Thing from the Planet

Pluton.

Years of cigarette smoke had turned the walls and the ceiling a dirty brown. Old men sat on red plastic cushions scarred with cigarette burns, the yellow stuffing poking through like pus oozing from an infected wound. In a corner four youths, all hard eyes and tattoos and body piercings, gazed stonily at me.

"Half of bitter please," I said. The bartender glared at me and slapped the glass down on the soaking cloth, spilling beer onto the bar. Jake Fist would have carefully explained to the guy the rules of polite bartending but I just said, "Thank you," picked up my glass and looked around the bar, taking care to avoid eye contact with anyone.

Agnes Golightly and her mum were in deep conversation with a man of about forty. Thin, dark, wearing a worn jacket with leather patches on the elbows, drinking a pint of Hofmeister and trying to look tough. The women were drinking Bacardi and cokes.

I stood at the bar sipping my beer. It was thin and flat and tasted of disinfectant and illicit cigarettes. No wonder the locals all looked bitter and twisted drinking this stuff. I read once about some sect in India who drink their own piss: they'd have felt right at home in The King's Ar s.

I reckoned that Agnes and her mum would either meet someone in the pub or leave with the thin man. Either way the odds were that they'd leave in a car and mine was at least ten minutes away in the rain. I decided to leave my beer (that wasn't the difficult part) and go back for the car, but the thin man was swallowing his lager and urging the women to drink up. Even as I stepped out into the rain I knew I didn't have a hope of making it back before they left.

The odds on what happened next are about the same as winning the National Lottery. As I ran into the deserted street a car came cruising down through the darkness. It was a taxi with his *For Hire* sign shining through the rain. I waved frantically and the taxi ground to a halt. "Where to, Guv'nor?" asked the driver.

I'd been in the detecting business for seven years and this was something I'd always wanted to do. A decrepit old Jaguar was nosing its way out of the pub car park. "Follow that car," I said.

"Are you windin' me up?"

"No, no, honestly," I said. "I need you to follow that car! I'm a private eye."

The cabbie looked at me wet, dishevelled, smelling slightly of beer. "Yeah right, and I'm Bing Crosby," he said. "What is this? Candid bleedin' camera?"

I watched the Jaguar's tail-lights disappearing in the distance. "You want the fare or not?" I snapped.

The cabbie shrugged. "You'd better not be taking the piss," he threatened, and screeched into a u-turn.

The King's Ar s vanished in the gloom. The streets became slightly less rubbish-strewn. Bits of brickwork peeped out from behind the graffiti; some of the windows had curtains instead of iron bars; we even passed the occasional garden that hadn't been concreted over.

Fifteen minutes later we came to a quiet leafy lane and the ancient Jaguar drew up outside a neat, single-storied detached house with a lawn and flower-beds, surrounded by a neat privet hedge. It was a comfortable affluent-looking residence, far removed from the delights of Brickford Terrace. Warm cosy lights shone from the windows. In the darkness a cat yowled and no one threw a brick at it. It was that kind of neighbourhood.

The thin man and the Golightlys walked down the driveway to the front door and rang the doorbell. A man appeared. He was dressed in a silk dressing gown, pale green with tasselled cords. He slipped an envelope to the thin man, who walked back along the driveway to his car, smoking a cigarette, shoulders hunched against the rain.

"Can you wait?" I asked the cab driver.

"Long as I'm not going to get shot," he grunted.

I sat in the back of the cab listening to the rain hammering on the roof, hoping that it might ease off a bit, but eventually I had no choice. I turned up my coat collar, stepped out of the cab, scuttled furtively around the pool of wet brightness cast by the streetlights and slipped over the hedge.

I'm not exactly totally enamoured of the detecting business, but there are a couple of things I dislike even more than the rest, one of which is prowling round in the dark hoping an aggrieved property owner won't hit me on the head. I've been arrested twice as a suspected burglar and I remember with no affection whatsoever being pulled out of a rose bush in the local park by a huge, unfriendly copper, when I'd been trying to photograph a forty-year-old schoolteacher giving extra-curricular biology lessons to his seventeen-year-old girlfriend. You should have seen the look on his face when I tried to tell him I wasn't some deviant sex maniac but actually a private eye on an important case. They let me out the following day with a warning.

I flitted across the lawn in the darkness and flattened myself against the bungalow wall. I crept around the corner and sank to my hands and knees until I was below the level of the window. Then I felt for the window-sill with my finger-tips, and slowly and carefully pulled myself upwards until I could see into the room.

The man who had opened the door was no longer wearing his dressing gown. He was kneeling on the carpet wearing long black stockings and a dog collar on a chain around his neck. Behind him, facing me and holding the other end of the chain, was a dowdy thirty-something woman, presumably his wife. She was wearing nothing at all.

Mrs Golightly had her back to the window and I had to admit that she had a very decent body. Especially when it was squeezed into a rubber corset which would have been tight on a Barbie doll, tastefully accessorised with black, see-through panties and thigh-length high-heeled boots with pointed toes. It might have been slightly erotic if I hadn't been kneeling in a muddy flowerbed, with the rain pouring down the back of my neck.

The kneeling man stared at Agnes Golightly. "I've been a bad boy," he said. "A very bad boy indeed."

"You certainly have, Cedric," Mrs Golightly said. She kicked him experimentally in the chest with the pointed toe of one of her black shiny boots. The man clutched his chest pitifully.

"Oooh, I'm such a naughty boy. I deserve to be punished, don't I?" he whimpered.

"Cedric, you're the baddest boy in the whole class," said Mrs Golightly, and with a right foot that David Beckham would have been proud of she booted him viciously in the stomach. I'd spent my afternoon fantasizing about tracking down dangerous blondes in high heels. Agnes definitely qualified.

Meanwhile Mrs Golightly's mother was sitting demurely on the sofa, respectably clothed in a green cardigan and a decorous long dress which reached from her scrawny throat all the way down to her bony ankles.

"Nice shot Agnes," she said, "and you, Nancy, pull his head up with that chain so's I can get him proper." She stood. "Right," she said. "Scene Two. Here's your whip, Agnes." She handed her daughter a wicked-looking black implement. "Now, just a minute while I get my depth-of-field sorted," she said as she deftly altered the settings on her video camera. I wondered if they had a director's chair.

I pulled my camera from my pocket and took five hasty shots. Even with the rain on the window and the lack of lighting there should be enough to convince Mr Golightly that his wife's bingo sessions had taken something of an unusual turn. I crept away through the rain, climbed over the privet hedge and made my way back to where my chariot awaited. I was soaked to the skin.

"Brickford Terrace please," I said.

The driver pulled away and drove silently for a few minutes. "Bleedin' disgustin' that's what I think," he said.

I shrugged. "Whatever gets you through the night," I said.

"No, not them," said the cabbie. "Not them perverts 'avin' a gang bang or whatever they was doing. I mean you. Sneaking around in folks's gardens and spying on them through their windows. It's nobody else's business at all what they gets up to in their own 'ouses. Stuff like that's completely private and you should be ashamed of yourself."

I said nothing, just sat wet and miserable in the back

19

seat wondering if there were any vacancies at the local undertakers.

"So what were they doing anyway? Orgy was it then?" asked my privacy-respecting cabbie.

Tom Collins, famous private detective, paid his fare and unlocked his car on the dark, deserted street. I noted with a mixture of puzzlement and relief that all the wheels were still there. I climbed in, switched on the engine, lights and windscreen wipers and drove slowly and silently back to my apartment in the rain. I felt in the mood for some soothing music on the car stereo but they'd nicked that two months ago.

When I got home I made myself a cheese sandwich and a cup of hot chocolate, took a CD off the shelf and fell asleep watching Bogie in *The African Queen.*

Chapter Four

Jake Fist sat on his usual bar stool at his usual bar. It was called Joe's. He sat staring into his Jack Daniels on the rocks and thinking about Suzie and the mess she was in.

It had been precisely ten months, three week and two days since she had walked down the aisle of the church holding on to Bruno Scarletti's large, hairy, well-manicured hand, wearing a dress of sparkling white: symbol of virginal youth and purity. In the wedding photos she stood out pretty as a picture against all the guys standing behind her, all dressed in black.

At the wedding party they played Elvis' brand new hit single on the gramophone. It was called Don't be Cruel. *Bruno was seen to be smirking in the corner listening to the words of the song. He did like a good joke, did Bruno.*

Bruno was neither especially young nor especially good-looking but everyone called him Mr Scarletti, shook him respectfully by the hand and walked away fast and careful like they thought they might get a bullet in the back. Suzie had heard the rumours going around about her brand new husband but Bruno told her it was just jealousy on the part of his business rivals.

He didn't tell her that his business was drugs, girls, protection, loan-sharking and the numbers racket. Or that his response to the jealousy was to break his rivals' legs with an iron bar.

21

So Suzie told Scarletti she wanted out. Bruno was an Italian and he didn't have a lot of happiness with a woman talking to him in this fashion so he told her that sure she had a way out: a permanent way. Which is why she had walked into the office of the one person in Chicago who hated Scarletti more than she did.

Jake Fist.

"So what's your plan?" she asked him as he dropped her off at his Great-Aunt Pauline's

"When I figure one out honey I'll let you know. But I can tell you that Bruno ain't gonna take this lyin' down. Apart from his wounded pride, if word gets out he couldn't even keep his own wife in order they'll start to wonder whether he's the right man to be holding down the Chicago job."

"So what do I do?"

"For now, you stay put and you stay quiet. I'll figure something out."

Then he'd looked at Suzie standing there with her blonde hair and her haunted blue eyes and he'd gone down to Joe's and sunk a few. That had been yesterday, the day after he'd paid back Willie the Weasel, the day he'd had his friendly talk with Bruno Scarletti.

He sat there on his bar stool in Joe's drinking and thinking. He couldn't keep Suzie stashed away forever but he could hardly trade her back to Scarletti and even if he did Bruno wasn't going to forgive him for killing the Weasel. Nope, whichever way he looked at it this was a problem with only one solution.

Somebody needed to die.

*

When I awoke it was still dark
    I'd had the dream again about my mother. I'd been playing with Terry, my elder brother, in the fields

22

leading down to the lake. The cows were chewing the grass and watching us as we ran past shrieking and yelling and playing at cowboys and Indians.

"Tea's ready, boys," she shouted in that thick Irish brogue, and we started to run back up the slope through the trees. Even as we ran I could see her body starting to crumble to dust in front of us, and I knew if I got to her I could save her, but my legs wouldn't run and my feet kept getting caught in the grass and when I got there she'd vanished and I knew she was dead.

I lay sweating in my bed, alone in the dark-ness.

We'd left Ireland when I was just seven years old. I'd heard lots of rumours that my father had killed someone in a drunken brawl in a bar, but I never knew if it was true and I would never have dared to ask my parents. Terry didn't know either, no matter how self-importantly he puffed out his chest and told me I was too young to know the truth. So we'd come to Manchester, where my dad got drunk every night and my mother pined for Ireland and wasted away and died. I lay in bed remembering how happy I had been in the tiny village in Ireland and how miserable I had been since virtually the first day I arrived in Manchester.

I'd managed to buy some milk at the weekend, and I decided to make myself a cup of coffee and a bowl of Cornflakes. The milk was off. I wondered how come they can't give you something that lasts longer than half a day, but in the end it didn't really matter because the Cornflakes were stale. I decided to go down to the local café instead. I showered and searched through my wardrobe trying to find something that was reasonably clean and didn't have any obvious holes. Eventually I pulled on a pair of tan trousers, a shirt that used to be white and went down the stairs.

My car was parked underneath a stunted tree which showed its displeasure at being left all on its own in a Manchester street by showering my bonnet with wet leaves. I started up the car and drove to my office with the engine banging and clattering. I would have to get it seen to before it fell apart.

For the hundredth time I dreamed that I was driving a Corvette, or a Mustang or an AC Cobra, anything really except this beaten-up old machine, but with the money I made out of the detecting business the nearest I'd ever get would be my model collection. I put aside thoughts of easing through the traffic in a 1935 Bugatti S-Type 57 Ventoux Coupe, and contented myself with trying not to hit anything with the Escort.

I parked the car, walked around the corner and dropped into my local café. I ordered coffee and while I was waiting picked up the newspaper and scanned the headlines but it was just the usual dreary stuff: Arsenal complaining about their fixtures for the new season and some TV starlet giggling at the camera and denying that she was one of them. I finished my coffee and drove to the office.

As usual there was nothing on the answering machine. The only mail was two bills and two reminders about two other bills which I hadn't got around to paying. I booted up my computer.

I can talk you through the complexities of the ignition system and engine components of a Plymouth Special Deluxe, but I had always viewed computers as some kind of alien life form until my mate Bill had insisted that I should drag myself kicking and screaming into the wonders of the 21st century. He'd patiently shown me the basic techniques: plugging it in, switching it on, composing and accessing e-mails. More complex techniques such as dialing into the world-wide web looking for vintage car sites and pornography I'd taught myself.

I did have, at the bottom of the tiny advertisement I carried in the local newspapers, an e-mail address and I have to admit that on the odd occasion it had actually brought me some business. There is however, one element of the computer for which I am eternally grateful: the digital camera. In my profession it's a blessing. Firstly because you can print out your dubious pictures instantly, yourself: secondly because you don't have to look into the stony eyes of the assistant in the photo shop every time you get a film developed. I plugged in my camera and printed out the photographs I'd taken the previous evening.

I was admiring Agnes' choice of evening wear and wondering how on earth she'd managed to shoehorn herself into that rubber corset when there was a knock at my door.

"Who is it?" I called.

It was Arthur Golightly.

"Morning, Mr Collins. So, anything for me then?"

I picked up the small stack of photographs and carried them over to the meeting table. On the table were a notebook, an ashtray, two toy cars (for the reconstruction of traffic accidents, or for husbands to play with while I searched for their wives), and a box of tissues for people who had lost their loved ones or their pets. Mostly they were used by those who'd lost their pets.

I switched on the overhead lamp and took the chair

25

opposite to Arthur.

"Last night, Mr Golightly," I began, "I followed your wife and her mother to a public house. There they met a man."

"'Ere, I 'aven't got all day," Arthur Golightly broke in. "Just give us the juicy bits - the stuff I can get me teeth in."

"You'd better see these then." I passed the photographs across the table.

Arthur Golightly seized the pictures. His eyes glowed. "Exactly what I thought." He took another long look. "Well, perhaps not exactly," he conceded.

"Look, Arthur, if you like I can recommend a good divorce lawyer," I said.

Arthur Golightly was still staring at the photographs. "Jesus," he said, "I don't think much of that one. Saggy, see?" He pointed at the dog-handler. "Never did like saggy women."

He looked up, puzzled. "Divorce lawyer?" he said. "What are you talkin' about? These are just what I need." He continued to examine the pictures. "Look at the way our Agnes is dressed here. Just wait till she gets home."

"You aren't going to do anything silly are you, Mr Golightly?"

"Well you might think it's silly but I don't." He leaned towards me confidentially. "You see, Mr Collins, me and the missus 'ave a bit of – you know what - about once every six months, and she's usually clippin' her nails or readin' a magazine or watchin' Coronation Street at the same time. So I'll show her these. It's quite simple. She can get her leather gear on for me and give it me good and proper like a married woman ought to do, or 'er and 'er mum can get their thongs and whips and stuff together and bugger off."

He rubbed his hands together. "Well, I'd better be off. Could be a long night tonight." He put the photographs carefully back into the envelope and slipped it into his pocket. "So how much do I owe you, Mr Collins? Don't worry, I've been saving up the fivers from her winnings. Knew they'd come in handy."

I showed him the invoice I'd prepared.

"Cheap at half the price," he said. He counted out a stack of crumpled fivers. "Cheerio then, Mr Collins."

"Good-bye, Mr Golightly."

It was nice to have a satisfied customer. For me, Arthur counted as a successful case. It hadn't taken long, I hadn't been stabbed or beaten up or arrested, and Arthur had paid in cash, the way I liked my clients to pay, because it eased the burden of donating a large chunk of it to the Inland Revenue.

I went round to my favourite cholesterol café, had greasy eggs, greasy bacon, fried bread, fried black pudding, fried mushrooms and chips. I could feel the arteries closing as I ate.

I'd been back in the office for a few minutes when I looked up to see the office door slowly opening. In the doorway stood a thin man with a sad, droopy face surmounted by a flat cap.

"Come in, Wally," I said and he shuffled in, the rain dripping from his cap and his mac. I've no idea what Wally's head looks like. I've never seen him without his hat. If he ever suffers serious head trauma the first thing they'll have to do is surgically remove his cap.

"Well?" I said.

Wally handed over his camera. "Easy Mr Collins. Never

suspected a thing," he said.

I plugged Wally's camera into the computer and printed out the photographs. Whichever way you looked at them there was no doubt about it. It looked as if Mr Masterson would have to have a long chat with his missus so they could decide whether she was a terrible slicer or a natural hooker. Yeah, OK it's the oldest joke in the book but in my job anything makes you smile you hang on to it.

I picked up the phone and called Mr Masterson. He agreed to come in later in the afternoon on his way home from the office. I paid Wally the agreed rate and he rushed off to put the money into his savings account at the bank. Or straight over the bar at his local pub.

I decided to check my e-mails. I deleted an offer to enlarge my penis; an invitation to watch American college girls performing live especially for me, (which would presumably have enlarged my penis without the need for surgery) and an offer of fifty per cent off a pre-erected garden shed (far too big for my window box). I was just about to hit the erase button on one of those suspicious messages that simply says 'Hi' when on an impulse I opened it instead.

Tom

Can you please call me?
I miss you.

Mary.

It came as a total surprise. It was four months since Mary had walked out and I had really supposed that that was the end of it. As I stared at the simple, short message I had absolutely no idea what I should do.

Mary was a woman who needed lots of affection. I had tried hard with flowers and the odd romantic dinner but I'm just not one of those types who kisses his woman every thirty seconds, holds hands under the table and spends his evenings massaging the back of her neck while handing out sympathy over the truly horrific nature of her day in the office. Don't get me wrong; I'm no Neanderthal, and I didn't go home pissed and beat her up, unlike the husbands and boyfriends of most of my clients. I'm not saying she should have been grateful just because I didn't knock her around on a regular basis. I suppose it was because she came from the south. They have higher expectations than women from Manchester.

I was thinking about Mary, remembering the tempestuous times we'd shared and wondering whether the companionship and the sex were worth all the rest of it when there was a knock at the door. I opened it to see Mr Masterson standing there. He was a thin-faced little man with a suspicious-looking moustache and looked as if he'd spent most of his life trying not to get beaten up by nuns and old ladies and social workers. I sat him down, explained to him that his suspicions had indeed been correct and that his wife spent quite a bit of her time practicing more than her golf swing. Then came another of the parts of being a detective which I hate: handing over the photographs. Some people want to cry on my shoulder, some want to beat me up for being a disgusting pervert and some seem to take a sort of masochistic pleasure in seeing their significant others involved in dimly-lit gymnastics classes.

29

Mr Masterson looked sadly at the photographs, shook his head and put them slowly into his pocket. I handed him an invoice and he wrote out a cheque for the agreed amount. He stood and put on his coat. I've seen it many times but I still couldn't help feeling for this quiet little guy whose boring comfortable life had just fallen apart. As he turned to leave he said, "It's just been one of them weeks, Mr Collins. First we get burgled and now this."

I went cold "Burgled?" I said, casually.

"Aye," he said. "Last night we think. Wife lost her purse and her watch and some cash we had hidden away disappeared. You're not safe in your own house these days."

It was on the tip of my tongue to ask if his wife was missing any of her knickers but under the circumstances it didn't seem a particularly tactful question so I kept my mouth shut. I wished him good-bye: he plodded down the stairs and as soon as the door closed behind him I stalked over to the phone and called Wally.

"Wally, I want you in my office now," I shouted.

So Wally was going straight was he? And just the previous day Mr and Mrs Masterson had been burgled while Wally was hiding inside the house taking photographs of Mrs Masterson's illicit amorous activities. I know that there are coincidences in life but this wasn't one of them.

When Wally arrived I had a few choice words with him. He swore he'd never touched a thing at the Masterson's house and I told him that I was a one-legged transvestite Kazakhstani pole-dancer looking for a serious relationship. I shoved Wally out of the office and contemplated the ending of yet another beautiful friendship.

And so ended another breathtakingly adventurous day in the thrilling life of Manchester's finest Private Investigator

Chapter Five

*K*arl Zieger had been Jake's partner in the old days, and he was as straight-up a guy as you could find anywhere in Chicago. But he and Jake had got to falling out and fighting, and eventually Karl had thrown it in and gone to work for a big outfit who specialised in protecting important people from getting themselves kidnapped or shot or both. Still it was Karl who Jake called when he needed help and he sure needed some now.

"Look, Jake," said Karl, "you're in this over your head. It's Scarletti's wife you're talking about here, not some five-cent chorus girl. Tell her to go to the cops or get her a one-way ticket to somewhere she can disappear."

"I can handle Scarletti," said Jake Fist.

"Yeah, maybe two years ago, but not now, Jake. Ever since what happened to Tanya you've been living in a bottle of whisky. You might think you're as quick as you used to be, but you're not, Jake. And one of these nights you'll be half a second too slow and you'll be dead. You either give up the booze, Jake or you give up this fight."

"Thanks for the advice." Jake slid his feet off the desk and deliberately poured himself another shot from the bottle.

Karl Zieger stood up, gripped the edges of the desk. "I'm not going to be around to bail you out, Jake. Just remember that." He strode *angrily from the room.*

Jake shook his head. He knew Karl was right, but hell, what was he supposed to do about it. He downed his whisky, stared out of his window into the Chicago night. Then he called Suzie. "If you're in trouble and you need somebody and I'm not around, call this number. His name's Karl. Karl Zieger. He's one of the good guys."

"You coming around to see me any time soon?" she asked.

"Uh, no," Jake replied. "Got a few things happening right now."

It had been a long slow day and Jake was hungry so he switched off the office lights locked the door and walked down the street. The news stands had some headline about some important meeting between Ike and that crook Dicky Nixon he'd picked for his Vice President. It was enough to drive any self-respecting American to drink.

Jake went to a steak house he used, sat with his back to the wall where he could see the street through the window and ordered himself a martini. Extremely dry. Extremely large.

He sat there at the table waiting for his steak and after a couple of minutes he stared at the empty glass where his martini had been and asked himself if he felt better. Maybe, maybe not. It was hard to decide.

So he decided to crook his finger at the waitress and order another.

*

It had been my father who insisted that my brother Terry, and I should learn to box. Terry was a natural: he'd inherited the family vicious streak, but I just stood there with my hands up, back-pedalling, trying not to get hurt. I just couldn't see the point of trying to beat someone up until they fell over and I certainly couldn't see the attraction in standing there while some hulking great thug kept hitting me in the face. My instructor was totally frustrated with me.

"I don't understand it, Tom," he'd say. "You're big and quick, you've got fast hands and terrific reflexes. You just don't seem to have the killer instinct."

My dad of course had another explanation. I was a nancy-boy and a miserable, snivelling coward and a bloody disgrace. Maybe he was right. I showered, dressed and went to the office.

My office is on the second floor over a shop. Someone with either amazing optimism or an admirable sense of humour had opened a small fashion boutique there, but it had been closed for over a year now. The empty room was guarded by a locked iron grille, and four forlorn, naked models stared through the grimy window like those dogs you see in the RSPCA ads waiting hopelessly for salvation.

I pushed open the door and made a mental note to polish up the stained brass plate with my name and profession inscribed on it. It was the same reminder I'd been giving myself for seven years. Hell, you can't rush these things. I walked up the narrow staircase to my office.

There was, as usual, nothing waiting for me and I sat there wondering what to do with the rest of the day. I had no clients, no money, no prospects and no dames, dangerous or otherwise lining up outside my bedroom door.

I went down the stairs, locked the door, walked to my car and drove to the gym. It's a mixed bag: hard-cases keeping in trim; apprentice body builders who spend fifty percent of their time looking at themselves in the mirror and the other fifty percent staring at my bottom in the changing rooms; serious fitness freaks, both male and female; bored housewives dressed in the smallest Spandex bodysuits they can find and getting totally pissed off because the serious athletes aren't interested and the bodybuilders are all homosexuals.

Usually I use the treadmill until I get fed up with it - generally about five minutes - then lift a few weights until I can work out my frustrations by prancing around the punch-bag and beating the hell out of it, trying to convince myself that I'm a real detective.

I changed and climbed onto a vacant treadmill. A couple of the women who use the place have given me the odd long stare or made the occasional suggestive remark. Whether they're married or single I wouldn't know, the gym gives them the perfect excuse to take their rings off, but I wasn't really looking for a new relationship. The end of my last one still hurt.

Mary was an accountant with a large firm called Mottley, Crust, Gump, Garrable and Frigget, or something similar. It's another cliché that accountants are really boring people, and it can't be said that Mary was particularly exciting – no naked free-fall parachuting or anything along those lines - but in a way that was why I liked her. She was extremely normal: she had a normal job, liked to watch the TV, attended Saturday morning aerobics classes, read romantic books about women who lose themselves in the bottomless pools of the dark brown eyes of real men, and enjoyed the occasional meal out with a glass of wine and me.

The problem was that Mary wanted the lack of thrills in her own life counterbalanced by a bit of excitement from the man she was with. When she first found out I was a detective she kept expecting me to come home with black eyes and bruises and tell her about chasing axe murderers over the rooftops. When she realized that wasn't quite the way it worked she changed tack, and suggested that if I was going to be boring I might as well be boring with something that had a pension and promotion prospects attached to it. So she nagged me to death about getting a real job as a bus driver or an insurance salesman. It had lasted for almost two years. I wasn't about to jump back on to that particular treadmill.

Since Mary walked out I'd been involved very briefly with a woman who'd sworn she was separated. Then one day she'd handed me my toothbrush and told me she didn't want to see me any more. Her dearly beloved had been serving five years for armed robbery and they'd let him out early for good behaviour.

In my professional capacity I've seen too much of what happens when builders and dockworkers come home unexpectedly to find their wives in bed with the milkman. I know all about the grief. Not to mention the grievous bodily harm. So though I can't say I was particularly enjoying it, I was, for the moment, celibate.

I finished my work-out, showered and bought myself a healthy sandwich made with real artificial wholemeal bread which I washed down with one of those drinks with names like Sporting Armpit, packed full of vitamins and electrolytes and tasting like carbonated camel's urine. Then I drove back to my office to wait for the next lost cause to stagger in off the street.

With nothing else to occupy my time I dialed up a website I use which has classic cars for sale. I don't know why I bother, I can't afford any of them but as I sat there, drooling over the old Chevrolets and Packards my office door opened. It was Wally Holden, white-faced and shaking as if he'd been stricken with malaria and I could smell the whisky on his breath from three yards away.

"Look, Wally," I said, "if it's money you want I don't have any and I'm not prepared to give you jobs if you keep robbing the clients. The next time they'll send me down as well as you. It's not a risk I'm prepared to take, Wally. And what the hell have you been doing. You look as if you've seen a ghost and you smell as if you've spent the night in a distillery."

He looked at me, a pathetic, abject piece of pure misery. "Mr Collins," he said, "I've seen a murder."

Now Wally was the kind of guy who would have given a lie detector an inferiority complex. Wally could put his hand on a stack of Bibles, look the judge straight in the eye, swear to tell the truth, the whole truth and nothing but the truth then come out with a fairy story that would have astonished Walt Disney. Which is why I just sat in my chair and waited for him to continue.

Wally stood there, fussing and fidgeting and gradually he told me his story. He'd been out riding his bicycle when he'd seen a car coasting to a standstill by the Barton Bridge on the Ship Canal. Being a prudent sort he'd decided to hide behind a pillar and watch as three men had jumped out of the car, opened the boot and emerged struggling with something awkward and heavy: something they'd pitched over the side into the water. Wally swore that he'd seen quite clearly what it was: a body wrapped in lengths of heavy chain.

"I swear to Gawd, Mr Collins, the poor bugger was still struggling. Crying and moaning too, I 'eard it with my own ears. Then he hit the water and slid under. I can't stop thinkin' about it, Mr Collins. It's drivin' me crazy."

37

Now when your average gang of thugs decides to dump a body they don't usually do it in broad daylight meaning that Wally's story must have taken place some time in the wee small hours when normal folks are in bed. Which would lead one to wonder why anyone would be riding a bike along the Ship Canal in the middle of the night but you have to be a bit patient with Wally. If you start to question him like a policeman he just shuts up like a clam.

"When did this happen, Wally?" I asked.

"Last night," said Wally, unhappily.

"And what time was this?" I asked.

He looked shiftily around the office. "Well it was quite late, actually," he replied. "At night," he added helpfully.

"So how can you be sure what you saw if it was dark?" I asked.

"Gawd Mr Collins, you know me," said Wally. "Eyes like a shithouse rat. And anyway the moon was going in and out of the clouds. I saw 'em like I'm looking at you now. And that's another thing Mr Collins. They was Chinese. They bunged the poor bugger in the canal then they got in a big black car and drove off."

"Look, Wally, there's only one thing you can do. You have to go to the police right now." I stood up. "Come on, I'll take you," I said.

He stood in front of my desk, wringing his hands and he said, "I can't Mr Collins. I would if I could but I can't."

We were of course now coming to what I believe is called the nub of the question.

"Wally," I said, "exactly what were you doing riding your bike under a bridge on the Ship Canal in the middle of the night?"

Of course it turned out that Wally had burgled one of

38

the pubs on the waterside. He'd been sneaking back to his bike with the cash from the till and a couple of bottles of scotch when he'd run into the late night bathing party.

"So I can't go to the cops can I, Mr Collins? They said the next time they'd give me ten years, but I've practically drunk both them bottles of whisky and hardly had a wink of sleep all night," he said, accusingly, "and when I did nod off I got these horrible nightmares. So I come to you."

"All right Wally," I said, "I'll sort it out."

"But what you goin' to do Mr Collins? You won't give 'em my name will you?"

"No, Wally," I said. "I won't"

I ushered Wally out of the office, hoping he'd do us all a favour and fall down the stairs and break his neck. When that didn't happen I picked up the phone and called Manchester Central Police Station. They put me through to a guy called DC Matthews who I remembered vaguely from my time in the Manchester police. I relayed to him the gist of Wally's conversation.

"Are you sure this is legit, Collins?" he asked. "There's going to be an awful lot of people very pissed off if we send a team of divers down and all we find is an old TV set."

"Look," I said, "the witness can't be said to particularly reliable but he insists that's what he saw."

"Who's the witness?"

"Sorry," I said. "I promised him I wouldn't give his name."

There was a silence. "OK Collins, I'll let you know what happens. But you'd better not be wasting our time," he said

I put down the phone and there was a tapping at the door. A little old lady in a black hat, black dress, black gloves crept cautiously into my office, peering over her shoulder to make sure she wasn't being followed. She inspected under the table for assassins, then cautiously took a seat.

"Good afternoon Mrs Green," I said. "How can I help?"

She leaned towards me and whispered to avoid being picked up by hidden microphones. "It's them next door. I think they've murdered somebody."

"And what makes you think that, Mrs Green?"

She stared around the room. "They were digging. In the garden. With spades."

Triumphantly she sat back in her chair

"Digging in the garden with spades," I repeated.

Gladys Green tapped her nose. "Burying the body," she said. "And it's not the first one. They've done it before."

"Mrs Green, last week you told me a young girl had been kidnapped by a villain in a van. It turned out it was her boyfriend picking her up for a weekend of illicit sex."

"Anyone can make a mistake," she huffed.

"And the week before that you thought the people at the bus stop had been abducted by a flying saucer. It was actually the Number 14 bus to Didsbury."

"Yes, but this time it's true," she insisted. "I heard this wild screaming, and then music playing really loud. To cover the noise. Again!"

"In that case I suggest you inform the police."

"The police," she cried. "But I told you the last time. Them's not real police. You can tell by their eyes. They're space aliens!"

I sighed. Based on my own experiences in the force, she could be right.

40

"Right then. I'll look into it at once," I said, ushering her out of the door. "Goodbye, Mrs Green."

Loonies, loose women and lost dogs. That's all I get these days.

I was by now thoroughly depressed so I decided to go home and play with my model cars. I shut down the computer and was preparing to leave when I heard a soft rapping on the door. Three visitors in the same day? If it went on like this I'd need to put in a turnstile.

"Come in," I said with a sigh. I turned to face the door waiting for another of life's sad victims to come creeping into my office.

Her hair was a dark, deep, shiny black with tiny pinpoints of light reflecting back like the streetlights in wet tarmac late on a moonless night.

Her dark brown eyes smouldered like the embers of a dying fire: her complexion was flawless; tanned and toned with haughty, high-set cheekbones. Her deep red lips were slightly parted as if she had just kissed her lover good-bye. She stood, framed in the doorway like something from a painting by Gauguin, an exotic, divine apparition from somewhere far away: China or Japan, or Thailand. Or maybe Paradise.

She looked around the room, at the old desk, the second-hand computer, the beat-up iron safe, the ancient filing cabinet and finally at me. I could see she wasn't impressed by anything she saw.

"Are you the detective?" she asked in a low, husky American drawl. It was like fingernails being dragged slowly down my spine. I imagined her arms around me and that voice breathing, "Good night lover," in my ear. I'd never sleep again.

41

"Sure," I replied shakily.

By this time Jake Fist would probably have had her on the office carpet but I just sat there with my eyes bulging and my mouth slowly opening and closing like a lovesick trout. Eventually I managed to get to my feet, and hurried around the desk

"Can I take your coat?" I asked.

She shrugged it off, revealing a black woollen dress that clung to her perfect body like a jealous barnacle. I carried the coat reverently to the nail behind the door and all the time a voice in my head was saying, "Please, please don't tell me you've lost your poodle."

She was breathing a little heavily, from climbing the stairs no doubt, and I tried desperately to look anywhere except at her small, beautifully heaving breasts.

I invited her to sit at my interview table. I was used to the nervousness, the stammering, the embarrassment, the averted eyes. Except this time it was me.

"OK to smoke?" she asked. I nodded. Yes, I know that it isn't allowed any more in offices but half the people who come to my office wouldn't be able to speak without a cigarette in their hands and as the only person affected is me I can't see it's much of a crime. Smoking's bad for you they say. It's one of life's little ironies that had I obeyed the no-smoking rules two days later I'd have been dead.

She found a pack of cigarettes, lit one and blew smoke into the air.

"What can I do for you?" I asked.

She tapped cigarette ash into the ashtray. "It's my cousin," she said. "She's disappeared and I want you to find her."

Somewhere in the distance a heavenly choir started

singing. I opened my notebook. "Could I have your name, please?"

"My surname is Wu. My first names are Mei Ling. My English name is Janet."

"And where are you from then Miss Wu," I asked. I was thinking somewhere in Cheshire or maybe a designer apartment in the city centre.

Her clear brown eyes looked at me over her cigarette. "I'm from Chicago," she said.

Of course. I should have guessed.

She undid the clasp of her Chanel handbag, reached in and took out a photograph. "That's my cousin," she continued. "Her name is Angel. Angel Wong."

I picked up the photo and now it wasn't just the heavenly choir. Seraphim and cherubim turned somersaults in the air. I stared solemnly at the picture. I was afraid to touch it in case my fingerprints ruined her beauty.

"She's very pretty," Miss Wu remarked casually. It was like saying that a Rolls Royce Corniche was ok for nipping down to the supermarket. Janet Wu crossed her legs and smoothed down her dress in a way that would have given Arthur Golightly a heart attack.

"Go on," I said. It was the longest speech I could manage.

"Angel and her husband had a silly argument. Something quite trivial apparently, but Angel's always been very difficult. Anyway when Johnny – that's her husband – came home she'd packed her things and gone. No note, no forwarding address, nothing."

I was a little puzzled. "Angel and her husband live in Manchester?" I asked.

"No, they live in Chicago, but Angel studied here, at

UMIST. When her husband had called up her friends and relatives and no one knew anything, he called the airlines. She took a flight to New York and then on to Manchester. She knows the town, she has friends here."

"Have you been to the police?" I asked.

"For what? She's a grown woman. If she wants to hide in Manchester what do the police care?"

She was right of course.

"Have you checked her phone records? Presumably if she's met up with old friends in Manchester she's been in touch with them?"

She shook her head. "There's nothing," she said.

"When did she leave UMIST?"

"Four years ago."

"Did she stay in touch with anyone?"

"Not that we know of."

There's a sizeable Chinese community in Manchester and they tend to keep themselves to themselves. They don't like outsiders, particularly nosey ones asking questions, but it would be worth the job just to keep Angel's photograph.

"OK, I'll take the case," I said.

My fees are fairly elastic. I try to decide how much the client can afford before I quote. This one was hardly living off food stamps. "It'll be fifty pounds an hour, plus expenses," I said as casually as I could.

She didn't bat an eyelid. Just opened her Chanel handbag and pulled out a wad of fifties.

"Five hundred up front be enough?" she asked.

I nodded.

"Find Angel and there's a bonus." She stubbed out her cigarette. "Five thousand pounds," she said.

44

I just sat there stunned. I said nothing at all. I didn't want to risk sounding like a parched duck. She counted out ten fifties and passed them across the table.

"Where do I get hold of you?" I asked.

She looked at me coolly, and I started to blush like a schoolboy.

"I'm staying at the Ritz," she replied, enjoying my embarrassment. It figured: the swankiest hotel in Manchester. Also the oldest, the worst staff, the lousiest food and the highest room rates; but it was slap in the centre and a chopstick's throw from Chinatown.

"Room 1501," she said. I dutifully wrote it all down in my notebook.

"I'll be in touch," I replied, trying to sound tough and efficient.

She stood up, slipped into her coat and walked out of my office, her tiny backside swaying like a field of wheat in a gentle summer breeze. I wondered if she practised in a mirror or if all beautiful oriental women naturally walked like that. I watched her walk away and once again I thought I heard the heavenly choir.

Or maybe it was just the sound of Jake Fist laughing.

Chapter Six

Another day of nothing. Jake had eaten a bagel at his desk for lunch, had spent the whole afternoon watching and waiting. He was prepared for just about anything Bruno Scarletti might throw at him except for the one thing that had actually happened. Nothing. So when the light started to fade he went down to Joe's.

Just about every boozed-up wise-ass that used the place would walk in and say, "Set 'em up, Joe," like they were the first person who ever thought up that crack, and Joe's face would slide into a big easy grin like he hadn't heard that thirty times a day for the last thirty years.

Jake sat there, drinking his Jack Daniels and remembering.

He'd had more women than he could count and he'd treated them all exactly the same. Real bad. Some liked it, some didn't but it didn't matter a spent bullet to Jake because he didn't give a dime about any of them. Then he met Tanya.

Jake had been laid out with just about every blunt instrument that could be cracked over his head, but nothing had ever hit him the way Tanya did.

They had held hands in public places, shared spaghetti for dinner, laughed at stupid drive-in comedies, snuck off and made love in the afternoons just like all those love-struck fools in the books and the movies. It had been two-and-a-half years ago now that Jake had come home late.

Tanya had short dark hair and they probably thought it was Jake lying in the bed in the darkness. They had stitched a neat line of bullet holes across Jake's best bed and his brand new sheets and his best feather duvet and straight through Tanya's chest. Scarletti had sworn he had nothing to do with it but Jake knew different.

And now Jake was hiding Scarletti's woman.

After a while Jake slid off his barstool, paid Joe and left. He was gonna go home, gonna be sensible but it was another night when sensible didn't work.

When he woke up the whisky demons were banging on the inside of his head and there was a couple of hours missing out of his life. He remembered deciding he'd have just one more at a cheap club used mainly by working girls and guys who couldn't afford them. After that it all became a little confused. He'd told himself to avoid two things: cheap booze and cheap women. He'd managed to get it wrong both ways. If Scarletti had come looking for him he'd have been dead.

Jake staggered out of bed, took a leak, brushed his teeth and stuck his head under the cold tap. Then he took a swig from the bottle to try to make himself feel better. It didn't work. Another perfect start to another perfect day, he thought: a bad hangover, bad breath and a bad conscience.

When he walked back into the bedroom the girl in his bed was sleeping as sweet and innocent as if she had no idea she was really a twenty-dollar hooker. He shook her by the shoulder. "Get up, get dressed and get out of here," he said.

She opened her eyes, sat up in bed, clutching the sheets over her breasts like she cared.

Jake threw her clothes to her, making sure she could see the number on the dollar bill he folded into the pocket of her shirt. He didn't know why he had to pick up the paid variety when there were hundreds of women out there who'd take him home for free.

47

He guessed it was just his way of repaying his debt to the society who'd raised him.

*

I lay in my bed in the early morning, in that pleasant drowsy state that lies half way between sleep and full consciousness, the sun leaking through the bedroom curtains casting light and shadows on the old faded wallpaper. Then I was jerked out of my reverie by the sound of the neighbours threatening to murder their kids unless they got up and went to school.

I lay there, fully awake now thinking about Terry, my brother. He'd joined the army; the last I knew he was in the SAS, though I never heard from him any more.

He was five years older than me and he'd been the apple of my dad's eye, mainly because he was just like him, big and tough and quick with his fists. I'd been happier with a comic book, and my father would sneer at me and tell me my mother had wanted one son and one daughter and that's what she'd got.

Of course, like all siblings we'd had our disagreements and our fights and Terry had given me more than one black eye, but on the whole he'd been good to me. He protected me as much as he could from the violence and the bullying that was endemic where we lived and also pretty common inside the house we lived in.

There was no grass where we lived in Manchester. There were no cows, no sheep. You couldn't walk through the green fields, alone and dreaming, down to the small sandy beach and the sea breaking endlessly against the rocks. It seemed as though the sun never shone, never set

48

in a blaze of orange and yellow over the purple hills. And I had no friends from the village school, from the farms to sit with in the evenings chewing on a stalk of wheat, talking of the small, simple things which governed our lives as the peat smoke drifted from the chimneys leaving its sharp, familiar smell in the air.

Apart from Terry the only friend I had in Manchester in those days was Maisie. Maisie owned a hotel-cum-boarding house in the next street. Some of the people who stayed there were pretty scary types, and it wasn't uncommon to see a police car racing up the street and some guy hotfooting it out of Maisie's place with a suitcase, but Maisie was a really good sort and she looked after me when Terry wasn't around and my father was in the pub.

The pub my dad used was called The Ship and if they ever hold a competition for the worst pub in England, The Ship gets my vote. Getting from the door to the bar without being mugged is an achievement in itself: having two drinks without someone picking a fight with you is virtually impossible. Unless, of course, you want to deal drugs, which they do quite openly every evening in the Saloon Bar.

One Sunday lunchtime Maisie had come out of The Ship with a couple of gin and tonics inside her to see me getting a kicking from some of the local hard-cases. I'd only been in Manchester for a week or two, and my Irish accent was just the excuse those guys needed to try to punch my lights out. Maisie had beaten them off with her umbrella, and taken me back to her hotel, where she'd sat me in the back room, patched me up with Dettol and Elastoplast, and fed me tea and biscuits. I was in a hostile, unknown place; a place I hated, where everyone seemed to

49

exist only for the sheer pleasure of kicking me around. When my brother was out, when my father was drunk, Maisie was the only person to whom I could go and I'd almost worshipped this strange, kind, fierce old lady.

She was where I went when I was in trouble, and she always treated me like she had that first time when I'd been seven years old, lying face down in tears in the street.

I shook the memories from my head dragged myself out of bed, showered, brushed my teeth and dressed. At least now I had a real case; a case that didn't involve straying spouses and lost dogs; a case that involved not just one but two beautiful oriental women. I sat at my breakfast table (breakfast?) with a cup of black coffee and took out the photograph of Angel Wong. She'd studied Management Science at UMIST, the University of Manchester Institute of Science and Technology, and even for a detective like myself it wasn't difficult to work out that maybe I should go there and ask some questions. I finished my coffee, left the cup in the sink and pulled on a coat.

My apartment is a conversion on the third floor of an old Victorian house. I went down the stairs and walked to where my car was parked in the street, glistening proudly under its coat of wet leaves and pigeon droppings. There was a piece of soggy paper under the wiper. Some kind-hearted soul was offering to rearrange all my debts for nothing and charge me only a tiny bit of interest on the whole outstanding amount. It's nice to know there are still some good people out there. I put the key in the ignition, listened to the rhythmic clunking noise of my engine starting up and drove to the university.

It was a cool, cloudy day but as I drove I wasn't thinking about the weather. I was thinking about Janet Wu and her little black dress. In my imagination she was walking towards me, her eyes full of gratitude because I'd found her missing cousin. The hotel room door closed softly behind me, her arms were around my neck, I slowly slid the straps of her dress from her brown, smooth shoulders. Then I almost hit the car in front. I pulled myself together and tried to concentrate on the traffic.

Maybe it was that acute longing for a little female company that reminded me of Mary. I decided that out of common courtesy I should at least give her a call, buy her a drink for old times' sake, and if she wanted to come over to my flat afterwards and rip off all her clothes, well that was OK too. But right now I was busy. Mary could wait until I'd checked out my latest case. Prioritise, I think they call it. Otherwise known as putting it off as long as possible in the hope that it goes away.

I thought again about the picture I had in my pocket. Even without that bonus I was rather looking forward to tracking down Angel Wong.

*

I arrived at UMIST, parked the car in a spot marked *STAFF ONLY* and introduced myself to the admissions tutor. I laid the picture of Angel on the table and told him I'd like to speak to one of her tutors: someone who had known her four years ago and might know who she was friendly with. He was about as enthusiastic as a man going to his own hanging. He pulled his lip and mumbled and stuttered about privacy and confidential affairs and so on. Eventually I told him that her uncle had died and left her ten million dollars, and I was working on behalf of the old man's lawyers. I managed to suggest that if the university was instrumental in finding her, she might turn generous. Five minutes later I was talking to a guy called Archibald. He was long and weedy with a yellow moustache and smiled at me sweetly. I could see that he approved of my shoulders.

"Yes," he said, "certainly I remember Angel. A remarkably beautiful girl. Could have been quite brilliant if she had put her mind to it. Six or seven of them stuck together, quite the best looking group of girls in the Department." He smiled and looked through his old class notes. "Of course, mostly they were overseas students and wouldn't be here any longer, but you could try these." He gave me two names. "They lived in this area, though I've no idea if they're still here now."

I thanked him and wiggled my bottom at him as I left. There's no harm in a bit of olde worlde courtesy.

I went to the records office and got their home addresses, then went back to thank the admissions guy and told him I'd put in a good word for him when the ten million came through.

The first of the two addresses belonged to a girl called Madeleine Jones, which didn't sound terribly Chinese to me but you never know these days.

I parked the car, rang the bell and was greeted by a Chinese lady of fifty or so, with a Welsh accent you could cut with a knife. She told me she'd married a man from Llanelli, a Mr Jones, which explained a lot. Madeleine didn't live at home any more. She'd married a guy from Hong Kong and gone to live there. Yes, she remembered Angel, a lovely-looking girl, but she hadn't seen her or heard from her in years.

52

Then I looked at the second name on the list. Meredith Tang, who apparently lived with her parents.

I arrived at a big prosperous-looking place sitting in a large garden with a Chinese pagoda and fat red goldfish floating lazily around in an ornamental pool. I pressed a button by the gates. When they eventually opened I drove along a semi-circular drive and parked in front of large double doors.

A middle-aged couple greeted me suspiciously at the door. I asked them if they were Mr and Mrs Tang and if they had a daughter named Meredith. They spoke to each other in Chinese. Then they told me they didn't know. I asked politely exactly what it was they didn't know. They didn't know if they were Mr and Mrs Tang; they didn't know if they had a daughter; or they weren't sure what her name was? After a while they admitted that they were in fact Mr and Mrs Tang and they did actually have a daughter. I pulled out the picture of Angel Wong and asked if they knew her. They gave each other hooded, conspiratorial stares then shook their heads and said they'd never heard of her. If they'd been taking a course at UMIST entitled: *How to Tell a Really Unconvincing Lie* they couldn't have done it better.

It was pouring with rain and I was getting soaked to the skin standing outside their ornately decorated door. It didn't take me long to realize these guys wouldn't invite me in if Manchester got hit by a hurricane, so I just walked in all by myself. The hall was covered in pictures of them standing in front of a big, red-and-gold Chinese restaurant and having their pictures taken with important people and Manchester City football players.

"Your restaurant?" I asked.

They looked at each other and down at the floor and muttered something that might have been "Yes."

"Could you give me the address of your daughter?" I asked. "Angel Wong was one of her closest friends. Maybe she'll know where she is."

They cast sidelong glances at each other and shuffled their feet and eventually the woman said, "She no live here."

"Look," I said, "all I'm asking for is your daughter's address so that I can ask her if she has seen Angel Wong recently. That's all. Now if you like I can ask my colleagues in the police force to come here and take a look at all your restaurant licenses, and my friends in the Department of the Environment to check if you comply with all the hygiene regulations, and my mates at the Inland Revenue to go over your restaurant's books and make sure you're not forgetting to put all the cash payments through them. Now, what do you want to do?"

The bit about licenses and hygiene didn't bother them, but the minute I mentioned the Inland Revenue they started to shake. I almost felt ashamed of myself.

"She don't live here any more," said the woman. "She go to United States."

"When?" I asked.

"We don't know anything," said the old guy and at that moment a young guy emerged, hard-eyed and tough-looking.

"What do you want?" he asked.

I repeated my story and he said something in Chinese to the old couple.

"They don't know anything," said the young guy standing pointedly by the door.

"Thanks for all your help," I said to the young guy. I stared at the middle-aged couple. "I meant what I said about the tax people," I said. "Better make sure you check your books."

There was a large puddle forming beside my car. I squelched through it and drove away. There was, I thought, definitely something wrong with the reaction of Mr and Mrs Tang. Something more than just natural reticence to talk to some nosy private eye. Why on earth couldn't they give me their daughter's address?

I bought lunch from the Ukrainian 24 hour mini-market, opened my office door and checked my answering machine. No calls, no mail, no visitors, no difference. I munched my way through my ham and cheese sandwich – two flavours of plastic between two layers of sponge and washed it all down with a warm Coca Cola. Then I picked up my phone and called Bill.

Bill was my best friend. To be honest, except for Maisie, he was my only friend. The first time we'd met was in the boxing ring where I'd accidentally nearly killed him. Persuading me to do really stupid things was probably his way of getting even. Like suggesting that he and I should sign up with the Greater Manchester Constabulary. It was fine for Bill: all that unarmed combat and interrogations and stuff brought out the worst in him and he was doing well now, rising steadily through the ranks of the cops. For me it was completely different.

Firstly I don't drink which is pretty much a mortal sin in the police force. I'd been lousy on the firing range, useless at any kind of combat and the thought of facing hulking great thugs late at night in darkened warehouses they were robbing at gunpoint - well, to be perfectly honest I wasn't terribly keen. About the only thing I'd been any good at was report-writing but in the Manchester police this doesn't compete with suspect-beating, thumping football hooligans on the head with your truncheon and general violence. So when it came to weeding out the unsuitables, I was number one weed.

You'd have thought I'd have learnt my lesson from that but no, once again I had to fall in with another of Bill's brilliant ideas. Having failed in the public sector, he explained to me, I should become a private detective. He'd feed me information and cases, help me out with car plate numbers and addresses and all the things that the police could get their hands on that I couldn't, and as soon as I had made a roaring success of it he'd join me. Pretty soon we'd be a sort of combination of Sherlock Holmes, Robocop and Securicor. That was seven years ago.

There's a pub right by the station which all the cops use but it's a bit daunting when you walk in there and all the off-duty cops start pointing you out to their mates: Tom Collins: the only person ever to be thrown out of the Manchester police for being reluctant to use violence. So I arranged to meet Bill at a quiet little boozer called The Lamb and Flag just outside the city centre.

I dusted the crumbs off my desk and turned to see if there was anything worth looking at on the computer. I had three new messages. They offered me a penthouse in Marbella, a new Mercedes and half a dozen horny housewives. I'd never been to Spain, preferred an old Mercedes and had had more than my fill of housewives.

I deleted them all and sat staring at the e-mail from Mary. I composed several replies and deleted each one. Then I wrote:

Dear Mary.

It would be nice to have a drink or dinner.
Please call me. My numbers are still the same.

Tom.

I sat there and dithered over erasing it yet again. Then by accident I hit the *Send* button. It was Fate, I decided.

I left my office and walked to the car park. Under my windscreen wiper was a circular issued by the Manchester Association of Lepidopterists. At least that's who I assumed had put it there. It said, *Exotic Eastern Butterfly. Urgently Requires Mounting.* I climbed into my Escort and drove to The Lamb and Flag.

Chapter Seven

*J*ake's nerves were getting frazzled by all the nothing that was happening around him. He'd far rather Scarletti's hoods came up the street with guns blazing rather than waiting around in this unreal quiet. Still tonight he had something else on his agenda: an appointment with a guy called Miller. Jake knew about the appointment: Miller didn't. Jake looked at his watch. A few minutes to midnight. Jake reckoned he had time for one more.

He thought back over the well-dressed, well-bred lady who'd walked into his office a couple of days before. Her name was Wendell. Her daughter had married a guy called Miller, son of a wealthy banker. Seemed he had two hobbies. One was playing poker, late with his friends. The other was beating up his wife.

After the meeting Jake had gone to an apartment block and taken the elevator to the ninth floor. There he knocked on a door. The woman who opened it was small and slim and pretty, or would be once the bruises had faded and the cut on her lip had healed. She looked up at Jake with puzzled, scared eyes. "Mrs Malone?" asked Jake

"No," she said. "I think you got the wrong address."

"This the tenth floor?" asked Jake.

"No," she replied, "this is nine."

"That guy in the elevator," said Jake. "Can't make it to double figures." He tipped his hat and left. Of course Jake didn't have the wrong floor. He was checking what he'd been told by Mrs Miller's *distraught, angry mother: whether her daughter really was getting beat up or whether Mrs Miller had her own private agenda. It wasn't that Jake didn't trust some of his clients. He didn't trust any of them. He picked up the shot in front of him and looked over the rim at Joe, polishing glasses.*

"Say, Joe, what do you reckon should happen to some rich guy who comes home once a week from the poker game and beats the shit out of his wife?"

"Well, personally I reckon someone ought to find a big ugly private dick and ask him to give this guy a polite talkin' to."

"You know what, Joe? That's what I think too."

At twenty after midnight he paid his tab, tipped his hat to Joe and drove to a smart street in a smart neighbourhood, parked outside of a smart apartment block and waited. Wednesday was poker night and Mrs Wendell reckoned they finished up around one.

There were four of them left the apartment, and they all walked to their cars. Jake climbed out of his Chevy, walked over to an Oldsmobile, opened the passenger door and stepped inside.

"What the hell you think you're doing?" said this guy with short, smart hair, an expensive grey suit and a blue and white striped shirt.

Jake hit him in the mouth.

The other cars were driving away and Jake could hear them shouting goodbyes, but Mr Miller couldn't reply because Jake was holding him by the throat.

"I got money, take it, it's yours," he gasped and Jake broke his nose.

After five minutes when he was crying into his own blood and his vomit Jake put his mouth close to his ear. "This is nothing, do you understand you miserable son-of-a-bitch." Jake took hold of his hand in his fist and squeezed, Miller writhing and gasping with pain. "You lay one more paw on your lady, and I guarantee that you'll never be able to pick up a poker chip ever again, you hear me?"

Miller just sat there, snivelling and sobbing, saying nothing.

"DO YOU HEAR ME?"

"Yes, yes," he stuttered, "I hear you."

"That's good," Jake said. He hit him one more time for luck, walked over to his Chevy and drove home. Sometimes he reflected this was a good business. You got to beat up some asshole and paid two hundred bucks for doing it.

He parked the car, checked his apartment for unwelcome surprises then went to bed with Betsy. He lay in the darkness smoking a Lucky Strike, wondering how much time he had before Scarletti made his move.

*

I ordered a tomato juice. Bill had a pint of lager. A couple of yobs playing the pool table kept throwing sly looks in my direction and grinning to themselves. In Manchester anyone over fourteen and drinking tomato juice is a poof.

I gave Bill a brief outline of what was going on and when I mentioned the name Meredith Tang he gave a low whistle and took a big gulp of his beer.

"Jesus, Tom," he said, "you've managed to land yourself with some big-time bad guys this time. Meredith Tang was her maiden name. She's now Meredith Liu. Her husband is a guy called Hamilton. We've been watching him for months now. We're pretty sure he's behind half the Chinese rackets in Manchester. He owns a Chinese restaurant and a club called The Yin and Yang club. They're both cash businesses, and seem to take in a lot more money than you'd expect. We suspect they're being used to whitewash the proceeds of drug deals. Brings a whole new meaning to the phrase 'Chinese laundry'."

"We know Liu and his boys are into distribution of E's, coke, heroin, whatever's flavour of the month, but they use the black gangs as front men. We think they also smuggle in illegal immigrants to work in the sweatshops. The Super wants to wait until we have enough evidence to put Liu away for ever, but he's very, very careful and all we've got so far is pretty circumstantial."

"He's about forty years old, immigrated to Manchester from Hong Kong. Usual background checks showed him as an upstanding model businessman, made his money in real estate. But since then we've heard rumours that the real money came from smuggling heroin down from Burma, through China and Hong Kong. Apart from that he was apparently known as a vicious little sadist who liked to do the real nasty stuff himself rather than just sending in the clowns."

He stared at his empty glass and I walked up to the bar and ordered him another pint. The lowlifes were giggling and smirking and making obscene gestures with their pool cues. Bill swigged his beer. "In any case, Tom my advice: stick to your missing pets and persons. These guys are way out of your league."

I sat there sipping my tomato juice and thinking. The people Wally had seen dumping the body in the ship canal were Chinese. I'd had had a beautiful oriental girl from Chicago walking into my office and asking me to find a missing person, one of whose friends just happened to be married to a person suspected of being Manchester's major Chinese gangster. Even a third-rate detective like me could see that there just might be some connection.

Bill put his empty glass down on the table. "Come on,"

he said. "This place is like a morgue."

As we left I stared at the yobs by the pool table. "Let's go, darling," I said to Bill, loudly. I wouldn't have bothered had I been with anyone else, but Bill was a natural in a fistfight and walking out with him gave me a nice warm secure feeling.

Bill looked at me, puzzled. "What did you say?"

"Nothing, Bill, nothing."

I was in a pretty thoughtful frame of mind as I drove home.

When I opened my front door there was a blue envelope lying on the hall carpet with my name on it. I smiled. I'd known Maisie for over twenty years and she still remembered my birthday. I opened the envelope and grinned at the scene on the front of the card. A bunch of riotous party-goers, skimpily-dressed women, bottles of champagne, couples having it away behind the sofa and in the broom cupboard. I took it up to my flat and propped it on the mantelpiece. I checked the sofa and the wardrobe but there was not a single bottle of champagne or half-dressed floozy in sight. Still, it was a couple of days before my birthday. Maybe things would change.

I sat on the sofa and looked around me. A tiny apartment with a huge mortgage; sixteen models of vintage cars; an eight-year-old TV with a stone-age VCR and a five-year-old CD player; four shelves groaning under a pile of books and outside a Ford Escort which, had it been a person, they would have turned off the life support system. That was it. The sum total of my thirty-one years on Planet Earth.

I tried to work out what to do about Janet Wu and Angel Wong and Meredith Liu and various other assorted

Oriental molls and gangsters. Bill had warned me to stay away from Hamilton Liu but on the other hand the sultry Janet had offered me five thousand pounds if I found Angel Wong. That should be enough for a new DVD player. Hell, I could even up-grade to one that recorded as well.

I walked over to my book-shelves and took down a book. It was *King Solomon's Mines*. I'd first read it with awe and wonder as a twelve-year-old and it's still one of my favourites.

The only good thing about my early days in Manchester had been the library. It was just a few streets away from where we lived and I'd practically lived there during opening hours, devouring anything and everything they had.

The English teacher at my school had been pretty good to me. I think I was the only boy in the class who would actually sit down and read a book without being chained to the desk and whipped with razor wire. She'd praised some of the essays I'd written and at the age of ten I'd begun to write a novel. It was about two boys who lived (of course) on a farm in Ireland and discovered an old gravesite in which was a skeleton wearing a crown, breastplate and jewellery. The tomb was full of fabulous gold and silver ornaments. There was an inscription on the tomb and by a great stroke of luck an old man in the village happened to speak and write fluent Amaraic or Sumerian or whatever it was (I forget now). It was of course a curse detailing terrible things which would happen to anyone who desecrated the tomb. This was nothing to do with the fact that I'd just finished reading about Howard Carter's expedition which uncovered the tomb of Tutankhamen.

63

Throw in a gang of thieves looking for the treasure, an evil cult looking to get their skeleton back and some weird supernatural banshee haunting the place and I thought I'd be the youngest and most successful author in England.

One night while I was absorbed in my novel, working by torchlight late in the evening my father had staggered drunk into my room. He'd ripped my hand-written manuscript from my hands, beaten me about the head with it and I'd never seen it again.

I cried for days. I tried to re-write it but although the story was the same the magic had gone. I put King Solomon back on the shelf and went to the Indian store.

"Hello, Mr Collins," said the ever-smiling owner, Mr Patel. "How is it going then in the detecting business?"

"Couldn't be better, Mr Patel. Shot three people, busted a drugs racket and now I'm going off to bed with a gorgeous Oriental siren."

"Excellent Mr Collins, dinner for one was it?"

I was tempted to buy a bottle of Jack Daniels but instead bought a boil-in-the bag meal. You just put it in a pan of hot water and wait for about five minutes. Even I could do that. I watched Elliot Ness in an old re-run of *The Untouchables* then dragged my weary body off to my lonely bed.

Chapter Eight

*I*t was like Custer before the Indians came swarming over the horizon, thought Jake. It was too damn quiet. Scarletti wasn't a guy renowned for his patience and it had been four days now that Jake had watched his back, watched his home and his office, watched every shadow, every guy who walked past, everyone who might be walking too quick or too slow or taking an intense interest in his cigarette or his newspaper. Nett result: nothing.

Jake looked at his watch. Time to call it a day and maybe say hi to Joe. It was already starting to get dark and Jake strolled to his office window and looked out into the street.

The guy that owned the grocery store opposite was an ex-cop called Mendez. He'd bought the store with his disability grant after he'd been shot and couldn't work no longer. He and Jake would shoot the breeze a little and Jake paid him to keep an eye on the street. Mendez kept notices in his window; stuff for sale, people looking for work and so on. Their code was simple. If Mendez saw something he didn't like one of those notices would be written in red ink.

As he looked down every muscle in Jake's body went tight as a wire.

He shrugged on his coat, slipped the safety off of Betsy, tip-toed across the room and threw open the door. Nothing. He walked down the corridor till he came to the door marked GENTS, kicked it open

65

and checked all the stalls. He tipped his hat to the guy standing at the urinal whose eyes were bulging out of his head staring at Jake's gun. If he'd had any difficulty taking a leak he sure didn't now.

Jake took the stairs instead of the elevator but there was no one hiding in the stairwell, no one waiting for him in the lobby. He nodded to the doorman and walked into the street. He wasn't afraid of a shot in the darkness, a black Buick tearing around the corner, two guys hanging out the window, guns blazing. Scarletti needed to know where Suzie was and for that he needed Jake alive.

Jake scanned the street and he would have seen it anyway, even without the warning sign: the car with the engine running a few yards past the entrance to the alleyway, the guy sitting in the driver's seat smoking his cigarette just a little too casually. Jake gave a big, mirthless grin and walked down the street.

He walked past the alleyway then flattened himself against the wall as the two guys came tearing round the corner. He hit the first guy with his left and as he doubled over brought his knee right up into his jaw. 'The old one-two' he said to himself as he round-housed the other guy with his right hand. The guy swayed but didn't go down so Jake took hold of him by the throat and smashed his head into the wall. He went down then sure enough.

Jake whirled on the balls of his feet but there was no one else hiding in the shadows. The driver of the car slammed the shift into gear but he stopped when he saw Jake Fist looking at him, his gun aimed at a spot just below the peak of his cap, just between his eyes. Jake strolled over.

"Don't kill me Mr Fist, I'm just the driver," he stuttered.

"Tell Scarletti when he wants to talk, make an appointment. I'm sure we can come to some accommodation," Jake said, softly. "And tell him the next guys he sends after me they won't end up in the hospital. They'll end up in the morgue."

"Yes sir, Mr Fist," said the driver, shaking like he had the *plague.*

"So what's your name, just the driver?" asked Jake.

"Bennie, Mr Fist. Bennie Marcello."

"Well, Bennie I suggest that after you've seen Scarletti you go home, lock your door and hide in a corner. Cos if I see you again, anywhere, anyplace then you're a dead man. Capice?"

The driver nodded vigorously.

"Ciao," said Jake as the car shot away in a cloud of burning rubber. Half a second too slow, eh? *he said to himself.*

Jake figured he'd earned himself a drink and that Scarletti wouldn't be making another try that night so he dropped into Joe's, perched on his usual bar stool and ordered himself a large JD on the rocks. Around him the guys sat drinking and smoking, talking and laughing, eyeing up Joe's pretty little waitresses, the married ones wishing they were single and the single guys trying to work out how to stay that way. Jake sipped his drink, thinking of how he'd gotten into this fight with Scarletti and his mind went back two-and-a-half years to a bone-chilling winter morning. He'd been sitting in his chair, dreaming, nothing on his mind except Tanya when this dame walked into his office. That had been the start of it all. A dame. He took another drink. Every bad thing ever happened to him had started with a woman.

*

Dennis Hemshall, Chief Constable of the Greater Manchester Police read the report on his desk.

Name:	Nguyen Van Duc, Charles.
Age:	Thirty-nine.
Marital status:	Single.
Occupation:	Office-bearer. The Heavenly

67

Tigers. Precise rank unknown.
Residence: Chicago.

There followed a long list of crimes, actual and suspected, including a few details as to how he had earned his nickname: Cheesewire Charlie.

Interpol had alerted them that a known, violent Chicago mobster was on a plane to Manchester so they'd put a couple of plain-clothes police on his tail. On his second night he'd gone into a club in Chinatown after eating alone and that was the last they'd seen of him until they'd pulled what was left of him out of the Ship Canal. The nightclub was called the Yin and Yang Club, owned by an ethnic Chinese called Hamilton Liu who they suspected was behind half of the organized crime in Manchester.

Attached was a copy of the autopsy report. Cause of death: drowning. He'd been alive when they threw him into the water, though only just. The body was covered in burns and bruises and lacerations, the face battered almost beyond recognition, and three fingers were missing from the right hand.

The Chief Constable initialled the report, added some comments of his own and asked his secretary to send it on. He ran his fingers over his rapidly balding pate. This was Manchester for Christ's sake, not Chicago. He had enough on his plate with the violent black gangs who terrorised Moss Side, and Cheetham Hill, not to mention trying to keep Manchester United's fans from fighting pitched battles with every other bunch of hooligans who came here during the football season.

He wondered what possible reason there might be for a Chicago triad member to be brutally murdered in

Manchester. The Chinese gangs tended to keep a low profile. They were more interested in making money than drawing attention to themselves. Still there was obviously something going on in his patch that he didn't know about and Hemshall, who had been a copper for thirty years didn't like the smell of it one little bit.

He picked up his phone. "DC Matthews," he asked, "this body in the Ship Canal. Who reported it?"

"Chap called Tom Collins," replied Matthews. "He's a local private eye. Used to be in the force."

"Tell McClusky to get him in. We need to know exactly what he saw."

"Well it wasn't him, sir. Someone else saw it. Collins won't tell us who it was."

"Well I'm sure McClusky can persuade him," said Hemshall. "As soon as you can DC Matthews."

"Yes sir, we'll pull him in at once."

*

I sat in my office wondering if it was too early in the morning to call Janet Wu. I wanted to ask her if she knew anything about her cousin's association with a woman married to a Chinese gangster. Instead I flipped through the phone book. There were quite a few Lius listed in the Manchester area but none with a first name of Hamilton. Then again if I were a violent criminal I wouldn't be advertising in The Yellow Pages. I returned the phone book to its accustomed place on the floor under my desk and called Chris Bateson. Chris was editor of the *Manchester Gazette* and over the years I'd given him a few bits of juicy gossip and in return he let me look through the newspaper archives for free.

"Chris," I said, "have you heard of a guy called Hamilton Liu?"

"Heard of him? Jesus, Tom, of course I've heard of him. He's into just about every piece of shit that goes down in this town. Drugs, girls, violence. Why? What do you know?"

"Right now nothing, Chris," I said. "Do you happen to have his address?"

"Look Tom I don't know what you're into here but If I were you I'd stay well away from this guy. Anyone gets on the wrong side of him is asking for trouble. There's no proof of course but there's at least two people who've disappeared after upsetting Mr Liu."

"Don't worry, Chris, It's nothing like that. Just need to ask his wife a couple of questions."

"Tell you what, Tom, since you're an old friend I'll do it for half price."

"Sorry Chris, I don't follow."

"This week's special, Tom. Your name in the Obituary column."

I laughed just like a real tough detective would. "Just give me his address, Chris. I promise I'll try really hard not to get killed." I had no idea then how true that would be.

After a few minutes Chris gave me an address about five minutes away from where I'd been slung out of the previous day. So much for Meredith having moved to the USA. "But just be careful, Tom. This guy's pure poison."

"I'll be careful, Chris," I replied.

As soon as I replaced the receiver the phone rang. I knew who it would be. I steeled myself, picked up the receiver, and as sweetly as I could I said, "Hi Mary, how are you?"

"Who the hell's that?" demanded an angry, nasal northern accent.

I hastily lowered my voice by several octaves. "Collins Detective Agencies."

"Is that Mr Collins?"

"Speaking," I replied.

"Oh good. Well, my name isn't Mary. It's Detective Constable Matthews of the Manchester Constabulary."

"And what can I do for you?" I asked.

"We'd like to have a word with you if we may."

"Regarding what?" I asked, guardedly.

"We found a body in the Ship Canal yesterday, Mr Collins. DS McClusky is very anxious to talk to you about it."

I sighed and looked at my watch. "Fifteen minutes be OK?"

"Yes, that would be fine," he said. "You know where the station is don't you?" and with that sarcastic comment he hung up. I sat there for a few moments staring at my desk. Of all the people they could have chosen to head up this enquiry the one person I did not want to see was Detective Superintendent Ted McClusky.

I drove to the station, parked my car, took a deep breath, squared my shoulders, walked in and asked for DC Matthews.

The desk clerk, obviously not a man used to the perplexing complexities of high technology struggled manfully with the internal telephone system for about ten minutes then, by some fortuitous accident seemed to get the right number.

Eventually Matthews appeared, showed me into

McClusky's office and took a seat. The office was grubby and small and unfriendly and had a peculiar, not quite definable smell: exactly like McClusky except that McClusky wasn't small: he was enormous. He was the same height as me but fat with fair hair, a red face and small, piggy, bloodshot eyes. He didn't bother to stand or shake hands or offer me a nice cup of tea and a digestive biscuit. He just sat behind his desk, his jacket over the back of his chair and his hands behind his head revealing two large dark damp patches of sweat under his armpits.

McClusky hadn't changed one bit since the day I'd first met him seven years ago when I'd left the comparative comfort of Police Training School for the delights of the Greater Manchester Police Force. He'd made no attempt whatever to conceal his absolute contempt for the poor saps he was supposed to be helping with their training and he'd positively hated me right from the very start. Even though it wasn't easy I tried not to take it too personally: McClusky hated everybody. McClusky was one of those guys who join the force because it gives them a legitimate reason to kick in doors, beat up suspects and generally act in a way which would get you ten years if you didn't happen to be wearing a blue uniform. In those days McClusky had been in the uniformed branch but since then he'd moved over to the CID basically, or so it was rumoured so that he could now do all the above in plain clothes, thus making life even more fun.

It was like being taken back seven years as he sat behind his desk, leered up at me and sneered, "Well, well, if it isn't big bad Tom Collins, Manchester's answer to Mike Hammer. Right Collins, you've got some explaining to do. There's a body in the water under the Barton Bridge just like you said. Been dead two days or so, so it looks like your informant really did see what happened. Now, you'll give me his name and address and you'll do it now or we'll throw you in a cell for obstructing the police in the course of their investigations."

"Look McClusky, that's privileged information as you well know, but I'm willing to give you my informant's name on two conditions."

"You don't give me conditions, Collins. We don't make deals with prats like you," he snarled. "Now I'm giving you thirty seconds to tell me what you know or else.."

"Or else what?" I interrupted. "Or else you'll find a sound-proof cell and a bit of rubber hosepipe? Go on then McClusky. I'll make sure it's in every newspaper in England. How a public-hearted citizen reported a horrible crime and your response was to beat the crap out of him."

There was a silence. McClusky leaned over the desk and I could smell last night's drink on his breath. At least I assumed it was from the previous night unless of course McClusky had decided to dispense with the milk at breakfast time and taken to pouring a couple of Boddington's on his Corn Flakes. "Don't play games with me Collins," he hissed. "Now, what's your bloody conditions?"

"Was there a robbery at a pub somewhere around the murder scene on Tuesday night?" I asked.

McClusky thought for a moment, then nodded his head. "Yes," he said. "The Green Man. Somebody robbed the till and stole four cases of whisky and a valuable computer."

I grinned as I thought of Wally trying to escape on his bike with two cases of whisky under each arm and a computer balanced on his head. "Well I suggest you go

73

back to the Green Man and arrest the landlord for insurance fraud, McClusky," I said. "It was two bottles of whisky, not four cases, and there was no computer. Anyhow that's not the point. The guy who saw the murder was the person who robbed The Green Man. He'll talk to you on two conditions. The first is that you guarantee you won't prosecute him for the theft. The second is that you don't lay a finger on him. You treat him just like any other citizen who's helping you with your enquiries, and there's to be a lawyer present at all times."

McClusky stared pure hatred at me, then rose to his feet and lumbered out of the room. Five minutes later he returned. "OK, it's a deal," he said. "Now who is it?"

"Sorry, McClusky," I said. "I'll take Hemshall's word, and no one else's." I smiled sweetly at him. "Not that I don't trust you of course Mr McClusky. Nothing personal."

I saw his shoulders tense and his right fist closing and for a moment I thought he was going to hit me, but he stood up and two minutes later I was being ushered into the office of Dennis Hemshall, Chief Constable of the Greater Manchester Police. He stared at me from behind his desk. I'd seen him just once previously, when he'd made an impressive speech to the new recruits at the training school, all about upholding moral standards and streets safe for citizens to walk down. Streets safe to walk down? In Manchester on a Saturday night? I doubted that he'd remember my face but if not I was sure McClusky would be only too keen to remind him that I was the wimp who hadn't made the grade.

Hemshall looked at me from his comfortable chair behind his large executive desk.

"Good morning Mr Collins," he said. "Firstly I must thank you for the information. However, as I'm sure you realize, it's imperative that we talk to the eye-witness. You know of course that in cases like this we can compel you to disclose what you know."

"Yes," I replied, "and it takes time and effort and lawyers and I don't think stealing a couple of bottles from a pub is something that really matters when you're looking at what may well be some kind of Chinese gang murder. In any case all it will do in the future is that in cases like this whoever sees something will just ignore it. At least this thief had the conscience to come forward. In any case the pub landlord's every bit as bent as the guy who robbed his pub."

Hemshall stared at me. "What do you mean, Chinese gang murder?" he asked.

When I'd reported the case I hadn't mentioned the Chinese angle. I didn't want anyone getting needlessly excited if it turned out that what Wally had seen was just someone dumping an old fridge or a sofa.

"My informant says the three guys who threw our man in the water were Chinese."

Hemshall raised an eyebrow, pursed his lips and looked at McClusky.

"Mr Collins, we'll take your informant's assistance into full consideration in dealing with the burglary. Other than that I can't promise anything."

"No deal," I said. "As you may or may not know I used to be in the force Mr Hemshall and I know perfectly well that that's the standard line you give anyone who won't co-operate. I also know it doesn't mean a damn thing. I've told my informant that he gets a guarantee that you won't

75

prosecute him and that McClusky won't beat him up. You give me that guarantee, I give you his name."

Hemshall thought for a few minutes then he said, "Very well, Mr Collins we have a deal. No prosecution. No strong-arm stuff."

I nodded my head. "Wally Holden," I said. "I think you know where he lives."

"Holden," snarled McClusky but Hemshall raised a hand and he fell silent.

"Is he certain these men were Chinese?" he said. "It was late at night. How could he tell?"

"Wally Holden's got 20/20 night vision," I said. "Comes from all those years of breaking and entering in the dark. He swears he got a good look in the moonlight and he swears they were Chinese."

As I was leaving I heard footsteps behind me and a great heavy hand grabbed my shoulder.

"One of these days, Collins," grated McClusky, "I'm going to sort you out good and proper."

"And a good day to you too, Mr McClusky. Don't drink too much lunch," I said.

I called Wally on my mobile and told him the deal. When he started whining I shut down the phone, climbed into the Escort and drove back to the office. I had a couple of calls to make.

Back at the office there was just one message on the answerphone. It was from Wally Holden saying that he was hiding in the pub and would only go to the police if I went with him. I walked back to my car and drove to The Red Lion, Wally's local. I picked up Wally who'd obviously been there for a long time, drove him to the police station and dumped him on the desk clerk.

"Aren't you coming in then, Mr Collins," he asked, his red eyes pleading at me from beneath his cap.

"Wally," I said, "the state you're in now you've no need to worry. They could hit you with McClusky's desk and you wouldn't feel a thing." I left him gibbering with terror and smelling like a second-rate brewery and drove back to the office.

*

I had lunch at my desk, wondering exactly what it was that Wally Holden had witnessed and what connection it might have to my enigmatic, sexy little Chinese client and her enigmatic, sexy little Chinese cousin. I called Bill.

"Bill," I said, "have they identified the body they found in the Ship Canal?"

There was a short silence. "I'm not sure if I'm supposed to tell you this, Tom but," he paused for a moment, "oh what the hell, it'll probably be in the newspapers tomorrow anyway. The guy's name is Charles Nguyen, otherwise Nguyen Van Duc, otherwise Cheesewire Charlie."

"Cheesewire Charlie?" I said.

"On account of his hobby. Strangling people with a cheese-wire. He was what they call an office-bearer in an outfit called The Heavenly Tigers. Know who they are?"

"No," I said.

"One of the big American Vietnamese gangs. Especially violent, extremely nasty. Anyway when we pulled him out of the Ship Canal he was weighed down with about fifty kilos of chains and his face would have been unrecognizable even if he hadn't been in the water. They beat the shit out of him, and for good measure they

77

chopped off three of his fingers. We don't know why he was here or what he was doing, but we think he might have been trying to put something together with Hamilton Liu. Whatever it was it must have gone badly wrong."

"How do you connect him with Hamilton Liu?"

"Guess the last place he visited before he vanished."

"The Little Sisters of the Poor?" I asked.

I could almost see Bill's wide grin down the phone. "The Yin and Yang Club," he said.

I paused for a moment, the receiver in my hand. "Bill," I said, "you say this guy was from one of the big American gangs. Where from, exactly?"

"Chicago," he replied.

"Thanks, Bill," I said. "I owe you." I slowly replaced the receiver and sat in thought for a few moments, then picked up the phone again and called Janet Wu.

"Hello," she breathed into the phone. I've heard about come-to-bed eyes but that voice was something else. If you could have bottled and sold it you'd make a fortune.

I asked her how she was and she told me she was fine and so on and so forth. Then she asked if I'd made any progress.

"Did Angel ever talk about an old friend of hers in Manchester, a girl called Meredith Tang?" I asked.

"No, I don't think so," Janet replied.

"Now called Meredith Liu," I continued.

"There was a silence. "Liu?" said Janet.

"Yes. She married a guy thought to be one of the biggest racketeers in Manchester," I said.

There was another silence. "No, I don't think I heard of her," said Janet slowly, and I could tell just from the way she spoke that she was lying to me.

78

"So what will you do now then, Tom?" she cooed.

"I'll have a word with her and let you know what happens," I said and put down the phone. I was absolutely sure that the name Liu meant something to the lovely Ms Wu and even though I might be a lousy detective it seemed to me that there were just too many coincidences piling up in what at first had looked a perfectly straightforward case.

I pulled out the picture of Angel Wong. Angel was Chinese. She was from Chicago. Janet Wu was Chinese. She was from Chicago. The dead man in the Ship Canal was Vietnamese. He was from Chicago. And one of Angel's closest friends was married to a violent Chinese gangster.

So why would there be some kind of Vietnamese hitman wandering around in Manchester? Why had Angel Wong left her husband and exactly why was Janet Wu looking for her? Who had murdered Cheesewire Charlie and why? And did I think it would significantly improve the life expectancy and pension prospects of some nosy private eye who got caught up in whatever the hell was going on here?

Dump the case, Tom, I told myself.

Yes, I replied, *but what about that five grand bonus?*

Reluctantly I agreed that five grand was not something I could afford to forget about but the part of me watching these negotiations, the part that told the truth, knew perfectly well that the reason I didn't turn round and walk away had an awful lot to do with a tight black dress, a figure to kill for and a voice that I can still hear now sometimes in the dark reaches of the night when the wind lashes the rain against my window in the wee small hours of the morning.

Chapter Nine

*I*t was a cold bright sunny Chicago morning, one of those blue-sky winter mornings when the city looks clean and fresh, the heavens as blue and empty as a chorus girl's eyes and the Chicago wind cuts through you like an open razor.

She was a real classy babe, one who knew how to walk and what to wear and which knife to use to cut the crust off of her smoked salmon sandwiches.

She was wearing a little white hat, a little white dress, little white shoes and a big white diamond the size of a cocktail cherry on her wedding finger. Jake had seen her somewhere before but he couldn't place it.

Faced with so much class Jake felt it only reasonable to take his feet off the desk.

"Yeah?" he asked politely.

She sat down. "I want you to find out what my husband's up to," she said.

Jake had heard those same words a thousand times in a thousand different ways but they always meant the same thing. He'd never been able to figure out why the only guys who cheated on their wives were the ones who had great-looking wives in the first place.

He'd had every colour, shade, variety and character of dame sitting in front of him with the same speech, and the one thing they all had in common was that Jake would have slept with them: every one of them. Quite a few he had too, but that was several other stories.

Jake pulled his notepad in front of him and waited.

"My name's Eleanor Mann," she said and suddenly Jake knew exactly where he'd seen her. On the front page of half of Chicago's newspapers. Her husband was a real estate tycoon, a wide, easy-talking nasty piece of work called Frankie who had built, bought or cheated his way into most of the tallest buildings in the heart of Chicago.

Frankie Mann was probably the biggest womaniser in Chicago. If Mrs Mann wanted evidence all she had to do was pick up any of the tabloids and cut out the pictures of Frankie dancing with some actress at three in the morning, or leaving some hotel with a Playboy centrefold, a big grin on his face and a statement to the waiting photographers that they'd been discussing some private business.

Eleanor was Frankie's third wife or maybe fourth, Jake couldn't keep up with it. She must surely have known what she was getting herself into.

"I'm worried, real worried," she said. "I think Frankie's getting in over his head. He's mixing with some bad people and I just have this feeling." She twisted her little white handbag in her perfectly manicured hands.

"Mrs Mann," said Jake, "with respect, Frankie's hardly the kind of guy who does business with nuns and preachers. I think he's pretty used to taking care of himself."

"I'll pay you twenty bucks an hour, plus expenses," she said.

For that kind of money Jake didn't give a damn whether Frankie was doing business with the devil.

*

I looked through my bedroom curtains. Nothing had changed. I shaved and showered and made myself a coffee. Maisie's card was sitting staring at me and it started me thinking about her, that strange, fierce old lady who'd been the only friend I had. In all the time I knew her I never once heard her talk about brothers, sisters, family members, her life before she somehow ended up in Manchester. The only time I did ask her I wished devoutly that I hadn't.

It was just a few days after she'd picked me up in the street, me just a kid sitting in her front parlour looking at the picture on her wall of a young, laughing woman and a shy man, standing stiff and embarrassed for the photographer. I wiped the cake crumbs from my mouth and asked, "Was that you when you were young, Auntie Maisie?"

She laughed and her eyes misted over as she said softly, "Yes, young Tom, that was me."

Another photograph showed the same man wearing a peaked cap and a uniform, and I asked her what had happened to him. She didn't answer; she just took out a bottle of gin and sat there staring into the distance with the tears rolling down her face. I was bewildered and didn't know what I'd done wrong. "I'm sorry, Auntie Maisie."

She pulled me to her and sat me on her knee and said, "Not as sorry as I am, Tom."

It was the only time I ever saw Maisie drunk, and afterwards she took the picture down. Even at that age I'd known never to ask her again.

I finished my coffee and drove to the office.

The rain was still falling as I parked the car and walked to the office. Normally I left my umbrella in the car and got soaked walking to and from the office or I left my umbrella in the office and got soaked walking to the car. This time it was in the office, and as I sat dripping water onto my desk I decided, not for the first time, that it would be a smart move to buy a second umbrella. It had only been seven years.

As usual there was nothing on the answering machine or the computer. I wondered how Wally had got one with my favourite policeman and if McClusky had kept his promise not to beat him to death with his truncheon. I picked up the phone and called him. Normally I wouldn't have bothered calling Wally in the mornings - his late night activities mean he generally doesn't wake up till the pubs open, but this time I kept the phone ringing till eventually he answered.

He complained that down at the station they'd kept him sitting in a room for two hours while they forced black coffee down him trying to sober him up. Eventually he'd given them the same story he'd told me. Then they'd left him going through mug shots of known Chinese criminals but as he said, it had been dark and he'd been some distance away. "The other thing, Mr Collins," he said to me, "not that I'm like a racialist or anything, but all I could really say was that they had black hair. They all look the same to me especially in the dark."

"And how are you getting on with my old pal Ted McClusky?" I asked.

"'E 'asn't changed a bit, Mr Collins. 'E's 'orrible, just 'orrible. He keeps tellin' me that he'll put me behind bars if it takes 'im the rest of his life. He keeps leanin' over me and shouting in me ear and tellin' me I ain't fit to live in a dog kennel."

"Has he beaten you up or threatened you, Wally?"

"Well, not exactly," he conceded.

"You should be happy," I told him. "From McClusky

83

that's the equivalent of patting you on the back and sticking a gold star on your witness statement."

I hung up, picked up the address given me Chris Bateson and headed out to talk to Meredith Liu. Maybe she was sheltering her old friend Angel Wong. Maybe she'd tell me where she was hiding. Maybe Janet Wu would be so grateful she'd invite me to snuggle down with her between the silken sheets of the king-sized bed of her hotel suite.

Hope springs eternal in the human breast. So said Alexander Pope and he should know. He was a four-foot high hunchback who spent his life writing poetry. He should have been a detective.

*

Dennis Hemshall, Chief Constable of the Greater Manchester Police Force was a man who enjoyed his breakfast. Now he sat at his desk in a rare mood of contentment. Though men were still beating up their wives, old ladies were still being burgled and mugged, drugs were still being dealt to schoolchildren, drunks were still hurling each other through shop windows and the general population was still being stabbed, shot and beaten over the head by blunt instruments, by Manchester standards things were generally calm and peaceful. Apart from the puzzling business of the Vietnamese gangster there hadn't even been a decent murder in the past few days.

As he was contemplating his day's labours his secretary walked in with a courier package. "I thought you'd like to see this at once, sir," she said.

Hemshall looked curiously at the parcel in front of him.

Even at his exalted rank it wasn't every day of the week that he received a *Top Secret* and *Personal and Confidential* direct from the Home Office.

The type-written message told him that three days previously a woman had taken a flight from Chicago to Manchester via New York. They were to find her, arrest her on any charge they could think of - crossing the street against the lights, wearing too much lipstick, absolutely anything - and hold her incommunicado. As soon as they found her he was to call the man who had signed the order. The Chief Constable was livid. The damned cheek of these people who sat in their offices in Whitehall, drawing their huge salaries for doing absolutely nothing. He, Dennis Hemshall, ran the Manchester constabulary, not some faceless civil servant sitting cosily in London. He was supposed to uphold the law, not break it, and he was damned if he was going to kowtow to some Whitehall mandarin, however senior.

OK, he'd look into the situation, but that was all. He wasn't to be dictated to by anyone, including the Home Office, and frankly, despite all this wonderful, new so-called fraternal co-operation between the world's law-enforcement agencies, he didn't give a damn about the Chicago police. He looked again at the information pack in front of him and the photograph of the person he was supposed to arrest. The Chief Constable whistled softly. She was a looker by anyone's standards.

She was twenty-seven years old; ethnic Chinese; five feet five; one hundred and ten pounds and an American citizen. Her name in Chinese was Wong Ka Wei. In English: Angel Wong

As I drove through the gates the first thing that struck me were the security cameras that turned and followed me along the driveway. I parked my Escort behind a 700 series BMW and tried to ignore the frenzied barking of two huge rottweilers leaping and drooling and tugging at their chains. I didn't think they wanted their tummies tickled.

A cold wind was blowing ragged clouds across the sky as I climbed out and rang the bell. The door was opened by a slim, muscular Chinese, barefoot, wearing black track-suit trousers and a tight white T-shirt from the sleeves of which tattoos of writhing blue dragons peeped out at me. He was around thirty-five years old and he looked as if he'd spent most of that time beating inquisitive detectives into a coma. He kept his right hand in his trouser pocket the whole time and I could see he had a gun or a cosh in there. Either that or what I had heard about Chinese men not being particularly well-endowed was spectacularly wrong.

"What do you want?" he said.

"I'm looking for Meredith Liu," I said. "I just want to ask her if she's heard anything from an old friend of hers called Angel Wong. They studied together at the University."

He stared at me as if he was trying to work out which part of me to pulverize first. Then he slammed the door in my face leaving me standing on the mat. It said Welcome.

I stood waiting, praying that the rottweilers' chains would hold until eventually the door opened again. "Are you same guy who came see Mr Liu's father yesterday?" he asked.

I nodded.

"Mrs Liu has heard nothing from Miss Wong for years," he said.

"Does she know where she might have gone, any other mutual friends in the Manchester area?" I asked, though I knew perfectly well I was wasting my time.

The Chinese guy looked at me. He took my arm in a muscular grip. "Do you see those dogs?" he asked me. I nodded.

"We feed them twice a day. Raw meat. It's quite a sight. You'd be amazed how hungry they get. We always get a little worried that one day they'll get loose and some poor innocent visitor will end up as a dog's dinner. Do you understand?"

Then, presumably because he couldn't think of anything else to talk about he slammed the door in my face again.

I took another look at the greeting on the mat then climbed back into my car. I was tempted to drive into the BMW and reverse into the rottweilers, but instead I negotiated my way carefully out of the driveway and drove back to my office.

I sat there at my desk and what I doodled on my executive notebook looked like this:

Conclusions so far:

Meredith Liu's parents are lying

The Chinese guy in Hamilton Liu's house is lying

Janet Wu is lying

Questions:

Do the Lius have something to hide?

Are they hiding Angel Wong? If so, why?

*What's the connection between Cheese-wire
Charlie, Janet Wu, Hamilton Liu and Angel Wong?*

If I find Angel, will Janet Wu take me to bed?

I thought fairly deeply about that last point, picked up my phone, called the Ritz and asked for Room 1501. That voice drifted down the phone, doing no good whatever for my state of unwilling celibacy. It was aural sex. Pure and simple. "Can we talk?" I asked.

"Sure," she replied. "Come on over." Before I could say anything more she hung up. I walked down to my car. This time the note on my windscreen offered me a discount price on a willing Latvian student, nineteen years old and never been touched. The handbill didn't specify whether the Latvian student was male or female. I guess in these unisex days it doesn't matter. I drove to the Ritz.

I was manoeuvring through the traffic when my trouser pocket started to vibrate. Someone was calling my mobile. Either that or the penis enlargement surgery was working. I didn't need to look at the caller's number to know who it was. I took a deep breath and hit the button.

"Hello," I said.

"Hi, Tom. It's me."

Driving a manual car through the centre of Manchester during an awkward conversation with your ex-girlfriend isn't easy. Without one of those fancy hands-free gadgets it's also illegal. When I'd almost rammed the car in front trying to change down left-handed, hold the phone in my right and steer with willpower and blind faith, I said, "Mary, it's impossible to hold a conversation on this phone and drive my car at the same time. I'll call you back in a few minutes, OK?"

There was a short silence, then: "You don't really change much, do you, Tom? When are you going to call me?" Her voice had dropped by about twenty degrees.

"Soon." I narrowly missed a forty-foot trailer truck. "Tonight. Look, I have to go."

I shut the phone down and concentrated on getting to my appointment in one piece.

*

The Ritz looks like the Victoria and Albert Museum except that most of the exhibits at the Ritz are older and covered with more dust. Outside stood an impressive array of Bentleys and Rollers. I resisted the temptation to valet park the Escort and stuck it on a meter instead.

The doorman looked as if he'd been kicked out of India in 1947 for being overdressed. He disdainfully threw open the huge glass door, looking pointedly past me as if it really wasn't his fault I'd managed to get in.

I walked in across the marble floors, past the unmanned Reception desk and the signs that said *Nous Parlons Francais, Noi Parliamo Italiano* and *Wir Sprechen Deutsch*. I looked for

89

the sign that said *English Spoken Here* but they didn't have one, presumably because no one spoke English. I walked unchallenged through the lobby and took the lift to the top floor of the hotel, the 15th. My heart was pounding like a schoolboy on a first date as I rang the bell.

Janet answered the door dressed only in the hotel's bathrobe. With her wet hair swirling about her face and shoulders and the loosely-belted robe showing off her lovely, dark skin she looked as if she'd just walked away from a photo shoot for *The World's 50 Sexiest Women*.

"Drink?" she asked.

Dumbly I shook my head. The room was a hell of a lot better than any hotel room I'd ever been in. I looked around at the antique-looking furniture, TV hidden cosily away in a wooden cabinet, cocktail bar, oriental carpets. The door to the bedroom was open and I could see the bed reflected in an antique mirror on the wall. It was bigger than my whole apartment. The bed, that is, not just the bedroom.

Janet Wu draped herself carelessly on the sofa and asked, "So, any news?"

I tried hard to pretend I wasn't interested in staring down the front of her dressing-gown and tried to remember why I was there. Eventually it came to me and I told her all about Hamilton Liu and his probable criminal/triad/murderous business activities. All the time I was watching her carefully. That is I was watching her face carefully. It wasn't easy. However it did seem to me that news about Hamilton Liu didn't come as a particular surprise. Then I told her about my visit to their house and the warm reception I'd received.

She sat up on the couch, the dressing gown gaping

invitingly. "Tom," she breathed, "Angel's my oldest friend. If anything happened to her I'd never forgive myself. Do you think she's in some kind of trouble?"

"No Janet, not at all, unless you can think of any reason why she might be staying with a violent Chinese gangster whose home is guarded by armed triads and rottweiler dogs," I snapped.

She gave me the soulful eyes treatment. "You're not scared, are you, Tom?"

Scared? Me? Tom Collins, the famous private eye? In the space of a few short hours I'd been confronted by savage dogs, muscular tattooed thugs, a dead Vietnamese gangster whose hobby was strangling people with a cheesewire, and Detective Superintendent Ted McClusky. So no, I wasn't scared. Terrified might have been a better term.

"Of course I'm not scared," I said using my best laconic, tough-guy detective impersonation. "I'm just keeping you informed as promised."

She aimed those great innocent eyes at me like searchlights and rose from the sofa. She spread her arms towards me and the cord holding her bathrobe loosely together slipped to the floor.

Like an automaton I walked across the room, took her in my arms and moulded my lips to hers while my hands caressed her small, perfect breasts. After a breathless few seconds she pulled away.

"I'm sorry, Tom, I just can't," she said.

I grabbed hold of her again but she pushed me away. "Not now, Tom," she said. "Of course I find you terribly attractive, but right now I am so worried about Angel that I couldn't possibly think of my own pleasure."

To be honest it wasn't her own pleasure that was uppermost in my mind but it seemed churlish to mention this when she was obviously so distressed about her best friend.

"No," she said. "Find Angel" - she looked down as if puzzled that her robe was loose, smiled coyly at me staring at that lovely body, put her hands on her hips and tossed back her head - "and then it's all yours, Mr big tough detective."

I took a long, long look before I turned my back on those soulful, calculating eyes, not to mention the rest of the package, and left the room closing the door carefully behind me.

I climbed into my car, stared into the Manchester night and wondered what I had got myself into. For Jake Fist it would have been par for the course, but I wasn't Jake Fist, and I wasn't deluded enough to think that a woman like Janet Wu had fallen for my manly physique, casual familiarity with the world's rich and famous and enormous bank balance.

Still, it didn't stop me staring though my windscreen in the rainy evening, thinking of her standing there, hands on her hips, flaunting that perfect body and hearing her voice over the sound of the wipers like a caress saying, "It's all yours, Mr big tough detective."

Chapter Ten

*J*ake called Tanya. "I'm gonna be late honey. Business," he said.

"What kind of business is this, Jake?" she asked. Any other woman had asked Jake a question like that he'd have put the phone down and found himself another woman, but he said, "It's a case, honey. Somebody messing around with the wrong people."

"Be careful, Jake," she said, and Jake said, "I will," and Tanya whispered, "I love you, Jake."

Jake put down the phone, picked up his cherry red Chevy convertible and drove out to Frankie Mann's place. He parked his car, leaned back in his seat, tilted his hat over his eyes and waited.

Frankie Mann had considerately bought himself a dark green Cadillac about as big as a city block, which made him a very easy target to follow. Jake tucked in behind him as the chauffeur drove carefully down Central heading south. It was dark now, and cold, with the wind blowing in off Lake Michigan and flurries of snow in the air.

Frankie's Cadillac turned left onto Garfield and Jake wondered what business a real estate developer would have in Little Italy. Eventually the car pulled up outside Antonio's, otherwise known as Fat Tony's. Frankie's driver hurried round the front of the car, opened the door for Frankie like he was royalty or something and Frankie strolled into the restaurant.

Your choice of restaurant depended who you were in the mob and which mob you were in. Fat Tony's was one of those hangouts with good food and long-time waiters who saw and heard nothing except the size of the tip. Tony had two guys permanently stationed by the door with heavy calibre machinery, just in case someone tried to come in without making a reservation or accidentally fired a machine gun through the window while his customers were eating their capelloni.

Jake ran through the list of hoods he knew who used Fat Tony's and tried to work out who Frankie could be meeting and why.

He stuck the car in first, slowly circling the block and then he grinned. He'd had three possible candidates in mind and it looked as if he'd chosen right. Two guys, one big and wide and looking even bigger in his heavy coat, and one skinny, dark, with thin lips and mean, vicious eyes were climbing out of a big black limo.

"Well, well, the Bear and the Weasel," said Jake to himself.

He parked the car and walked into a pizza place where he was reasonably sure that no one who used it particularly wanted to shoot him, sat down and ordered himself a hot pizza with extra pepperoni and extra peppers and a half a bottle of chianti.

The Bear was Bruno Scarletti, the top mobster in central and west Chicago and right now in an uneasy truce with the guys who ran the east side. Willie Malone was his leg-man, a crazy half-Irish half-Italian who'd kill you without thinking about it. He'd been known to take a knife to anyone who used his nickname to his face: Willie the Weasel.

So what would they be doing talking with Frankie Mann?

Jake finished his pizza and his wine and ordered coffee. He gave it a half-hour then paid, left and started to cruise the streets, waiting to see whether Frankie went home to the loving arms of his dear lady wife or had something else on his mind.

*

94

It was probably some deep-seated Freudian longing for something Oriental. In any case I bought myself a Chinese take-away, took it back to my apartment and sat there sucking on egg foo yong, spare ribs and fried rice. I stuck Part One of *The Godfather* on the DVD but I couldn't concentrate at all on the screen: all I could think about was Janet Wu. Every sensible piece of me told me to drop the whole business, but like most men, it isn't my sensible bits that have the final say. I stared mechanically at my TV set, briefly wondering if the Latvian student was free for an hour or so. Then it came to the part in the movie where they strangle the guy in the front seat of the car. That got me to thinking about Cheesewire Charlie and I picked up the empty food trays, threw them into the bin and paced up and down my room wondering what I should do.

There was only one bit of this case that I liked the look of; the bit in room 1501 at the Ritz and if ever Jake Fist had seen trouble in letters twenty feet high, she was it. Bill had warned me to stay away, Chris Bateson had warned me to stay away and a Chinese thug had threatened to feed me to his rottweilers if I didn't stay away. I still fancied Janet Wu, I still fancied Angel Wong and I still fancied up-grading my lousy DVD player though it might be a bit difficult to operate the remote control if they cut three fingers off my hand and threw me in the Ship Canal. Eventually I picked up the phone. There was only one sensible course of action which was to call Janet Wu and tell her I was off the case.

So that's why I called directory enquiries and asked them for the address of The Yin and Yang Club.

I'm a fairly big guy and the gym keeps me in pretty good shape. My hair's cut short and I often get mistaken for a policeman, which can have its advantages and disadvantages.

I was pretty sure the Yin and Yang Club wouldn't be too keen on having someone they thought might be a copper walking through the door. (It's different if there's a bunch of you. They know that a gang of off-duty cops drink more and spend more than sailors on shore leave, but that's another matter), so I decided to disguise myself as a visiting businessman looking for a good time. I tried out my American accent, (sort of Humphrey Bogart with a bit of Al Pacino thrown in) and decided it wasn't too bad. I had one good suit, a genuine almost-new Armani that I'd picked up from a closing down sale at a second-hand shop. It very nearly fitted.

I chose a white open-necked shirt and my only good pair of shoes, drove down to Chinatown and parked in a multi-storey which was open twenty four hours. I figured I might be late.

The bouncer stopped me at the door of the club and I gave him the 'hi there I'm in from the States and looking for a bit of action, know-what-I-mean' spiel.

"You need to be a member," he said, in the dead, flat monotone of someone who isn't really sure where he is, whether he's alive or dead.

"So how much is membership?"

"Twenty quid including one drink," he replied.

I gave him the money and he pushed a ledger at me.

I wrote: *Name: Jake Fist*

   Place of Residence: Chicago, USA.

I sat at a table in a large dark room and looked at the drink list. The main reason they keep these places so dark is to make sure you can't read the prices. They had the world's finest tomato juice (it must have been – it was certainly the world's most expensive) but Jake Fist would probably set himself on fire before he'd order a tomato juice so I ordered a Jack Daniels and water.

When it arrived I wasn't sure whether to pour the water into the drink or to take it neat and wash it down, so eventually I poured half the water into the bourbon. As I raised the glass to my lips I realized that this was the first time I'd ever actually tasted the stuff that Jake Fist put away by the bucketful. I took a cautious sip. It wasn't bad. I took another. To be honest it was pretty good.

The room was decorated in that style known as Chinese bad taste. Golden plastic dragons; red paint; glittery cheap chandeliers. Business didn't look to be too good. The room was empty apart from a couple of tough-looking Chinese guys deep in conversation over a bottle of brandy and four drunk guys in suits and ties with half-dressed bimbos on their laps ignoring the signs on the wall that said you weren't allowed to touch the girls.

The music was loud and monotonous, two bored half-naked girls dancing around chromium poles at the sides of an empty stage. I was wondering exactly what I was supposed to be doing there when a pretty, skinny little Chinese girl dressed in two pieces of string came over, sat uninvited on my lap and began to wriggle.

It had been bad enough watching Janet Wu taking her clothes off. This I didn't need. I tapped her on the shoulder and said into her ear, "Will you please stop that."

She turned to look at me and said, "Why? You don't like?"

"Yes, yes, I like," I said.

She grinned at me and said, "Yes, I know." It must have been like sitting on a tent pole.

"Can't we just talk?" I pleaded.

"OK," she shrugged. "But it's same price."

We talked nonsense for a while and I bought her a drink. "You want another?" she asked, pointing at my empty glass. I hadn't even realized I'd finished it.

I shrugged my shoulders. "Why not?" I wondered what Janet Wu would say when all this lot went on my expenses. I figured she could afford it.

The dancer's name was Candy. "Sweet to eat," she whispered in my ear, giggling.

"So what you do?" she asked me.

I was about to give her my 'American in town on a business visit' story then I decided that I might as well tell her the truth and see what happened. "I'm a private detective," I said.

Her eyes widened and for a moment I thought she'd run, but she just looked at me for a while then said very softly, "Can you help me?"

I replied. "It depends if you can help me."

"How?"

"I'm looking for someone. A Chinese woman. I think she might be hiding out somewhere around here." She looked at me in silence. "I'll pay," I said.

She sat on my lap, motionless thank God. "Can you meet me when I finish work here?" she whispered.

"What time is that?" I replied.

"Three o'clock."

Three o'clock! I looked at my watch. It was half past eleven. I didn't fancy hanging around in this dismal dump for another three and a half hours.

She saw my expression. "Or you can buy me," she said.

I asked her what she meant.

"You can take me out from the club. It cost fifty pounds. After that you can negotiate with me what you want and how much to pay."

"OK," I said and she stood up and walked away to talk to someone at the bar.

Second Chinese takeaway of the evening I thought. I threw down the rest of my second Jack Daniels, feeling it burn all the way down. I could see why a bored private eye might take to this stuff.

I signalled for my bill. I wondered why it took two of them, one waiter and one gorilla in a black bow tie, to bring it over. When I saw it I knew. Reluctantly I peeled off two more of the notes that Janet Wu had given me and asked for a receipt.

The receipt said: *The Yin and Yang Chinese Restaurant and Night Club*. I suppose that made it easier for your businessman to claim as legitimate expenses from the company accountant than if it said: *Girlie Bar and Clip Joint*.

Candy appeared dressed in jeans, sweater and a shapeless black coat and we walked out into the night. I took her to the car park and sat her in the passenger seat.

She told me that she had been smuggled in illegally from China with her mother and brother. Her father had died in a mining accident and this was the only prospect they had.

Candy's mother was working as a cleaner, her brother packing stuff in a warehouse, and Candy… well, Candy was earning money any way she could.

They owed thousands of dollars to the guys who brought them in, and were paying off their debts as best they could. As if that wasn't enough they were charged a fortune for their rent, food, clothing and other costs, and unless they could come up with some quick money they were virtually slaves for life.

"Why don't you just go to the police?" I asked. She told me they'd just be sent back to China, and all the money they'd spent would be wasted. In any case they'd borrowed from friends and relatives in China, and they in turn were in hock to loan sharks, so if they didn't send a regular amount back their friends would get a beating if nothing worse.

I'd read about this kind of thing in the papers, but it still wasn't a pretty story. I asked her if she knew who was behind it, and she said it was the Lius although they were far too smart to get involved personally. Then she asked me who I was looking for. I passed her the picture of Angel Wong.

"She very beautiful," she said, and I agreed with her. She handed back the picture and I had the impression she knew more than she was saying.

"Her name's Angel and I think she's hiding in Manchester. I think she might be in some trouble and she's an old friend of your boss."

"My mother is a cleaner," said Candy. "She have many, many friends. The girls too. I will ask. And how much is she worth, this pretty Angel?"

"To you," I said, "five hundred: cash."

She looked at me in amazement. "How I know you tell the truth?" she said.

"I'm sorry, I don't have any guarantees," I said, "but when I make a promise I keep it."

She looked at me for a while. "How can I contact you?"

100

I opened the glove compartment, tore a slip of paper from the notebook I keep there and wrote down my name and mobile number. "Call me. Anytime," I said.

She took the slip of paper, looked at it for a moment, then folded it and slipped it into her purse. It was very dark and silent in the car park. Candy looked up at me. "So how you feel now?" she asked.

"Sorry?" I wondered what she meant.

She put her hand on the inside of my thigh and started to giggle. "I think long time since you have a girlfriend."

"No, er, it's OK," I said, weakly, but she was exploring now, and even though a part of me didn't want to go through with this another part was of a very different opinion.

"It's OK," she whispered. "For you is free."

I couldn't do it. It was one case where the flesh was willing – desperate might have been a better term – but the spirit was weak.

"No, Candy," I muttered, unwillingly.

"But why not?"

Reluctantly I took her hand away from my trousers. If she'd offered me a free demonstration of her professional skills before telling me her story, well, that may have been different but I just felt too ashamed to be another in the long line of those who exploited these poor, desperate people.

"So you don't think I pretty?" she asked.

"No, yes, look Candy yes I think you're pretty it's just that…"

Candy shrugged her shoulders, obviously totally unable to comprehend this odd behaviour, gave me a small, sad smile and opened the car door.

"See you later," she said.

I grabbed her by the hand and said; "I don't think it's safe for you to walk around here at this time of night. Come on, I'll drive you." Hell, under any normal circumstances I certainly wouldn't have been wandering around Chinatown on my own at this time of night, and I couldn't let this little skinny slip of a girl do so. I started the engine, drove out of the car park and Candy gave me directions. We headed south for a few minutes then, in a dingy, depressing side street she told me to stop.

It was dark and deserted. She put her hand on the handle of the door. "So what is really your name?" she asked.

"My name's Tom; Tom Collins," I replied. "I wrote it on the paper you put in your purse."

"In the club they told me your name was Jake Fist."

"But that was just a fake name. It doesn't mean anything," I stammered. "Sometimes, as a detective you have to give a false name."

She looked at me with that heart-breaking look that says, *I am seventeen years old and I have already heard all the lies in the world.*

"Goodnight then Tom, or Jake, or whoever you are," she said. She took a good look around before walking quickly away into the shadows. I don't know whether someone was out there, watching, but obviously she couldn't take the chance they'd seen me drop her off: start asking who I was.

I sat there, staring through the windscreen for a while. Part of me wanted to go grab Candy and get her to finish what she had started; the rest of me felt utterly ashamed of myself. Over it all I was furiously, terribly angry with the

102

people who traded the lives of these poor innocents. I put the Escort in gear and as I drove I tried to push away the sight of Candy's sad face by trying to think of a grateful Janet Wu slipping out of her bathrobe and walking towards me, naked with five thousand pounds in her hand.

I parked the car and went back to my flat. I locked the door, cleaned my teeth and collapsed into bed. I tried manfully to sleep but I just lay there in the darkness thinking about Candy and Janet Wu. That didn't help me sleep either. Eventually I fell into a kind of waking dream where I was sitting in my front room reading a good book when the doorbell rang. Standing at the door was a crestfallen Playboy model and three of her friends. Some heartless villain had stolen their handbags and all of their clothes leaving them completely naked except for their high-heeled shoes. They wanted me to investigate the crime but the dastardly criminal had taken all their money. They couldn't think how they could *possibly* pay me.

For some reason I didn't even once think of my promise to call Mary.

Chapter Eleven

*F*rankie's Cadillac eased into the traffic and moved north before he turned into Cemak, then West 22nd and pulled up in East Walton Place. He tossed his keys to the attendant and strolled through the double doors into the lobby.

Jake grinned. The Drake was one of the best hotels in Chicago and it didn't seem likely that Frankie was calling in for a quick cocktail on his way home.

Jake parked the car. He knew every desk clerk in every decent hotel in Chicago and quite a few in places that weren't quite so up-market as the Drake. It took him five minutes and five bucks to establish that Frankie had booked himself into room 1501 calling himself Johnny Harris, and that as yet there were no other guests in his room, male or female.

As Jake was pretty sure that Frankie would be expecting some chorus girl, and as he wasn't being paid to check out the amorous side of Frankie's activities, he decided to call it a night. He was heading across the lobby when he saw the doorman pulling open the huge glass doors. Jake looked at the guy coming through the doors, turned his back and walked swiftly into one of the phone booths. He took the phone off the hook pretending to make a call while the guy walked to the desk.

A couple of minutes later he put down the phone and buttoned the *same desk clerk.*

"The big guy, dark coat, fedora, just came in. Which room did he ask for?" The desk clerk stared at him. Jake slipped him another five spot and the desk clerk said, "He asked for Mr Harris' room, Mr Fist."

Jake drove home with a whole lot of questions in his head. Eleanor Mann was right that her husband was meeting with some dangerous people. First Bruno the Bear and Willie the Weasel; and unless Frankie had decided he preferred men in uniform to dames in their birthday suits, why would he be having a meeting late at night in a hotel room with Lew Kraski, the deputy chief of police?

*

I woke late and for a second I'd forgotten about Janet Wu and Angel and Candy but it didn't take long to remember. I had a headache from the drinks and I lay in bed and thought over my previous day. A beautiful naked woman; drinking Jack Daniels in a seedy nightclub; an exotic dancer on my lap; a missing woman who might or might not be hiding out with a bunch of vicious criminals and me in bed with a hangover. I was starting to feel like a real detective.

That was when I remembered I had promised to call Mary - twelve hours and two oriental women ago. The excitement I had been starting to feel was laid waste by the guilt. I checked my phone for rude messages. Nothing but the little light blinking to show the battery was running low. Should I call her? Arrange to meet? Did I really want to do this, revisit the memories of the complaints and the fights and the long accusing silences? It wasn't an easy decision to make on an empty stomach so I decided to put it off till after breakfast.

I shaved, showered and dressed and checked in at my usual café, but the bacon and greasy eggs and crisp fried black pudding and sausages didn't slide down so easily today. I sat there drinking far too much of their horrible, sweet thick coffee and thinking.

As a boy I'd had no clear idea what I wanted to do with my life. I'd been a pretty reasonable student but not good enough to go on to university and in any case I couldn't have afforded it. I'd not been too bad at sports either but nowhere close to good enough to make a living out of it.

Then when I was fourteen my mother had died. I guess my old man must have loved her in his own way, though he had some fairly strange ideas of how to demonstrate it. In any case after the funeral he went completely to pieces.

At least when she'd been alive he'd made a pretence of working, though he never lasted very long at anything, but afterwards he just signed on the dole, stayed at home slumped in front of the TV and drank away every penny that the government gave to him. Terry went away in disgust and joined the army and I was left on my own.

I did part-time jobs until the day came to leave school at fifteen and then I worked on various building sites where they laughed at me because I couldn't operate a pneumatic drill, didn't yell obscenities at every fat slag, schoolgirl and grandmother that walked past and wouldn't drink ten pints of beer every lunchtime.

Then I got a job in a bank, which I hated so profoundly that I felt ill every morning, standing waiting for the bus in the rain, and only kept because I dreaded having to stay at home with my father. I stuck it out for four years, even got myself promoted. Then one day some money disappeared and I was given the boot even though I knew absolutely nothing about it.

A few weeks later my father achieved his ambition of drinking himself into a six-by-two plot in the cemetery and I moved out of the council house and rented myself a flat. I was still only twenty-one. I worked in factories, department stores, anything to pay the rent until the day Bill signed us both up for the police.

Now I was approaching my thirty-first birthday and I still didn't have the faintest idea what I wanted to do when I grew up. In the meantime I was a private eye who didn't drink, didn't like violence, was afraid of walking around in the dark and whose career highlight to date had been busting a twelve-year-old kid with a dog-ransoming racket. Now that I had a real case, the kind of case for which I'd sent up prayers to Jake Fist, a case involving real gangsters with proper gangster names and stunning oriental molls, I was considering having a heart-to-heart with McClusky and abandoning it. So I sat there wondering what to do about Janet Wu and what to do about Mary and I thought it would probably be better to go find Wally, go with him to the Red Lion and drink myself unconscious.

At ten o'clock, after finishing my third cup of coffee and having come to absolutely no decisions about anything I paid the bill and walked down to my office. I thought of calling Janet Wu but what did I have to tell her? That I'd run up half my advance in a girlie joint? I decided I'd call her anyway, just to hear that voice but when I got through to her room there was no answer. Those rich bitches, I thought, never out of bed before lunchtime. I left my name and number and asked her to call me.

I booted up my PC and logged on to my e-mail. The in-box contained the usual exhortations from the usual suspects, and just one real message.

Tom,

> *You're a bastard. And a lily-livered, weak-kneed bastard at that. If you don't want to see me, why don't you just say so instead of pissing me about?*
> *Yours ever – your ex and forever ex girlfriend – the one you frequently said you were in love with, you miserable liar.*

> *P S You're also a rotten detective.*

I read it again – twice - to see if I could find some hidden declaration of love in there somewhere. I couldn't.

Mary thought she'd had a terrible childhood, though it didn't sound too bad to me. She was from a middle-class family down on the Sussex coast, and had grown up, in my view perfectly normally, with a father who retired to his study most nights with his books and a mother who cooked and washed and cleaned and doted on Mary's older brother. I could connect with that, but at least her father hadn't beaten her up twice a week when his horses didn't win.

She'd been sent to ballet classes and horse-riding classes and one of those holidays where you go and stay with a French family for a few weeks, but she said all of it was just to get her out of the way. As far as she was concerned she had been totally starved of any real love or affection. She should have tried living in our house.

She'd had half a dozen boyfriends but nothing worked out and at first we'd got on really well. She was

108

undeniably attractive and made love in a desperate, demented way that took me by surprise. I found it extremely sexy until I was so exhausted I had to keep stuffing myself with vitamin pills and pretending I was on late surveillance. We discussed our lousy childhoods, competing over whose parents were the worst, and even though I'm not really very good at the relationship sort of thing it did occur to me that slagging off our parents was not a particularly healthy basis on which to build a long-term future. When she reached the last time she'd shown her drawings to her mum and her mum couldn't be bothered to look at them, and when I ran out of times when my dad gave me a smack in the mouth, what else were we going to talk about?

I sat there composing e-mail apologies and lies. Eventually I picked up my office phone and called her number.

A voice said: "You have reached the offices of Grumble Fossit, Cluck and Snidgeley." After an electronic pause Mary's voice said, "Mary Gilroy," and the dalek continued, "is not available right now. Please leave your message after the tone."

"Mary," I said, "I'm really sorry about not calling you. I was just completely run off my feet. I'm not trying to upset you. Can we meet for lunch tomorrow?" I didn't feel up to an intimate dinner for two and Saturday lunchtime felt safe enough to avoid a plate of spaghetti in the face and/or sex in the car. I named a nice little Italian restaurant I knew she liked, and asked her to call me back. It was called Antonio's, or Fat Tony's; I had once taken her there for a ruinously expensive Valentine's Day dinner. Romantic Tom! I'd even bought her red roses.

*

They'd checked every hotel, boarding house and flophouse in Manchester, and no one had checked in using the name Angel Wong. None of the taxi drivers who served the airport remembered picking her up. She'd walked off the plane and vanished.

The bio data showed that she'd studied Management Sciences at the University of Manchester Institute of Science and Technology, so two DC's had gone over there to check known acquaintances, previous addresses, anything that might give them a lead. Now the Chief Constable was sitting behind his desk facing two nervous, sweating junior officers who were not used to speaking to someone of his exalted rank. "So, findings up to now please, gentlemen?" he asked.

DC Matthews reported that only two of Angel's Wong's known acquaintances were still resident in Manchester, one of whom was a harmless old lady whose daughter had married and gone off to Hong Kong. The other was married to a guy suspected of being the biggest gangster in the North of England. Matthews refrained from making any smart remarks about which of the two he thought might bear further investigation. The Chief Constable reflected that it was the second time that Hamilton Liu's name had cropped up in the last few days. Once in connection with the dead Vietnamese in the Ship Canal and now with the mysterious Angel Wong. He wondered whether he could get a warrant for a raid on Mr Liu's premises, not that he had any hard evidence.

"But there's something else, chief."

110

The Chief Constable was known for his equable temperament. He was unfailingly polite and courteous, hardly ever lost his temper or raised his voice and was said to be capable of dismembering a body with a smile on his face. Now he looked mildly at Matthews. "And what would that be?" he asked.

"There was someone else there yesterday, sir, asking the same questions. A local guy, said he was a private eye."

"What do you mean asking the same questions?"

"Same as us, sir. About this Angel Wong. Any friends, known acquaintances, possible addresses and so on and so forth."

"Did you get a name?"

"No, sir, they didn't think to ask, but we got a description. Sounds like Tom Collins, sir."

The Chief Constable looked at his watch. It was a few minutes after ten in the morning. Tom Collins, he thought, was popping up a little too often of late. "Ask DS McClusky to step in on your way out," he said.

Matthews and Pike - who had not uttered one single word in the entire interview - pushed back their chairs and headed gratefully out of the office.

*

I wandered over to my meeting table and idly played with the cars. One was a black and silver 1936 SS Jag Tourer, the other a red 1931 Cadillac V-16 roadster; but these were just cheap die-cast toys. At home I had a collection of model cars that I'd started on my ninth birthday; I'd bought some but mostly built them from kits and lovingly painted them. Everyone's got to have some kind of a hobby and whatever Mary thought, this was more harmless than drinking or joining a gang of street thugs.

Problem is; collecting model cars is a bit like stashing a huge pile of girlie magazines under the bed. The more you have, the more desperate you are to get your hands on the real thing. I wonder how many times I've sat at the wheel of my Escort imagining it was Jake Fist's Chevy.

I sat there, running the model cars back and forth across the table-top and wondering what to do about Mary, and whether I should ditch Janet Wu and her little black dress and her five thousand pound bonus. Luckily I was saved from actually having to make a decision by the ringing of my phone.

"Good morning, Mr Collins. DC Matthews here. Do you think you could pop down to the station?"

"What's this about?" I asked.

"Probably better if we discuss that at the station Mr Collins," he replied. "Ask for me. You'll be pleased to know that your interview's with DS McClusky again." I could almost hear him grinning down the phone. "Do you think you could be here by ten thirty?"

I looked at my watch. It was ten fifteen. At least in the Manchester police they give you plenty of warning. I left my office and drove to the police station.

You see it all the time in those so-called lifestyle magazines, how minor events can trigger off earth-shattering eruptions:

My Cat Pissed on the Carpet and I Met the Man of My Dreams.

My Girlfriend Dumped Me and Suddenly I Was on a Plane to

Mongolia.

If I Hadn't Listened to That Tom Jones Record I Wouldn't be a Millionaire.

It's true. A trivial occurrence or a minor decision really can trigger a life-changing event. In this case, had they chosen anyone else, anyone at all other than Detective Superintendent Ted McClusky, I would probably have told them the truth, and things would have turned out very differently indeed.

McClusky was a loud, rude, aggressive bully, which is in itself not uncommon in the police force but the thing that really got to me was the general air of satisfaction he displayed at the discomfiture of all around him as he bawled and swore, scratched his crotch and armpits and bathed happy, secure and totally satisfied in the knowledge that everyone hated him and there wasn't a damn thing they could do about it.

I hadn't lasted long in the force, but long enough to develop an absolute and utter loathing for McClusky. The feeling was mutual. As far as McClusky was concerned I, the one who hadn't had the guts to stick it out in the force, was a form of life so low that I was hardly worth scouring the bottom of his shoes for. I think, in McClusky's pecking order I came just above dirty old men molesting schoolgirls, and well below pimps, muggers, violent thieves and serial murderers.

"Still sleeping with your teddy bear are you Collins, you bloody useless wimp?" he said.

I could smell the stale beer on his breath, and my first instinct was to turn around and walk out. Instead I said, as mildly as I could, "Nice to see you again too, Mr McClusky. What do you want?"

"I want to know what you're up to, Collins. You keep turning up here like a bad bloody penny. First it's a Chinese gangster, tortured and drowned, now it's a Chinese tart."

I raised my eyebrows. "Chinese tart?" I said, innocently. "I never eat them."

He glared at me venomously and threw a photograph across his desk. "Who's that then?" he said contemptuously.

I immediately recognised Angel Wong. It was the same photograph that Janet Wu had given to me. I pretended to study it closely for a few moments, then shook my head. "No idea," I replied. "Your girlfriend?"

His face went even redder with rage, and he leaned over his desk. "Don't you take the piss out of me, you little prat, or I'll fit you up and you can see what it's like being an ex-copper in Strangeways." Strangeways is Manchester's prison. It isn't a very nice place, especially if you are, or used to be, a cop.

"You've been down to the university asking questions about someone called Angel Wong. That's her," he said pointing a finger at the photograph. "So you'd better tell me what you know and you'd better not give me any shit."

"I had a phone call from a firm of lawyers in London," I said, recalling the story I'd concocted for the university tutors. "They told me they were looking for a woman called Angel Wong. Her uncle had died and left her a lot of money. They're going to send me an official letter of appointment, a photo, and some money, but I haven't received it yet."

114

"So what the blazes were you doing asking questions round the bloody university, then?" he bawled.

"They told me she used to study at UMIST. I was just conducting a few preliminary investigations," I replied. "That's what I am, you see, McClusky: a private investigator. People hire me to go out and investigate things. Privately," I added, for the avoidance of any possible future misunderstandings.

His bloodshot eyes stared at me from his fat, round face.

"What's the name of the law firm?" he hissed.

"Parker, Froom, Leggit and Crop," I replied. He threw me a piece of paper. "Write it down," he said. I wondered how long it would take them to find out that the company didn't exist.

"Telephone number?"

"Sorry," I said. "I didn't ask."

He stood up and leaned over the desk putting his face an inch from mine in a blast of halitosis. "You're a lying little sod, Collins, but don't think you can put one over on me. I've eaten bigger men than you for breakfast. When that letter arrives, if it ever does, you bring it straight here. Immediately. You don't read it, you don't even open it. Understand? And if I find out you've been lying to me, which you bloody are, of course, I'll throw you in jail for wasting police time and misleading us in the course of an investigation. And if I happen to hear about you snooping around asking questions about Angel Wong I'll make you wish that your bloody mother had strangled you at birth. Which is what she should have done in the first place. Now, get out of my office."

I stood up and walked as casually as I could away from

McClusky. It was only as I was walking across the street that I realized that my hands were clenched so tightly in my trouser pockets that a fingernail had drawn blood from my palm.

I climbed into my car and on the way back to my office I fantasized about me, McClusky, a dark alley and two feet of lead piping. I parked the car and went to the local pub for a meat pie and a soda water, sat on my own in the corner and wondered what I'd got myself into. No matter how long I thought about Janet Wu and her little black dress and Janet Wu falling out of her bathrobe and Janet Wu with five thousand pounds in her hand and Janet Wu with her lips pressed against mine I knew I was not equipped to handle Chinese gangsters and Heavenly Tigers and people with names like Cheesewire Charlie, not to mention Ted McClusky with a hangover. Reluctantly I decided that I had to agree with Bill: whatever was going on it was out of my league.

Chapter Twelve

*K*arl hung his hat on the hook and sat across the desk from Jake.
"Busy?" asked Jake.

"Not so you'd notice," Karl replied.

"Let's go get a coffee," said Jake.

They walked out of the office, took the elevator down and waited as the doorman pushed open the heavy wooden doors. Outside the wind was howling through the streets of Chicago.

Jake sat drinking his coffee strong and black and while Karl spilled sugar into his mug Jake filled him in on the Bear, the Weasel and the Deputy Chief of Police.

"Know what I've learned on the streets, Jake?" said Karl, stubbing out his cigarette. "There's two things that matter in this life; money and sex. And in ninety percent of cases, the money's there to buy the sex. There's some dame buried in here somewhere, Jake. If there ain't, I'll eat my desk."

"Yeah, but Frankie Mann's had more public dates with more dames than Errol Flynn," replied Jake. "Why would his old lady start getting jealous over another one?"

"Why don't you go ask her?" said Karl.

Jake drove to the big mansion where Frankie Mann stayed over the odd night when he wasn't in a hotel room. He reckoned a busy guy like Frankie wouldn't be home in the middle of the morning.

The front doors were twice as high as Jake and three times as

117

wide. A snooty, uniformed flunky conveyed Jake through to an expensive-looking lounge with pictures on the walls of ancient Greeks killing each other in front of bare-breasted ladies who didn't look worth it.

Eleanor Mann sat alone behind a coffee table in a tight black skirt, nervously fingering the beads around her neck. Jake figured each one would keep him for half a year. He told her about Frankie's evening.

"Did anyone else go to the hotel room?" she asked impatiently. When Jake told her he hadn't stuck around long enough to check for later arrivals, she looked positively disappointed.

"Look, Mrs Mann," said Jake, "not wishing any disrespect or nothing, but Frankie's got himself something of a reputation. You asking me to keep a check on all his visitors, male and female?"

She gave him an icy stare and said, "Mr Fist, if I want a list of my husband's girl friends I don't need to pay you. I can just pick up the newspapers. I have told you that my husband is into something I don't like and I want you to keep an eye on him. That's all." She stuck a cigarette in her mouth and snapped a small gold lighter.

"I told you Mrs Mann: Frankie met two Italian gangsters in Fat Tony's; then Lew Kraski in the Drake. Scarletti's mean and dangerous, and Kraski's as bent as a wire coat hanger. That's all I know, unless you can help me out a little."

She sat thinking, then she said, "I think maybe he's looking at a casino."

Jake stared at her. "A casino? In Chicago? He doesn't have a snowball's chance in hell."

"That's all I know," she said, and Jake stood, picked up his hat and left.

He drove back downtown, thinking about how a casino in Chicago would go down with the mob who ran Las Vegas. Frankie could be storing up an awful lot of grief.

118

Except Jake didn't think so. Eleanor Mann had small, even, pearly white teeth, and Jake thought she was lying straight through them.

*

I opened my office door and checked my answer-phone for messages. There was just the one. It asked me to call back Detective Superintendent McClusky at my earliest convenience.

I'm extremely careful who I give my mobile phone number to and I certainly wasn't going to give it to McClusky. Thinking about it reminded me that the battery was almost gone, and I plugged it into the battery charger I keep on my desk.

I picked up the phone and called McClusky. He advised me that the firm I'd given them didn't exist, and I expressed my surprise and disappointment that I'd been the victim of some cruel and heartless hoax.

He told me that if I knew what was good for me I'd come to the station and tell them the truth. I said I'd be on my way as soon as I had the time.

I then took several deep breaths, picked up the phone and called Janet Wu. After a short pause that voice started up again. I didn't know what business Janet Wu was in but whatever it was I reckoned she could make a lot more on one of those telephone chat lines.

"I've just had an interview with the police," I said. "Seems they're looking for your cousin too. Now, why would that be?"

There was a silence down the line, then she said, "Tom, what did you tell them?"

"Nothing," I grunted. She gave a sigh of relief.

"You won't tell them about me will you?" she breathed. I mumbled something about client confidentiality.

"You see, Tom," she said, "I just got off the phone with her husband and he says that he thinks Angel might have been kidnapped. And of course if the police get involved it could make things terribly complicated.

"So why didn't you call me and tell me?" I said. "Listen, Ms Wu, when my clients come into what could be a vital piece of information I expect them to let me know about it. In most circumstances clients who hide things from me very rapidly become ex-clients. Do you understand?" There was a short silence. "So perhaps you'd like to tell me the truth," I said. I didn't know then that oriental beauties and the truth are absolute strangers to each other.

"What you said about Hamilton Liu, Tom, we think Angel may have gone to meet Meredith and now, well, we think they might have kidnapped her."

"Why would they want to do that?"

"Angel's husband's very rich. Maybe for the ransom money?"

It was of course all a complete pack of lies and I knew I was just delaying the inevitable when I said, "If that's the case, Janet, then the only thing to do is to go to the police."

"Tom, why don't you come over and we'll talk it through?"

Yes, of course, I thought. Much better to do it face to face. The thought she might drop her bathrobe on the floor again never even occurred to me. Honest. I checked my watch: it was just after one-thirty. "OK, I'll come straight over."

"Give me time to get dressed, Tom," she giggled. "Maybe a couple of hours or so. Look, I have to go now

120

there's someone at the door."

The phone went dead and I sat down at my desk. I had a couple of hours to kill so I booted up my computer and looked at some vintage car sites. After some time looking wistfully at beautiful bodies I couldn't afford I picked up my detective story and read about Jake Fist and Eleanor Mann, but I just couldn't concentrate. After a while I gave up on Jake and went to sit at my interview table. I sat there, running the model cars back and forth across the table-top and contemplating a future of lost dogs, lying spouses and long lonely nights. I decided I should do something dynamic and meaningful, so I stood up and emptied the ashtray into the bin. I was thinking about going completely overboard and emptying the bin when the office door opened.

There were two of them. They were both Chinese, one thin and well dressed and the other built on similar lines to my safe. The skinny one had his hands in his pockets. The other guy's hands were hanging down about four inches below his belt and I could see that he was just aching to hit someone. I looked around the room. There was no one else to hit but me.

"You the detective?" asked the skinny guy.

"No," I said, "I'm the cleaning lady." That's the problem when you spend your time with stories about hard-nosed American private eyes. You just can't help the smart answers.

The other guy was short and wide and solid, but he was also extremely fast. I hardly saw him move as he sank his right fist into my stomach. I collapsed onto the floor gasping like a stranded fish.

"You've been sticking your nose into where it don't

belong," said the skinny guy, and his colleague booted me in the ribs. It was like being hit by a hammer. This guy and Agnes Golightly would have made a great team. I couldn't breathe, I couldn't speak and I couldn't see much either because my eyes were full of tears. Gradually the mists cleared and I staggered to my feet holding onto my table for support.

"So you find Angel yet?" asked the skinny guy. He had pale flat eyes like a toad.

"No," I gasped.

"Any idea where she is?"

"No."

"Good," he said, and nodded at the big guy, who, I realized with horror, was pulling a gun from his pocket.

There were two conflicting feelings running though me as I realized what was happening. The first was a terrible, knee-trembling fear, almost a sickness in the pit of my stomach. The second was a stone-cold, icy clarity.

Tom, said the voice in my head, *unless you do something and do it now you have two seconds to live.*

The ashtray was by my hand. It was a big heavy stone model, the type made for the serious smoker. My office is tiny. The big guy was standing only a couple of feet away. At this range I couldn't miss. The ashtray hit him across the bridge of his nose and he fell backwards as if he'd been shot.

The big guy was struggling to get to his feet and I took two steps and kicked him as hard as I could in the face. He gradually collapsed sideways, like one of those buildings you see sometimes on the TV when they get demolished in a controlled explosion, but I was too busy to watch him because now, the thin man had a gun in his hand.

122

I leapt at him and grabbed his wrist as he pulled the trigger; the report of the gun boomed loud in my ear. I hit him with a vicious left jab to the nose and he staggered back, dropping the gun on the floor. The big guy was shaking his head in a confused fashion and I knew that in a fair fight he'd kill me so I dived for the gun, grabbed it, and covered them both.

"You," I said to the skinny guy, " kick that gun over here." Very deliberately I pointed the other gun at his head. "And be very, very careful." I was amazed at how steady I sounded.

The skinny guy was clutching his nose. Blood was dripping slowly on to his nice suit and his clean white shirt. The big guy was shaking his head and moaning as his colleague kicked his gun across my office carpet. I was watching him like a hawk and if he'd tried anything at all I'd have shot him. Basically because I was scared to death.

I kept the gun in my right hand, and with my left I knocked the phone receiver off its cradle.

"Who are you calling?" asked the skinny guy.

"Calling? The police," I said.

"I wouldn't do that if I were you," he said.

"Oh yeah," I replied. "And why not?"

He fished a packet of tissues from his pocket and dabbed at his nose. "You were lucky today," he said, in a flat, emotionless voice. "You go to the cops; we kill you. You stick your nose in our business; we kill you. You ask any more questions about Angel Wong; we kill you."

He flicked a hand at the big guy who was dragging himself to his feet and they began to back warily out of the room.

"Where do you think you're going?" I asked, tightening

my finger on the trigger.

"What are you going to do? Shoot us?" he sneered.

I stood there clutching the gun but he was right of course. I could hardly shoot them both in the back. I heard them clattering down the stairs, walked to the window and saw them climb into a big black Toyota Crown parked outside on the double yellow lines. I watched as it vanished into the distance, then I collapsed into my chair trembling like a leaf. There were flakes of white paint on the carpet from where the bullet had buried itself in the ceiling. Now I knew why in the stories all the private eyes had bottles of whisky stashed all over the office.

After a few minutes I picked up the second gun from the floor and put it in the office safe. The other I shoved into my pocket. It gave me the same comfortable feeling as having Bill beside me in a fistfight.

This had gone far enough for me. It was a matter for the police now: to hell with Janet Wu and both her offers. I wasn't equipped to handle gun-toting Chinese gangsters. This was Manchester, not Chicago, and real life, not Jake Fist. I'd been sitting happily in my office doing no one any harm when two thugs had walked in off the street and tried to kill me.

I'd told Janet Wu I'd go over to the hotel but it seemed a whole lot more sensible and a whole lot safer to drive over to the station and throw myself on the tender mercies of Ted McClusky. I was just shrugging on my coat when I saw my office door slowly opening.

No Olympic diving champion in history could have competed with me as I threw myself headlong onto the floor at the side of my desk, wrestled the gun out of my pocket and trained it on the door, waiting for the chatter of a machine gun or even a grenade to roll through the opening. It was Gladys Green.

She looked at me lying on the floor with a gun trained on her and said, "Getting some practice in, Mr Collins? Can't say I blame you, there's all sorts out there these days. Why, when I was a young girl you could walk anywhere, any time of the day or night and be as safe as houses, but nowadays, they're just waiting around at bus stops and in dark alleys in broad daylight, just waiting to murder you in your bed and rape you too, like as not, even if you're an old woman. Why, my friend Matilda, Tilly we call her on account of she's a bit deaf, well, she said that she'd have been raped in her own garden if she hadn't had t' presence of mind to threaten him with the hosepipe. And talking of gardens…"

"Please, please Mrs Green," I gasped, pulling myself to my feet. "Not now. I'm very busy."

"Aye, while innocent people are getting murdered in their beds," she sniffed. "And what about my neighbours? You promised you'd come and have a look, and now they've gone and done it again. Another one. Last night."

"Another one what?" I squawked. I had visions of a carload of Chinese thugs setting fire to my office while I sat there making small talk with Gladys Green.

"Burying bodies. Next door. In the garden. With spades." She spoke slowly and with great emphasis, as if she was talking to someone foreign, deaf, or extremely dim. Or all three.

"Oh yes, I remember," I gabbled. "But I've got to go. Right now. It's a lady," I said. "A beautiful lady getting murdered in her bed. I'll be round as soon as I can."

"Aye well just make sure you do or I'll have to call the

police," she said.

"Yes, yes, you and me both."

My office chair was lying on the floor where I had knocked it over in my panic-stricken dive, and the phone was still off the hook, but I didn't care.

I pushed Gladys Green out of the office, turned out the lights, locked the door, took the stairs three at a time, slammed the outer door behind me and almost ran to my car.

I jumped in, hit the ignition and drove out of the car park watching anxiously for large black cars with open tinted windows and the barrels of machine-guns poking through them, and trying to work out the best way to ingratiate myself with McClusky. I mentally ticked off what I had to offer him: two armed thugs, almost certainly working for Hamilton Liu; a car licence plate number; an unlicensed gun in my pocket; a gorgeous Chinese chick holed up in the Ritz.

That's when I started to think about Janet Wu. It seemed hardly fair to take on the case, pocket her money and just throw her to McClusky. Whatever she'd done wrong I didn't fancy her chances stuck in some prison with a bunch of Manchester dykes propositioning her in the showers. The more I thought about it the more I realized I owed it to her to give her a warning before McClusky came looking for her.

Which is why I decided to stop off at the Ritz and tell her that I was off the case. If I'd taken thirty seconds to think about it I'd have known I was motivated solely by the desire to see her naked one more time, but I didn't stop to work it out. There were plenty of times afterwards when I wished I had.

126

Chapter Thirteen

*J*ake sat in his office with a glass in his hand. It helped him think. Right now what he was thinking about was Eleanor Mann. Jake knew as well as anyone the first rule of any decent private eye: when your client comes in and asks you to investigate something the very first thing you do is to investigate your client. He put the top back on the bottle, took the elevator, climbed into his Chevy and drove to the offices of The Chicago Gazette.

Jake had a deal with The Gazette. He'd tip them off if anything was happening that he thought should be brought to the attention of the great American public and they'd help him out with back numbers, inside information and so forth.

Jake went through the back issues till he came to the wedding of fine upstanding real estate developer Frank Ernest Mann and his little lady, Eleanor Scott. It was the fifth time Frankie had promised to forsake all others: the fifth week-end that must have intruded on his real estate development schemes. You needed to wonder why he bothered.

Jake took the elevator to Bart Stanton's office on the fourth floor. Bart was editor of The Gazette and he and Jake got on pretty good. Jake had given Bart enough info over the years to run a few headlines that had upset just about everybody in Chicago, which was the way Bart liked it.

Bart laughed out loud at the prospect of anyone obtaining

permission for a casino in Chicago, not unless they were planning to assassinate Mayor Daly first. But he did know something about Eleanor Mann. The rumour ran that Dillinger Scott, Eleanor's rich banker father had run into a spot of trouble. Fast cars, slow horses, trustworthy hookers, that kind of thing. Frankie Mann had bailed him out. Apparently Dillinger Scott didn't really have any collateral to back up Frankie's loan except for a rich spoilt only child: a real good-looking daughter, twenty years younger than Frankie.

Of course he wasn't just going to give his daughter to Frankie so's he could get himself laid. What kind of a father did Frankie think he was? No, Frankie was only allowed to screw the pretty blonde nineteen-year-old if he did it legally and legitimately and put a goddam gold band on her finger.

"So what, in the great wide scheme of things does that mean?" asked Jake. "And why is Eleanor Mann after her husband and why was her husband talking with Bruno the Bear, Willie the Weasel and the deputy chief of police?"

Bart had no idea but Jake had seen that look in his eyes before. Like a bloodhound scenting something rotten floating on the wind.

*

I parked my car on a meter, threaded my way through the cars and buses and taxis and trucks, and walked up to the imposing front doors of the Ritz.

The doorman was still gazing disdainfully over my head, trying to spot the Himalayas or the Taj Mahal. The Reception desk was still devoid of human life and I walked to the lift and pressed the button for the 15th floor.

The doors opened smoothly. My heart was pounding like a jack-hammer as I wondered what Janet Wu's response would be to my news. Whether she'd sit me down and soothe my fevered brow as I told her of my heroic intervention with brutal, gun-toting thugs. And whether I should tell her I was ditching the case before she'd held my trembling hand or afterwards.

There was a *Do Not Disturb* sign hanging on the door but I ignored it, rang the bell and waited, rang and waited again. There was no response. A short, dark-skinned woman in a maid's uniform was cleaning the next room. I summoned up my American accent again, told her that I'd locked myself out of my room and could she please open the door for me. She looked at me as if I was speaking in Swahili and it occurred to me that if I had, I'd probably have stood a better chance of being understood. Eventually however, she worked out my sign language and opened the door with her pass-key.

The room was empty: the door to the bedroom was closed. I knocked at the bedroom door, waited for a second then opened it and walked in.

I had wanted to see Janet Wu naked one more time but not like this. Each of her hands was tied to one of the bedposts and a hand towel was stuffed into her mouth, held in position by a broad piece of tape. There were ugly red burn marks on her breasts, and the white silk sheets were now a deep, dark red. I grabbed at her wrist looking for any sign of a pulse, but I knew I was wasting my time. She was very, very dead.

I took a huge deep breath, walked into the bathroom and stood there, leaning over the basin, trying hard not to be sick. I had never seen a dead body before except for my mother, lying sadly in her coffin in our front room, and she hadn't had her throat cut.

I stared into the washbasin and there were two thoughts

going round and round in my head. The first was Janet's throaty voice down the line saying, "Let me get dressed first, Tom," and then, "there's someone at the door." That someone at the door must have been the person who killed her. The second was the last thing I'd said to Gladys Green, a throwaway quip as I'd bustled her out of the office. "It's a beautiful lady," I'd said, "getting murdered in her bed."

I tried hard to be calm, to think through exactly what I'd done and what the hell to do next. I had come up to her room without asking at reception, had gained access by asking the cleaning lady to open the door.

The only other person who'd seen me entering or leaving the hotel was the Indian doorman and he seemed to have a professional pride in taking no notice of anyone. But one thing was certain. If anyone came in now, my goose was plucked, gutted, stuffed, trussed up and baked to a crisp.

I opened the door a crack and peered out. The cleaning woman was in the next room. There was a good chance she hadn't really taken a good look at me and there was nothing else to connect me with the dead woman. Then I remembered leaving my phone number on her answering machine.

I tiptoed across the room and picked up the phone. It had one of those voice menus which tells you how to retrieve, access, reply to and finally delete your messages. I heard the recording of my voice on the answerphone half a dozen times before my panic-stricken fingers managed to hit the right buttons.

I took a towel from the bathroom, walking past her body while staring at the wall, and cleaned the phone of fingerprints. I left the room, leaving the door to close behind me and wiped my fingerprints from the door handle. I walked to the lift and pressed the call button. Carefully I cleaned away my prints with a tissue.

The lift took an age to arrive. On the way down it stopped at virtually every floor. People walked in and smiled at me and I felt as if I had a huge neon sign plastered on my forehead reading MURDERER.

I walked across the hotel lobby as casually as I could, amazed that no-one stopped me. I was sweating as if I'd run a marathon. The Indian doorman was still staring away into the far, far distance and, with my head averted, I pushed through the door and into the street.

I gratefully swallowed huge lungfuls of Manchester smog, climbed into my car and drove away as fast as I could while being desperately careful to break no traffic rules.

I hardly knew what I was doing as I drove, on auto pilot back to my apartment, but all the time a voice was screaming in my head: It's not supposed to be like this! It's fine in the books and the movies but not in real life. Nobody's supposed to die!

I parked my car against the kerb, shakily inserted my key into the door, climbed the stairs to my flat and locked and bolted my front door. I sat in my apartment, sweating and shaking, and trying to stop seeing that beautiful body spread out across the sheets. The realisation of what I'd done began to dawn on me.

I may have been the last person to see her alive, except for the people who'd killed her. I'd gained unauthorized access to her room, interfered with a crime scene, removed evidence, failed to report a murder. And she had been tortured. With a burning cigarette, or cigar. Why?

The ringing of the telephone interrupted my reverie. My first instinct was to ignore it, but instead I picked up the receiver and in a voice I barely recognized as my own I said, "Yes?"

"Tom," said Mary's icy voice down the receiver, "I don't know if you think it's a game or something, but if it is, I, for one, am sick of it."

I stared at the phone in amazement. A game? What was she talking about? "I'm sorry, Mary," I croaked, "I've no idea what you mean."

"I've been calling your phone for the last hour and you simply don't answer. Is it just me that you don't want to talk to, or do you have some kind of a problem with the whole human race?"

I was completely baffled. I reached into my pocket for my mobile phone and then realized that, in my mad panic to escape from Gladys Green, I'd left it on my desk.

"I'm sorry, Mary," I said again. It occurred to me that I was doing an awful lot of apologizing for someone who'd just invited her to lunch. "I've left my phone in my office. By mistake," I added, for avoidance of doubt.

"Oh," she said sarcastically, "a forgetful private detective. That's not very good is it?"

I stared at the phone. I'd been assaulted, threatened with guns, shot at, found my client dead in her bed. Grief from my ex was something I definitely didn't need.

"Anyway," she continued, "I accept your kind invitation. I will see you at Antonio's tomorrow at 12.30 and please don't be late." There was a pause and she said in a softer voice, a voice I remembered from our early days, "So is this a confirmed date, then?"

I stood there staring at the phone. "But Mary," I wanted to say, "I've got to go to the police. I really don't think that I'll be able to make lunch tomorrow, as they'll probably arrest me for murder."

"Hello," she said, "Are you still there, Tom? What on earth's the matter with you these days?"

Everyone's heard of Parkinson's Law and the Peter Principle and so on but I think there should be another principle enshrined in the English language. This would be called Collins' Law. It would say that whenever you are faced with two choices, one of which is eminently sensible, (go immediately to the cops and fling yourself on the mercy of Ted McClusky), and one of which is clearly monumentally and totally insane, (forget about gorgeous dead Orientals and people trying to murder you and go and have a pleasant lunch with a bad-tempered, spoilt, sarcastic, utterly unsympathetic ex-girlfriend), then you always take the insane option.

"OK, it's a date," I croaked and slowly put the phone down.

I sat on my sofa, staring across the room at a model of a maroon Pontiac convertible, trying to wrestle with what had happened to me. I thought of the two thugs who'd come to my office. They'd asked me if I'd found Angel Wong. It was Janet Wu who'd hired me to find Angel, Janet Wu who knew my name and my office address. There was one logical conclusion. The guys who'd paid me a visit that morning had tortured her to find out who and where I was. Afterwards they'd killed her. Then they'd tried to kill me. But why?

And what the hell was I supposed to do now?

133

Chapter Fourteen

Jake had a burger and a couple of martinis for lunch and went back to his office. He was just hanging up his hat when the phone rang. "Yeah?" *he said.*

"Jake, Bart. Look, this may or may not mean anything but Frankie Mann's latest squeeze is some wannabe actress called Melissa Francis. She's in some musical showing down The Gaumont called Let's Kiss it All Goodbye. *Apparently Frankie's one of the show's backers.*

"Know anything about this broad?"

"Nothing much. Young, pretty, usual stuff. But you wanna know what they call guys who invest in these kinda half-assed shows?"

"What?"

"Angels. Kinda funny don't you think, Jake; Frankie Mann's an angel?"

"Anything to do with me he'll be talkin' to one shortly," said Jake and put down the phone.

He drove down to The Gaumont and looked at all the handbills and posters advertising the show. It was a musical. Jake had never seen a musical in his life and he didn't intend to start now. He picked up a handbill and had a look at the stars. There was Melissa Francis in short shorts and long legs and a big smile on her pretty face. She looked familiar somewhere but Jake couldn't place it. So he

134

went to Joe's.

He had a couple and fished the handbill out of his pocket.

"Getting' into the shows these days?" asked Joe with that big wide grin, "or getting into one of them showgirls?"

"Neither, Joe," said Jake, looking at Melissa Francis and her high heels and her long legs.

Suddenly the JD kicked in, gave him that kind of insight that doesn't come when you're stone-cold sober. "No, no," he murmured. "That can't be right."

But just to be sure he had another Jack Daniels and another long look at the girl.

There was no doubt about it.

*

Sleep didn't come easy that night as I fought with the bed sheets, wondering how I'd got myself into this mess. When I did finally drift off I kept dreaming of Janet Wu lying dead in the hotel, and Chinese gangsters trying to kill me.

I tossed and turned and started thinking about Mary. I still wasn't totally sure whether I wanted a return to the situation we'd had, but at four in the morning, with the rain beating on the windows and a mind full of dark shadows, it can be awfully lonely sleeping alone. She'd been OK at first, with the private eye stuff. I think she thought it would be glamorous and exciting, but when she'd realized the sheer boredom of it all she'd kept on and on at me to do what she called a proper job. Like working in a bank, or delivering milk, or being a schoolteacher.

Eventually she'd given me an ultimatum. Either Tom Collins, Private Detective, had to go, or she would. I'd prevaricated until one day I'd come back from spying on a married man and his boyfriend in a car. She was gone. No note, no rabbits boiling on the kitchen stove, nothing.

I missed the companionship at the weekend and the fact that she could put together a mean Sunday roast. I missed the sex too. I still hadn't worked out whether I actually missed her as well.

I could understand her concerns about my present situation and future prospects, but I couldn't work out why she was so opposed to my hobby. After all it wasn't doing anyone any harm. I had sixteen classic cars on display in cabinets and shelves in the front room. She'd been so caustic about them that eventually I'd moved them all into the spare bedroom.

"Model cars are for little boys, Tom," she kept saying. "Not for grown men. And it's no use dreaming that one day you'll have a real one, not unless you get a proper job."

I just think that she didn't like affection or attention being lavished on anyone or anything except herself, or maybe she was just jealous that however miserable my childhood had been, at least I'd managed to preserve the tiny part of it that I'd liked. As a kid, my model cars were my refuge, the things I'd hold onto while hiding in my room with an aching backside or a throbbing ear from one of my dad's tantrums.

Mary had left home at the age of eighteen and had never been back or contacted her parents since. She thought that because they hadn't instigated a nationwide manhunt, it was just another sign of their total lack of interest. I explained to her that the police weren't interested in runaway teenagers unless there was some prima facia evidence of foul play, and in an case at eighteen

136

she was an adult and could do whatever she liked. It made no difference.

I thought about my models, now restored to the front room, and admitted to myself that there was another possibility. Maybe Mary was right. It was just another sign that I'd never grown up. And then of course there was Lindy. Lindy who I still thought about, dreamt about, whose sad accusing eyes I saw sometimes in the corner of my room as I struggled to sleep.

At six in the morning I gave up the struggle, got out of bed and plugged in the electric kettle.

I still had no milk so I walked down to the local store. The ever-cheerful Mr Patel smiled at me from behind the counter – he and Mrs Patel have solved the mystery of how to work twenty-four hours a day and never sleep. "My goodness, Mr Collins," he said. "Bright and early this morning."

"Well, Mr Patel, those gorgeous oriental sirens don't make their own breakfast," I told him.

I bought milk and a newspaper and walked back to my flat. Despite a careful check I couldn't find any Oriental sirens anywhere. I put coffee in a cup, milk in the coffee, and picked up the paper.

The front-page news was all about a murdered woman in a top city hotel. Only she wasn't Chinese. She was an American of Vietnamese extraction. Her name wasn't Janet Wu either. That was the name she'd used when she checked into the hotel but her real name was Nguyen Li Binh, also known as Jenny. The Vietnamese are like the Chinese in that they put their surnames first, which meant that the woman I'd known as Janet had the same name as the guy they had fished out of the Ship Canal. All of which made me none the wiser.

The news report said that the police had several leads and that they were anxious to interview a man, thought to be an American, who had been seen leaving the room. He was described as being over six feet tall, broad, with short dark hair, aged between thirty and forty. I looked gloomily in the mirror. Apart from the stubble and the bloodshot eyes it was a perfect description of me.

I drank more coffee and tuned in to the early news on the TV. There was an identikit picture of the person the police wanted to talk to. I was heartened to see it didn't look much like me. Or to put it another way I hoped it didn't look like me. If I looked like that I'd shoot myself. There were also photos of two Vietnamese men the police were anxious to trace in connection with the murder. The news switched to the day's big soccer games, so I took a long shower and prowled around the apartment trying to work out my next move. The questions were buzzing round my head like a swarm of hornets

I had to go to the police, but with what? I sat down with a piece of paper and a pen, and pieced together the facts.

A woman saying that her name was Janet Wu had walked into my office and told me she wanted me to find her cousin, Angel Wong.

Angel's friend was married to Hamilton Liu, a suspected Chinese racketeer.

The police were also looking for Angel Wong

138

Two Chinese had threatened me with guns. If anyone needed *proof there was a bullet in the ceiling of my office.*

'Janet Wu' was actually a Vietnamese called Jenny Nguyen.

She had the same name as a man who'd been found murdered and dumped in the Ship Canal.

Jenny Nguyen had been murdered, probably by the same guys who'd tried to shoot me in my office.

Next I tried to work out where I stood in all this.

I'd lied to the police when they asked me about Angel Wong.

I'd failed to inform them about two Chinese who'd tried to shoot me.

I had been to Janet/Jenny's room on the Thursday afternoon and again on the Friday, both times without making myself known to the hotel desk.

I'd removed evidence and I'd failed to report a murder.

I was walking around with an unlicensed gun in my pocket.

I looked at it from every possible angle and there was just one simple, straightforward answer: make a clean breast of things. I decided to call Bill and tell him I was on my way over to the station to throw myself on the tender mercy of Detective Superintendent Ted McClusky. My hand was hovering over the receiver when the phone rang. I hesitated, then it occurred to me that maybe it was Mary calling to say she couldn't make lunch. I grabbed the receiver.

"Is that Mr Collins?" It was a throaty, foreign voice and for a second I thought it was Janet Wu. Then I realised it was Candy, the dancer from the Yin & Yang club. "I've been trying to call you," she said. I cursed as I remembered that my cell phone was still sitting on my office desk.

"Yes, this is Tom Collins," I replied.

"I got your number from the directory. I thought you might be in some trouble," she said.

Trouble? Me? No, of course not. Just two guys trying to kill me, the police desperate to get their hands on me; my client dead in her bed and me up to my neck in a murder.

"No, Candy, there's no trouble," I replied. "What can I do for you?"

"I have some information," she said. "Can you meet me?"

I thought for a moment. Angel Wong was obviously the key to this whole business. The police seemed extremely keen to discover her whereabouts, and if I could deliver her to McClusky, it just might help to save my neck.

Once again Collins' Law came to the rescue. It was simple. All problems were solved. I'd go meet Candy; find out where Angel Wong was hiding; take Mary to a nice spaghetti lunch at Fat Tony's; go to the police; hand over Angel Wong; explain all about the dead girl and the gunfight in my office, and with any luck I'd be home free by Sunday. It does make you wonder whether sometimes evolution takes a few paces backwards.

"Where do we meet?" I asked Candy.

"The same car park," she replied. I looked at my watch. "I can be there in half an hour," I said.

"OK," she said, and I could hear the fear in her voice as I put down the phone.

I'd promised Candy five hundred pounds if she could lead me to Angel, so I took my jacket and counted out what was left from Janet Wu's advance. Two hundred and fifty pounds. I cursed, went downstairs, took my car and went to the bank, where I drew out four hundred pounds, leaving very little behind.

My client was dead, I was being chased by a bunch of murderous Chinese gangsters, I was on the run from the police and I was losing money on the deal. Not for the first time I wondered whether I was in the right business.

*

The four policemen sat round the desk. The Chief Constable, DS Ted McClusky, DI Mathews and Inspector Bill Waters.

"DI Matthews, could you please fill us in with what we know at this point," said the Chief Constable pleasantly.

"Yes sir," replied Matthews. "First. There's a Vietnamese gangster from Chicago pulled out of the Ship Canal. He's been murdered. Main suspect, in fact only suspect right now, is a Chinese called Hamilton Liu, who, we think, is engaged in various criminal activities including drugs, prostitution, illegal immigration and money-laundering."

"Second. There's at least two more Vietnamese from the same gang who we know are in Manchester. We've put out their photos. No response so far."

"Third. There's a woman called Angel Wong the Home Office are desperate for us to trace. She used to go to UMIST, together with a Chinese woman called Meredith, who's married to Hamilton Liu. Angel Wong lives in Chicago."

"Fourth. There's a dead woman in the Ritz Hotel. She's also Vietnamese; she's also from Chicago. She's been tortured and murdered."

"Fifth. There's a local P.I. called Tom Collins who's been asking questions about Angel Wong. Told us a cock-and-bull story about some London law firm who don't exist. A man was seen entering the murdered woman's hotel room around three o'clock yesterday afternoon. Description may or may not have been Tom Collins. He was seen by a cleaning woman and by the doorman. We've shown them Collins' picture, but neither of them can give us a positive i.d."

Matthews leaned back.

"So what's going on then, McClusky?" asked the Chief Constable.

Ted McClusky didn't feel well. Ted McClusky had a monumental hangover. Saturday was supposed to have been his day off and he did not appreciate at all being made to get out of bed, to come into a meeting with the C.C. especially looking and feeling like this.

"There's obviously something going on between this Hamilton Liu and the Vietnamese, though I can't see what it could be. Can't be turf wars. As far as we know, the Vietnamese aren't active here. Could be some spillover from something in Chicago, but we don't know anything about that either. It would help if we knew who this Angel Wong is and why they're after her."

142

"They won't say," replied the Chief Constable. "Just keep telling me to arrest her. And Tom Collins. What's he up to? You're supposed to be his mate Waters. What's going on?"

"Tom came to see me a couple of days ago, sir. Told me he was looking for Angel Wong. He didn't tell me who'd hired him," responded Bill Waters. "Said she was a friend of Meredith Liu. I told him that Liu was trouble, and warned him to stay away. That's all."

"So next steps?" said the Chief Constable.

"We've already got a watch on Liu's residence and his restaurant and his night club, though we don't know what we're supposed to be looking for," responded McClusky. "Next step is to pull in Mr bloody Collins. He was supposed to come over here yesterday but he never showed up."

"And Miss Angel Wong?" queried the CC.

"We've drawn a total blank," replied McClusky. "She seems to have vanished. Maybe Collins can point us in the right direction."

"Very good," replied the CC. "Let me know what Mr Collins has to say. You might treat that as urgent Detective Superintendent."

"Priority sir. We'll bring him in at once."

*

When I arrived, Candy was waiting for me. It was cold and wet, the wind whistling down the streets and blowing old newspapers around the car park. Manchester in September. Candy looked thin, frightened and half-frozen, and in daylight looked a damn sight younger than she had in The

143

Yin & Yang Club. She climbed, shivering, into the car.

"You promised me five hundred pounds," she said in the frightened, pleading voice of someone who has been given lots of promises and never seen any of them kept.

I counted out ten fifty-pound notes. Her hands were shaking as she folded the money and pushed it into the pocket of her overcoat.

She gave me a slip of paper with a name and address written on it. The name was Hamilton Liu: the address was the place I'd been slung out of on the Thursday afternoon.

"Are you sure she's here?" I asked.

She nodded her head, her eyes wide and terrified. "The Lius have two maids. One of them is a friend of my mother. There's a Chinese woman from America. She's locked in a room on the first floor. She's being kept a prisoner."

"Do you know why?" I asked. She shook her head. She was watching constantly through the car windows, as if afraid she might have been followed.

"I have to go," she said, and began to get out of the car. Suddenly, she smiled at me and if she hadn't been quite so thin and frightened she would actually have been extremely pretty.

"Thank you for the money," she whispered, and hurried away across the car park.

I watched her walk away; her head bent forward into the collar of her raincoat, taking short, defeated steps across the concrete.

"Candy," I called after her. She turned and stared at me. "Be careful," I said. She gave me a brief, strained smile and vanished. When you think about it, all those stereotypical pieces of advice are actually just so much horseshit, and I was to remember that one later.

Through my grimy windscreen I could see three pigeons fighting over a cigarette butt. A fat man with car keys in his hand was standing next to a rusty, decrepit old Cortina, swearing at a cowering, red-faced woman. She was carrying three shopping bags while trying to hold on to a scruffy, snot-nosed little girl. The little girl was crying. On the wall of the car park, a public-spirited citizen had thoughtfully written out a warning to everyone, in red spray paint, that Kenneth was a wanker. I started up the Escort and drove away.

What I didn't know of course was that as I left the car park DC Pike was standing at the door of my flat with his finger on the buzzer. After a while he stopped trying and turned to DI Matthews.

"What do you reckon?" he asked.

Matthews shrugged. "His car's not here. Maybe we should try his office."

*

I drove slowly home, wondering what I should do with the information Candy had given me.

Had I been five minutes earlier I would have been arrested, frog-marched into a police car and dragged round to the station. There, I would have faced the extremely unpleasant prospect of interrogation by Detective Superintendent Ted McClusky, in a foul mood, with a terrible hangover, probably followed by being thrown into a cell with a murder charge round my neck.

Compared to what actually happened it would have been a walk in the park.

145

Chapter Fifteen

*J*ake woke, checked he hadn't been shot in the night, had him a *cigarette and a black coffee and drove to the offices of* The Chicago Gazette. *Bart gave him a guy to help, a thin, nervous junior about seventeen years old whose name was Jed. He looked as if he'd have a heart attack every time Jake looked at him.*

"What are we looking for Mr Fist?" he asked, his voice trembling. Jake told him he wanted any information he could find on three things. One was Mr Dillinger Scott, friendly neighbourhood banker, failed gambler and father of Frankie Mann's newest wife. The second was Frankie Mann, including his chequered career history and frantic social life. The third was Frankie's latest squeeze: Melissa Francis.

After an hour or so Jake left him to it and dropped in on Bart Stanton.

Bart looked at his watch, looked at Jake and took the bottle off the shelf behind him.

"Found anything?" he asked.

Jake shook his head. He didn't want to tell him his suspicions about Melissa Francis, least not yet. He wanted to be sure what he'd seen.

Bart poured them both a shot. "You know I got people out all over town, Jake. Well one of 'em's a beat-up old wino working for The Plan-ning Commission. How he keeps his job is one of life's little mysteries, but there you go. Anyhow I asked him if there's anything big in the wind, anything that might be linked to Frankie Mann. Guess what he told me?"

Jake shrugged his shoulders.

"There's a rumour going round that the cops are looking to move to a new place, somewhere more modern, more comfortable, maybe out on the east side."

"So?" asked Jake.

"Where's the police HQ right now, Jake? You oughtta know. You've been there enough."

Jake lit up a Lucky. "Just behind South Michigan. Corner of South State and 16th."

"Yeah, right, and it takes up a whole city block. Some two-storey fifty-year-old heap right in the heart of downtown. Think what you could put there, Jake. Fancy shops, restaurants, twenty floors of swanky offices. Any developer gets his hands on that piece of land at the right price stands to make an awful lot of money."

"And Frankie Mann's a real-estate developer having late-night meetings with Lew Kraski, the deputy Chief of police," said Jake

"And Lew Kraski's got two more years before he retires. Could be setting himself up one helluva pension plan," said Bart

It was there again, on Bart Stanton's face that old newshound look when the scent of carrion comes floating down on the wind.

*

So Angel Wong was being held at the home of Hamilton Liu: maybe for ransom, maybe not. In any case it had nothing to do with me any more. Janet Wu was dead, along with my five grand bonus and my new DVD player and

147

there wouldn't be any repeat of her soulful eyes staring at me, her bathrobe hanging open, saying: "It's all yours Mr big tough detective."

No, what this big tough detective was going to do now was to drive to Manchester central police station, ask to see DS Ted McClusky, tell him the whole, unexpurgated truth and hope that he'd be merciful and kill me quickly. But that pleasure could wait a couple of hours. First I was going to sit in Fat Tony's and buy Mary an expensive lunch. I also decided that if there was ever a good moment to break all my non-alcoholic promises then this was it. I'd treat us to a pre-lunch martini, a decent bottle of Chianti and for good measure a grappa or two to follow. Then I'd go and breathe on McClusky.

As I eased into the familiar street where I'd lived for the past four years I saw that there was another car I hadn't seen before parked in my spot but I didn't think anything about it, just parked a few yards further down. You're probably slowly starting to grasp now the reasons why I'm such a lousy detective. Anyway I unlocked the door to the hallway and walked up the stairs. I opened the door to my apartment, stepped inside and felt something cold and hard boring into the back of my head.

I sometimes think that what I should do in my spare time is to put together a book of handy hints for anyone dumb enough to want to become a private eye. One of those hints would be that when there's a bunch of gangsters threatening to murder you and you notice a strange car parked outside your apartment, it might make some sense to take some elementary precautions. Another hint would be that before walking into a room you should check behind the door because that's where the bad guys always hide.

I cursed myself for a fool as I stood with my hands in the air, while the guy behind the door removed my gun and car keys from my pocket. Did I think that someone like Hamilton Liu wouldn't make another try for me just because he'd failed once? Did I think that someone who could do something like that to Janet Wu would have any qualms at all about shutting up some nosy private eye? On the mantelpiece I could see the cheery card Maisie had sent for my birthday. I wondered if I'd live to see it.

"Let's go," said an American voice in my ear. We went down the stairs, the barrel of the gun making a dent in my head.

There was a Chinese-looking guy standing by the car. He looked vaguely familiar, but I couldn't place him. This guy produced yet another pistol – I hadn't seen so many guns since I was about eleven years old watching John Wayne win World War Two single-handed. He pushed me into the back seat with the gun sticking in my ribs, while the guy who had been hiding behind my door started up the engine. Then I realized where I had seen him before. He was one of the two men whose photographs I'd seen on the TV that morning; the two Vietnamese the police were looking for in connection with Janet Wu's murder. But Hamilton Liu's gang were Chinese, so who were these Vietnamese guys? The Heavenly Tigers? But in that case what did they want with me?

As we drew away I saw another of the gang climbing into my car. I wondered why. They already had a car and mine certainly wasn't worth stealing. However another of the pieces of advice I would offer to would-be detectives is this: if in doubt, keep your mouth shut. I said nothing at all

149

as the two cars threaded their way through the Saturday lunchtime traffic.

I stared through the car windows at the bustling city streets. Shoppers thronged happily into the stores to spend money they didn't have on things they didn't need, or as gifts for people who didn't want them. Soccer fans crowded into the pubs to get as much beer inside them as they could, so they wouldn't be able to remember whether they'd won the game or not. I wondered if anyone vaguely suspected that a few feet away was a terrified private eye being kidnapped by a couple of homicidal Vietnamese.

I winced as I thought of Mary, sitting in Antonio's, waiting for me to show up, but on balance I'd rather be in her situation than mine. It was difficult to feel sympathy for her, quietly seething in front of a nice plate of ribs while I was sitting in a car with a gun in mine.

We drove through Moss Side, through streets of terraced housing, past boarded-up houses and vandalized cars, and stores where you received your purchases through slits in the steel bars that protected them. We turned into a council estate with hard-eyed blacks standing around, staring at us as if we were white slavers with a bunch of coloured beads. We eventually came to a halt outside a group of decrepit blocks of flats.

I was ordered into a lift covered with graffiti and stinking of urine, and taken to the seventh floor. I was thinking wistfully about Fat Tony's spaghetti carbonara as we picked our way along a filthy, rubbish-strewn corridor to a small council flat.

Inside were a couple of ancient mis-matched sofas, a table with the remains of a Chinese take-away and a one-bar electric fire. Three more tough-looking Orientals sat at the table, playing cards and smoking cigarettes by the flickering light of a TV with the sound turned off.

They sat me on a sofa and stared at me with expressionless, flat, black eyes while the guys at the table continued to play cards as if seeing someone brought in at gunpoint was such a normal occurrence that it wasn't worth even inquiring who I was. The guy who'd brought me in, who seemed to be the leader, handed his gun over to one of the card-players and both men disappeared.

I sat there and tried hard to concentrate on watching an old black-and-white movie on the TV instead of staring at the hard-eyed, silent guy sitting a few feet away from me, the gun in his hand aimed somewhere between my mid-section and my groin.

It must have been a couple of hours before my captors returned. They had a brief conversation with the guys at the table. Then they turned to me.

The one I'd recognized was about forty years old, slim, and looked as though he could kill you with one hand while eating lunch with the other. The second was younger, solidly built and had that easy walk that you see in boxers and athletes. He took the gun from the guy who'd been watching over me, pointed it at my forehead, steady as a rock and said, "Who killed Jenny?"

"I don't know," I said. He shook his head, stood up, walked over and put the barrel of the gun in my right eye.

"Let me explain something Mr Collins," he said. "In Chicago there is a Vietnamese gang named The Heavenly Tigers. They are one of the most ruthless and feared gangs in the whole of America. All of us here are members of that gang. My name is Nguyen. Jenny was my sister. Is this making sense to you?"

151

It's difficult to nod with a gun in your eye. "Yes," I croaked.

"We know you went to see Jenny in her hotel the day she was killed. I hope for your sake, Mr Collins, that you can tell us who killed her; because if I think for one moment that you had anything to do with it, I will personally make sure that by the time I am through with you, you will be begging me to let you die. Now tell me again that you don't know anything."

"I think I can help," I said shakily.

He took the gun out of my eye, walked back and sat on the sofa. "Talk," he said.

I told him how she had come to my office and hired me to find Angel Wong; how the two thugs had tried to shoot me and that I suspected that they had killed her. Nguyen asked me for a description and he and his colleague talked briefly in a strange language.

"The fighter is a man called Ah Luk," said Nguyen. "Also known as Lucky. He's a hired killer. Congratulations, Mr Collins. Not many people can claim to have hit him and lived. The other man is Hamilton Liu. Have you heard of him?"

I nodded.

"A few weeks ago one of our emissaries came to England: also called Nguyen." He smiled at me and I was reminded of a picture I'd once seen of a hungry barracuda. "We like to keep things in the family, Mr Collins. Nguyen had a meeting with Hamilton Liu. We have mutual enemies in Chicago, a Hong Kong triad outfit who are trying to establish an operation here in Manchester which would severely impact on Mr Liu's business. We proposed terms to Mr Liu, but he did not seem to think they were

152

acceptable, so he had Nguyen murdered. Now we are going to show Mr Liu how The Heavenly Tigers deal with anyone who crosses them."

I swallowed hard. "Look," I said, "I didn't have anything to do with any of this. Your sister was my client. Why would I want to kill her?"

Nguyen stared at me with black, unblinking eyes. "Where is Angel Wong?" he asked.

"I don't know where she is," I lied desperately. "Janet, Jenny that is, just said she'd run away from her husband: I was supposed to find her."

Nguyen stood up and I thought, why am I protecting Angel Wong? I don't know anything about her. I stared at Nguyen and before he could stick that damned gun in my eye again I said, "But I have an idea."

Nguyen sat down.

"I think she may be at Hamilton Liu's house."

"Explain," said Nguyen curtly.

I told him how I'd met a dancer at The Yin & Yang Club. I didn't say that I knew definitely, just that she'd told me she'd heard someone was being held at the Liu's residence. There was an animated discussion in the same strange language, presumably Vietnamese.

"Do you know where this place is?" asked Nguyen.

I shook my head. "No," I replied.

With a sardonic smile on his face, Nguyen said something that made my blood run cold. "Then we will show you the way," he said.

He rapped out some commands. The two guys who had been playing cards left the room. They returned with a couple of large calibre handguns, two sawn-down pump-action shotguns and enough ammunition to wipe out half the population of Moss Side.

"You are going to drive us to see Mr Liu, Mr Collins," said Nguyen.

I stared in horror, then, for reasons I don't understand I said, "In that case let's not be formal. You can call me Tom."

It was a Jake Fist response. Nguyen's face cracked into a huge smile. "Perhaps you're not as big a coward as I supposed," he said.

Don't you believe it, I thought as we headed for the lift.

Nguyen threw me my car keys and we all climbed into the Escort. I didn't know then that the description and number of my beat-up old heap was in front of every copper in Manchester after I failed to show up at the police station. If I can give some advice to the young villains out there it's this: plan your bank heists, or whatever crimes you want to pull, for a Saturday during the football season when all the coppers are at Old Trafford trying to prevent the Third World War from breaking out between Manchester United and Leeds, or Liverpool, or Tottenham Hotspur. When I think about it now I still can't believe that I drove through Manchester on a Saturday afternoon through all the surveillance cameras, then out to Hamilton Liu's, and not a single police officer or patrol car spotted us. Just born lucky I suppose.

As I started up the car engine I made another mental addition to my book. This would say that if you are ever invited to drive a gang of heavily armed homicidal maniacs to a gunfight, then it's probably best to tell them that you'd rather not do it because you've got a headache. My manual for budding private eyes will be called *Detecting for Dummies*.

Chapter Sixteen

*T*he young guy must have been up half the night, Jake reckoned. He had a stack of cuttings and clippings and pictures going back years.

Dillinger Scott had been the owner of a prosperous banking business called Upstate Savings and Loan. Scott's first wife had had a mental breakdown and he'd stuck her in a home where she'd died shortly afterwards, leaving him free to marry a younger, better-looking, and presumably saner version. Eleanor Mann's mother was the second Mrs Dillinger Scott. She'd been a socialite, twenty years his junior, and every bit as good-looking as her daughter.

Eleanor Scott had then married Frankie Mann: his fifth walk down the aisle. Three of his wives were divorced; one was dead.

Jake leafed through the stuff about Frankie's third wife. She'd married Frankie at nineteen years old. One year later she'd been driving her car down a quiet road, late at night, when she'd lost control and carelessly driven herself over a cliff and into a river. She'd been dead when they pulled her out. There were no suspicious circumstances, except that no one seemed to have thought to ask why she'd be driving alone, in the middle of nowhere, in the middle of the night.

The police and the coroner had ruled accidental death, and the book had been closed. The officer in charge of the case had been a guy *called Lew Kraski.*

Then Jed passed over a short article about Melissa Francis.

Jake called Bart and asked him for a favour.

"Sure," said Bart. "No problem."

Jake left Jed going through the back copies, picked up a pass which said he was a staff reporter for the Chicago Gazette *and drove out west.*

*

It was a pretty little place, with a lawn out front and a yard out back, with a big happy-looking dog yapping at him as he stepped out of his car and rang the bell. A middle-aged woman answered the door.

"Mrs Drabowsky?" asked Jake. She nodded. Jake showed her his press card and told her he'd like to ask some questions about her daughter as they were planning to feature her in one of their forthcoming issues. Mrs Drabowsky was only too happy to help.

It seemed that Irene had been abandoned as a child, and the Drabowskys, who seemed as nice a couple as you could find, had adopted her, the fourth of six kids they'd given a home to. Jake listened patiently to details of her childhood and her early career. He dutifully wrote it all down, while Mrs Drabowsky fed him two cups of coffee and half a dozen of her home-made cookies. After an hour or so he managed to escape. He tried not to feel like a heel as he crumpled up the notes he'd so laboriously taken and stuck them in the trash.

He turned the key, cranked the starter with his foot and drove back to the offices of The Chicago Gazette. *He reckoned it was time to talk to Greta.*

*

One of the Vietnamese gang had stayed behind in the lousy flat. Nguyen climbed into the front seat with three more in the back and began to give me instructions on how to get to the Liu's place.

"It's OK," I said. "I know where it is." I drove along in silence.

"Can I ask you a question?" I ventured.

"Sure," replied Nguyen.

"Who is this Angel Wong and why are you looking for her?"

"As Jenny told you, her husband is a mutual friend and we would like her to return to him."

"And that's all?" I said, incredulously

"That's all," he replied. I didn't bother trying again. I could see that was all the information I was going to get.

It was late afternoon, the sun sinking in the sky in a big red fireball. The rain had stopped and I thought it looked like a beautiful evening for a gunfight.

We arrived at the double gates at the entrance to the Liu's place, with Nguyen crouched down out of sight in the passenger seat and the three guys in the back doing the same. "Wind down your window and say, 'I have a message for Mr Liu from Good-bye Johnny,'" he hissed.

I spoke into the microphone as instructed and to my surprise the gates began to open.

"What now?" I whispered.

"Pull up to the front door, get out, and ring the bell. And please don't try to warn them. I'd hate to have to shoot you, now that we've become such good friends."

The rottweilers were obviously pleased to see me again, barking and leaping against their chains and howling like werewolves on a full moon. "What happens after I ring the bell?" I said.

"I suggest you run away as fast as you can, Tom," he replied mockingly.

*

Across the street an excited young plain-clothes constable was talking into his microphone.

"It's a red Ford Escort." He read off the serial number. "The driver answers the description of Tom Collins."

There was a short delay, and then an angry voice sounded in his ear. "Wait till he comes out, then follow him. Don't stop him outside Liu's place. We don't want them to know they're being watched. As soon as he stops, arrest him: and Pike,"

"Yes sir?" said the constable.

"You lose him, and you'll spend the rest of your life cleaning out the station's shithouses. Understand?"

"Yes sir," responded Detective Constable Pike.

*

I drew up behind a Mercedes and the same black Toyota that Liu had used when he came to my office.

I got out of the car, quaking with terror. Reluctantly I approached the door, but while I was still a couple of yards away it opened, revealing my old friend Lucky Luk. He didn't look at all pleased to see me. I was wondering how I was going to run away, with Lucky pointing an automatic at me, when there came the flat 'whump' of a shotgun. Lucky's luck had just run out. He was blasted straight back through the door, and then the Vietnamese opened up like

158

an invading army.

I started to run, difficult with legs like jelly, when I heard a hideous, savage yowl, and saw crazed eyes, flashing teeth, and a hundred and fifty pounds of black hatred flying at me through the air There must have been some release mechanism for the rottweilers. I almost pissed my pants in terror, grabbing at the hound's throat as I fell backwards into a flowerbed.

I was screaming and fighting for all I was worth, when I became aware that the dog was not moving. I shoved it away, and crouched on the ground to see Nguyen grinning at me from behind the Mercedes, sliding a new magazine into the butt of a huge automatic.

While in an unmarked car DC Nigel Pike was screaming into his mike; "Jesus Christ, it's like the Wild West here. Handguns, shotguns, automatic weapons. There's at least six people shooting at each other. We need an Armed Response Unit. Urgent! Repeat: urgent!"

*

I heard a shout, and saw one of the Vietnamese stop in his tracks, clutching at his stomach as he fell. Glass was flying everywhere as the windows were shot out. From inside the house Liu's men were blasting away into the gardens and the shrubbery.

The noise was indescribable: yells, and screams and gunfire coming from all directions. I was on my hands and knees, trying to hide behind my car, when a woman came haring round the corner: tall, dark-haired, clutching a bag in her hand, and running like an Olympic sprinter; or at least how an Olympic sprinter might have run, wearing

159

jewelled Ferragamo sandals with four-inch stiletto heels.

"Help me, please help me," she shouted at me. I grabbed her hand and pulled her down behind my car.

I opened the door to the rear seat. She crawled in and I clambered into the driver's seat, turned the key in the ignition, and levered the gear stick into reverse while trying to keep my head down below the dashboard. You should try it – it isn't easy. In the mirror, I saw someone racing out of the house holding a huge handgun. In total panic I floored the accelerator. The car shot back in a roar of screaming tyres and flying gravel, and the gunman screamed as the car hit him. I swerved that car flat out backwards through the gates into the street. If there had been any traffic we would have been dead. As it was we narrowly avoided a police car with headlights blazing and sirens screaming, racing down the street at about a hundred miles an hour. I fishtailed along the road, sweating and swearing, and trying not to smash into the garden wall. I drove away like a maniac, dodging flashing headlights and police cars roaring by me, as I hung onto the steering wheel, dedicating my life to doing good works in a monastery if, by some piece of sheer blind luck, I ever got out of this alive.

"Shit, that's Collins," shouted DC Pike but he had an armed man in body and face armour, crouching down beside his car, screaming at him, "Who's in there? How many are there? What weapons do they have? Come on man, we need to know!" while gunfire, and screams, and the sound of breaking glass ripped through the fading September evening.

Not that Pike could have followed Collins anyway. When the first shots had rung out, he'd leapt out from his car and hidden behind it. Now, there was no way in hell he was going to climb back in, and drive through that lot.

Armed police were taking up position all around the house. A CID officer ran towards him, crouched down, and grabbed the mike. Over the noise of the gunbattle, and through the static, Pike heard McClusky's voice saying, "I'm on my way now." He crouched in misery thinking that maybe driving the car through a hail of bullets might, after all, have been preferable to what he'd have to go through when McClusky arrived.

*

I drove the first few hundred yards like a madman until I began to calm down, and to realize that somehow, I'd managed to come out of it in one piece. I slowed down, and turned to look at my passenger, who was sitting in the back seat, a Luis Vuitton shoulder bag grasped tightly in her hands. She looked up at me remarkably calmly for someone who's just been driven backwards at eighty miles an hour through a remake of *Gunfight at the OK Corral.*

"Have we escaped?" she asked.

"Yes, I think we have," I replied, as casually as I could.

"My name's Angel Wong," she said.

"Yes, I know," I replied, with police sirens screaming in my ear as another half a dozen cars raced past, bound for the Liu's place.

"Where are we going?" asked Angel.

"The nearest police station," I replied.

"Please, please don't do that," she cried. "They'll kill me for sure."

"Who'll kill you? The police?" I responded.

"No, look, is there somewhere we can go; somewhere safe where I can explain?"

That's when the Collins' principle began to kick in. In my defence I was scared to death, starving and I didn't know whether I'd killed the guy I'd hit with the car. The very last thing I needed at this point was twelve hours in a police interrogation room with Ted McClusky. I also wanted to know what, exactly, I'd got myself into and the person who could supply those answers was sitting in the back of the car. My apartment wasn't safe, neither was my office but there was one place I knew where we could safely hide out for a while. I drove to Maisie's.

Maisie's was in an area fairly close to Piccadilly in what had once been a fashionable part of town with smart Victorian homes owned by the gentry and staffed by the poor but honest working classes. It was now a rundown place full of dingy apartments and cheap hotels, peopled by drug dealers and petty criminals and drunks – the poor and totally dishonest classes who had never done a day's work in their lives.

I rang the bell of a four-storey Victorian block with a cheap sign outside saying, The Belvedere Apartments. It was a place you could rent a room for an hour, a day, or the rest of your life and nobody asked any questions at all as long as you paid in advance.

A short, fat woman with a mass of blue hair opened the door a crack, peered suspiciously out, then flung it open. She embraced me in a hug that would have broken the ribs of a grizzly bear.

"Tom," she gasped, in delight, "how have you been keeping? Come on, come in."

She looked past me at Angel Wong and raised an

eyebrow.

"I need a couple of rooms Maisie."

She studied me with a critical eye. I was filthy and wet from lying in assorted lawns and flower-beds and I hadn't realized that my trousers and shirt were stained with blood, presumably from the rottweiler. In contrast, Angel looked as if she'd just had a tough afternoon shopping at the Arndale Centre.

"I think you'd better come in," said Maisie. She turned and I noticed how very slowly she walked, how very old she looked.

"Maisie, first I need to park the car," I said.

I wondered how badly McClusky wanted to speak to me now, after the quiet suburbs of Manchester had been turned into something resembling Baghdad on a bad night. Sitting behind the big wooden gates in Maisie's yard the Escort would out be of sight of anyone who happened to be looking for it: like the entire Manchester police force.

Maisie was far too old a hand and had far too much experience in dealing with people on the run from the Law to think that I was simply concerned about keeping the local villains' hands away from my hub-caps. She gave me what they call an old-fashioned look and tossed me a key. I ran round the corner, and unlocked the massive padlock holding together the gates which opened into the paved yard at the back of Maisie's guesthouse. I parked the car, pocketing a little souvenir Nguyen had thoughtfully left on the dash and walked back into Maisie's feeling a little more comfortable. Not a lot, but a little.

I went past the tiny front desk into the rooms at the back where Maisie was sitting opposite Angel Wong. She was dispensing hot, sweet tea from a pot which seemed to be permanently full like those magic vats of porridge or Guinness in one of those Irish fairy stories my mother used to read to me.

"I've only got one room, Tom. But the bed's big enough for two." She cocked an eyebrow at me.

"I'll take it."

Slowly and with an obvious effort she led us up the stairs into a large room with heavy old brown wooden furniture, a sagging double bed, a shower and toilet. She gave me the room key and a key to the front door, something she didn't do for anyone else, but the one thing she did insist on with everyone was money up front. You couldn't blame her. Some of her clients did moonlight flits; some never had any money in the first place and some went out for long walks, for health reasons and never came back.

I paid her for two nights and sat on the bed. I was completely exhausted but at least I felt safe. For a while anyway.

Angel sat on a chair looking disdainfully around the room. She was dressed as if she was about to go to an expensive cocktail party, and looked completely out of place in this third rate flophouse. "I'm going to have a shower," she said, disappearing into the bathroom.

I went down to get soap and towels from Maisie. I asked her if she could put on any food: I hadn't eaten the whole day.

"There's a Chinese down the road but you can't go out looking like that," she said. "Go and lie down for half an hour, Tom and I'll get something sent up to you."

Gratefully I lay down on the bed. There was something I was supposed to do, someone I was supposed to call, but

164

I couldn't remember what it was and seconds later I was asleep.

*

McClusky and three members of the Armed Response Unit gazed grimly at the shattered remains of Hamilton Liu's house. The shooting had stopped. They were loading the bodies and the wounded into ambulances. One of the wounded was Meredith Liu but there was no sign of her husband. Neither was there any sign of Tom Collins or his car. Armed men were searching through the house but it seemed that there was no one else there.

"Know what it's all about?" asked one of the officers.

"Not really," replied McClusky through his teeth. "Some kind of gang war but we haven't the slightest idea why. Hemshall's taken personal charge of it," he said, gloomily.

He turned his back on the wreckage and walked across the street to where Detective Constable Nigel Pike was standing by his unmarked car. "What happened to Collins?" enquired McClusky, conversationally.

"Sorry Super, he got away," replied Pike. "I couldn't do anything, sir. The ARU needed me here as only I knew what was going on."

"How, exactly, did he get away?" responded McClusky.

"In his car, sir. Came backwards through those gates like a bat out of hell: nearly hit a squad car and then drove down that road," Pike pointed a finger, "like the devil himself was after him. There was a woman in the car too. Couldn't make out much, except she had long dark hair."

"Chinese?" enquired McClusky.

"Not sure, sir. Could have been."

McClusky stood with his hands in his pockets and

165

gazed at the young constable.

"Do you know how many toilets there are at Police Headquarters, Pike?"

"No sir," replied Pike, unhappily.

"Well you will soon, Pike. You'll know all of them. Personally."

McClusky walked slowly back to where an armed officer was standing in front of the smoking ruins of Hamilton Liu's house, turning over a dead rottweiler with his foot.

Chapter Seventeen

Greta was about sixty years old and had been The Gazette's *gossip columnist for years. Anything she didn't know about Chicago's high and low society wasn't worth knowing. She was about five feet tall, chain-smoked Lucky Strike cigarettes, kept a bottle of Old Crow in her office drawer and had a memory that would have made an elephant pack its trunk and head for the high hills.*

She loved to see Jake because she thought he was about the only person she knew who was nearly as tough as she was. It also gave her an excuse to pick up two tumblers, open her drawer, and pour them both a shot that emptied half the bottle.

They shot the breeze for a while, and then she said, "OK Jake, what's on your mind?"

"Frankie Mann," said Jake. "I hear one of his wives went swimming and forgot to get out of the car first."

It seemed that Frankie's third shot at the sacred rite of matrimony had been called Claudia. The story went that she'd told Frankie his old habits would have to stop. When it became obvious that Frankie had no intention of playing the faithful husband, Claudia had decided that she may as well play the part of the unfaithful wife. Apparently, the night she died, she'd been on her way back from a liaison with one of half a dozen guys she was openly sleeping with.

Frankie was distraught.

Jake took a drink, nodded his head. He'd figured it would be

167

something along those lines.

Greta and Jake had another shot and Jake asked her what she knew about Eleanor Mann. Greta lit a new cigarette from the stub of the old one.

Dillinger Scott, Eleanor Mann's father had a public reputation as a well-respected banker and public benefactor, sat on the boards of school governors, made highly visible donations to charities, and generally made himself out to be Santa Claus with a heart.

Privately he was known to foreclose on anyone if it made him a buck and have his loans repaid in any way that got him the money. It was also rumoured he was involved with financing stolen property, and that in the thirties he'd made a bundle in the illicit booze racket.

Since then things had gone downhill with his bank. It was currently rumoured that he was on the payroll of Frankie Mann and had been ever since Frankie had started bedding his daughter.

"And I presume that Mr Scott, our upstanding banker, having married for the second time had given up on his whoring ways and was now faithful to his young and pretty new wife?" said Jake

Greta laughed so hard she nearly spilled her drink. "Jeez, Jake, you kiddin' me? He had VIP cards in just about every brothel in Chicago. Half the hookers in town had him on their Christmas list. They reckoned he couldn't get a hard-on without a fifty dollar bill in his hand."

"So what did his little lady do then, left sitting home at nights, sad and bored and all on her lonesome?"

Greta gave Jake a big grin. "There was a guy called Dean Larkins. Big handsome son-of-a-bitch. Played for the Chicago Cubs, until one day, for no apparent reason, they traded him to Washington. It was round about the same time that Eleanor Mann's mother was hospitalized for a few days with a 'ladies' condition'. The rumour ran that the 'ladies' condition' resulted in a brand new bawling little baby. Who definitely wasn't the old man's."

Jake sat there smoking, and drinking Greta's Old Crow, and worked out that if the story were true, that little baby would now be about twenty-five years old. The same age as Irene Drabowsky who'd been adopted at the age of three weeks.

Greta tossed the empty bottle into the bin, gave Jake a big hug, and told him to come and see her some more.

As Jake drove away he was reflecting on a few things. There were only two things worth the trouble according to Karl: money and sex. And there seemed to be an awful lot of both surrounding Frankie Mann and his associates.

Karl had also said that if there weren't a woman at the bottom of this case, he'd eat his desk. It looked as though his desk might be safe for a while.

*

I lay on the bed in The Belvedere dreaming of those days when I used to sit contentedly in Maisie's back room with a drink and a slice of cake, or a great hunk of shortbread in my hand, while assorted villains, escaped convicts and axe-murderers booked themselves in for a night's sleep. When I opened my eyes Angel Wong was walking out of the bathroom in a brand new outfit, looking ready for a night out at the Oscars. I wondered what I would grab hold of if I were running for my life. I certainly didn't think it would be a Louis Vuitton bag and a complete change of designer clothing.

Then Maisie was knocking on the door, with a tray loaded with food, but she'd also brought me a pair of jeans, a shirt and some socks from the discount shop and a pair of Nike trainers. "Off the back of a lorry," she grinned.

"Maisie, I swear when I win the Lottery, half of it goes

169

to you," I said. She gave me that big grin of hers, all red cheeks, wrinkles and false teeth, and said, "You'd better, Tom Collins."

We ate spare ribs, fried rice, sweet and sour pork, chow mein – all those Chinese dishes that were invented in England or the USA. Whether Angel Wong thought it was authentic Chinese or not she wolfed it down like a concentration camp survivor.

It was my turn in the bathroom. I showered, changed into my new clothes and went down the stairs to see Maisie.

Maisie was in both senses of the word my oldest friend. She could provide you with virtually anything, from a woman for the night to a false passport and a ticket to Puerto Rico but there were two things she wouldn't touch: drugs and guns. She was sitting in her parlour with a drink in front of her and as she looked up at me I saw all the lines and wrinkles that the years of struggle and care had etched deep into her face.

"So how much trouble you in this time, Tom?" she asked.

I shrugged. "Plenty, Maisie."

"You want to tell me any of it?"

"No."

"Up to you, Tom." She took a sip from her drink. "So I guess you didn't come down here to make small talk?"

"No Maisie. I'm just too tired right now. I came down to see if I could beg a drink from you."

"Don't remember you being the drinking type, Tom," said Maisie.

"I wasn't Maisie," I replied. "Until about half an hour ago. Right now a large scotch would certainly help."

She poured for me and for herself, her hand trembling and we sat there in a companiable silence sipping at our drinks. "It's not the first time you've sat there in trouble, Tom," Maisie said after a while. "But it's been a long time."

I finished my whisky and put the glass on the table. "Yes, Maisie," I said, "and I still think about those old days, and you're still the person I come to when I need help." I stood up and hugged her to me before I went upstairs to talk to Angel Wong and try to find out what the hell was going on.

*

Angel Wong sat on the bed. She looked a little pale, but pretty much in control of herself, looking at me with big luminous eyes and half a smile on her face. I thought she was probably the most beautiful woman I had ever seen.

"OK," I said, as gently as I could. "Now could you please tell me what the hell all this is about?"

"Look," she said quietly, "it's very late, and I'm very tired. Can't we do this tomorrow?"

I was tired too, but I wasn't prepared to wait any longer. "No," I said.

I stood at the foot of the bed, staring at her, her face illuminated by one of the cheap bedside lamps Maisie had thoughtfully provided in case you woke up in the middle of the night with your true love beside you, and decided you'd like to read a book.

She looked at me for a moment, trying to decide exactly how serious I was, then tossed her head, and said, "My husband is a businessman in Chicago. He's very rich, but he's very, very difficult to live with. A few days ago we had

171

this huge fight."

I looked at her Louis Vuitton bag, and her simple, shortish, black silk dress that was probably worth about the same as the earnings of a small country. Her watch was an antique-looking lady's Cartier; she had thrown her simple fur stole on the dresser. Her Ferragamo shoes were parked side by side, beside the bed. I wondered what she and her husband had to fight about. Probably she didn't like the colour of the carpets in the new Mercedes.

"Anyway I decided to go away for a few days, to think things over, so I went to stay with an old friend from my student days called Meredith Liu."

"Well, after a while I began to realise that Meredith's husband was mixed up in some pretty nasty rackets, so I thought I'd move out and stay in a hotel. That's when I discovered I was being kept virtually a prisoner. I tried to ask Meredith what was going on, but she wouldn't talk to me. I didn't know what was happening." At this she began to cry, and I had to admit it was a pretty good performance. I pulled a crumpled tissue from the box by the bed, supplied free by Maisie for those evenings when you can't afford any company, and handed it to her.

"I think that they'd decided to hold me to ransom. As I said my husband's very rich. I was sitting in my room, with a guard watching me, when suddenly I heard one of Hamilton's guys screaming something about Goodbye Johnny. I heard a gunshot, my guard ran out of the room, and the next thing I knew it was like the fireworks going off on the Fourth of July. So I took my chance."

"I've never been so scared. I just grabbed my bag, and ran out the back door." She looked up at me then with those big dark eyes, and said, "And then you saved my life.

172

I haven't said thank you to you yet, for that."

I have to admit that tired and angry though I was, it did fleetingly cross my mind to wonder just how grateful this Angel could be, but I pushed those unworthy thoughts aside. "Who on earth is Goodbye Johnny?" I asked.

"I'm not sure. I think he might be a Chicago gangster."

So why would they be expecting a Chicago gangster to show up in a quiet Manchester suburb? I thought back over what Nguyen had told me, about their mutual enemy in Chicago. It still made no sense, and neither did this pretty little thing sitting in front of me.

"So what about your cousin, Janet Wu?" I asked, "Or should it be Nguyen Li Binh?"

She looked at me with those hooded eyes that could mean any damn thing she wanted them to. "I don't know what you mean," she said.

I'd picked up a newspaper from downstairs, and I threw it at her. "That's the woman who hired me to find you," I said. "She said she was your cousin; your best friend. Now she's dead."

Angel stared at the newspaper and the photo of Janet Wu or whatever her name was. "I'm sorry," she said, "I've never seen her before."

For a moment I thought that perhaps she was telling the truth. I realized then how tired I must have been.

"Yesterday morning," I continued, "after I tried to talk to your friend Meredith and her husband two Chinese paid me a visit in my office. They asked me if I knew where you where. Then they tried to kill me. Then I find the woman who hired me to find you dead in her hotel room. The next day I'm kidnapped by a gang of Vietnamese, armed to the teeth and out for revenge and guess who they're looking

173

for? You! And you tell me that all this is because you ran away from your husband?"

"I'm sorry," she said, "I just don't know."

None of it made any sense to me but I was dog-tired, and I'd had enough of being lied to by beautiful oriental women. The next day I was taking the whole thing to the police.

I walked into the bathroom. I'd already had one shower but that had been a matter of necessity. This time I stripped off my clothes and stood gratefully under the hot water. It was the first time I'd felt relaxed since Janet Wu had walked into my office. I closed my eyes, letting the water pour over me, beating on my head, drowning out the problems of the day when suddenly the awful realization hit me. It was as if someone had turned on the cold-water tap. I'd left Mary sitting on her own in Fat Tony's and now, several hours later I still hadn't called her to explain. Maisie had a payphone at the bottom of the stairs but I was tired, wet and naked and didn't feel at all inclined to get dressed again. Neither was I too happy at the prospect of fifteen minutes of torrential abuse from Mary.

Then reason came and helped me out. It was late and I was tired. Mary would be tired too. What we both needed was a good night's sleep. I'd wait till the morning and call her then, when she would be in a better frame of mind. Did I mention somewhere the possibility of evolution taking a few steps in reverse?

I walked back into the bedroom, wearing my boxer shorts. Angel stood out like a sore thumb in her elegant, expensive clothes in this shabby room. She was staring out of the window. Luckily it was dark and raining, otherwise she might have seen what the rest of the street was like. I checked the chain was on the door and climbed into bed, watching Angel's eyes widen as she saw what I held in my hand.

"I didn't think English people were allowed to have guns," she said.

"They aren't," I replied. "Goodnight Angel."

I settled gratefully back on the old, well-used mattress. The last thing I remember was half opening my eyes to see Angel slipping out of her designer dress. It didn't matter a thing. She could have performed an erotic *pas-de-deux* with a boa constrictor while dancing on my spine naked in her stilettos. I'd have slept through the whole performance.

Chapter Eighteen

*J*ake picked up the phone. "Fancy lunch?" he asked.

"Sure," said Bart Stanton. They met at a steakhouse, a real old-fashioned place that did nothing fancy, just served up a steak the size of Manhattan done any way you asked.

"Usual, Mr Fist?" asked the waiter.

Jake nodded. Bart Stanton ordered his burned to a crisp on the outside with the heart still beating in the centre. It's called Chicago blue and Chicago's still the only place they do it right.

"I did some more checking on your good friend Mr Mann," said Bart, sucking down his martini. "Seems he's making waves about buying a piece of real estate out east. There's a little resistance to the sale by some parties but apparently after a few soothing words from Little Paolo they see the error of their ways."

Little Paolo – Paolito Campioni was the guy who ran the gangs on the east side. Him and Bruno Scarletti were holding hands and blowing kisses to each other, at least for now.

"So that would explain why Frankie was talking with Bruno," said Jake, waving his hand at the waiter for a couple more martinis. "And why do you think he wants this piece of land?"

"Who knows? But by a sheer coincidence seems just about the same size as the police HQ on South Michigan."

"So what you gonna do then?"

"Have a word with Mayor Daley. He thinks there's anything going on here he doesn't know about he'll kill it stone dead."

176

"But doesn't that leave Frankie Mann with a big parcel of land in the east side and nothing to do with it?"

Bart Stanton grinned. "Sometimes, life just ain't fair, Jake," he said as his steak arrived.

They ate in silence. It's a kind of insult to interrupt a good steak for small talk. Occasionally the waiter filled up their red wine glasses. Eventually Jake pushed away his plate. The two men drank some wine. Then Jake said, "Read your own newspaper today?"

"Of course. What did I miss?" asked Bart.

Jake fished a copy out of his pocket and folded it up to show Greta's section, the gossip column. Frankie Mann was steering Melissa Francis away from another stellar performance at The Gaumont.

"So what?" asked Bart. "She's an actress. She puts on one show before the curtain goes down, another one after. It ain't the first time and it won't be the last. So what's the big deal?"

Jake leaned back with his cigarette. "Take a good look at Melissa Francis, Bart," he said, "assuming you can still see straight with all that booze inside you."

"Booze?" laughed Bart Stanton. "Jesus Jake, I'm a newspaper-man. That doesn't even qualify for starters." He studied the picture of Frankie and his broad. "Sorry Jake, this doesn't mean a thing to me."

Then Jake passed him a second photograph. "Mean anything now?" he asked.

Bart stared at the picture and realization dawned. "Holy hell, Jake, what's going on here?"

"I'll let you know as soon as I know myself," replied Jake.

He put the two pictures back in his pocket then. Frankie Mann with Melissa Francis and Frankie Mann with his dear lady wife.

*

177

For a moment, when I woke up I was unsure where I was. A strange room, a gun in my hand and a dark-haired oriental beauty lying beside me in the bed. It wasn't my normal start to a working day. I looked at my watch. It was still only eight thirty. I climbed out of bed and went to the bathroom.

When I walked back into the bedroom Angel Wong was sitting up in the bed with the sheets pulled decorously round her shoulders. I went to the wardrobe where I'd hung up the clothes Maisie had brought me, took off my boxers, and dressed. I figured that Angel had definitely seen a naked man before in her life and if she hadn't, well, she didn't have to look.

I put on my brand new Nike trainers which were at least two sizes too big, but still better than the mud-stained, blood-stained shoes I'd worn the day before.

I sat on the bed trying to look tough and said. "OK Angel, now we're going to try one more time."

"Can I go to the bathroom?" she asked.

"No, you can use the bathroom when I'm satisfied you've told me the truth," I said. That, I thought was exactly the way Jake Fist would have played it.

"Bathroom first, truth afterwards," she said, throwing back the sheets. She was wearing a tiny white bra and pants, wrapped around a body that would have left Claudia Schiffer sobbing. Five minutes later she returned, and climbed back into bed.

"There's a guy called Johnny Wong. He runs all of the Chinese rackets in Chicago. He's known as Good-bye Johnny because that's the last thing a lot of people have heard him say. He fronts his rackets with a real estate business, you know, buying and selling big houses and apartments, property development and so on. I used to work for him until he started to come on to me. He started to get heavy with me." At this point she gave me those big soulful, virginal eyes, "until one day I couldn't take it any more. So I left. That's why I had a fight with my husband. He wanted me to stay and I didn't."

"I thought you said your husband was a rich businessman. Why would he want you working for a guy like Goodbye Johnny?"

She shrugged. "I don't know how he got rich," she said, "but I think he owed Johnny."

"So why did you go to Meredith Liu?"

"I just thought they'd help me out," she said, "but they wanted me to give them all the information I could about Johnny. I think they were going to blackmail him."

I sat on the bed thinking that this definitely sounded nearer to the truth than her previous effort. Then again, she'd had the whole night to think something up.

"So what did you tell them?" I asked.

"I told them a few things – unimportant stuff," she said, "but they were starting to get impatient."

"And threatening to rip your pretty little finger nails out?" I offered.

She nodded her head. "Something like that."

"So who was this woman Janet Wu, and why would she want me to find you?"

"There's a Vietnamese mob in Chicago called The Heavenly Tigers. They and Johnny are always at each other's throats. Maybe they thought they could trade me back to him or something. I really don't know."

At least that part checked out.

"I told you last night that two Chinese came to my office and tried to kill me. One was Hamilton Liu, the other was a thug called Lucky."

"Yes, I know," she said. "I heard Hamilton screaming at Ah Luk. I never saw anyone so angry in my life. He told Ah Luk to bring you to him, or he'd have Ah Luk's head served to him on the dinner table."

"Well he can't do it now," I said. "They shot him last night."

"Yes, but Hamilton's got plenty more men, Tom."

"Well with any luck they shot Hamilton Liu as well," I said. "And even if he managed to stay alive, right now he'll be sitting in a prison cell."

The previous night's shoot-out must have made the front page of every newspaper in England. I wanted to know exactly what had happened and exactly where I stood in all this, but there was no TV in the room and no newspapers.

"No, they didn't kill Hamilton. He wasn't in the house last night," said Angel. "He went out with two of his men just before you arrived. I saw them leave."

"Yes, well, he'll have more on his plate than me to worry about right now," I said grimly.

Angel looked at me over the bedsheets. "Do you understand the Chinese concept of face, Tom?" she asked

I shook my head.

"Face is kind of like the Italians when they insist on "respect", but it's a lot more than that. You can take away a man's wife, his money, but you can't take away his face. You've punched Hamilton in the mouth, beaten up his guard, taken his gun away, thrown him out on the street. Hamilton's lost face real big time."

"Which means what?"

"Which means that whatever else has happened, he'll be looking for you and he won't stop till he finds you."

"So what happens if he finds me?" I asked

"He'll kill you," she replied.

"And if he finds you?"

"He'll kill me, too," she answered.

"And the Vietnamese gang?"

She shrugged her shoulders. "I don't know. Kidnap me; hold me for ransom, torture information out of me; kill me."

"And Goodbye Johnny?"

"He'll probably kill me as well."

It was a typical dark, cloudy, Manchester morning; the kind that has you wondering how far down it is from the balcony to the street. I felt much better now.

"Look, Angel, the only thing we can do is go to the police," I said.

She shook her head, violently. "No, you can't. They'd never let me testify, never," she said. "They'll find a way to stop me. You want to go to the cops, you may as well shoot me now."

I thought about that for a moment. It was definitely an option. "So what do you want me to do?" I asked in exasperation.

"Take me to the airport. Let me get away. I have money, I know where I can go."

"Angel," I said, "there's a dead woman, God knows how many dead men, three Chinese gangs running around trying to murder me, or you, or probably both of us, and all you've done is tell me a pack of lies. Can you please give me one good reason why I should help you run out on this whole mess?"

She stared directly at me, with the kind of look that would have burned a hole in the shield of the space shuttle.

"You could always come with me," she said.

I had visions of white beaches and exotic cocktails, and Angel Wong stretched out in front of me in a tiny white bikini. I couldn't handle it: not at this time in the morning. I swallowed hard, stood up.

"Look, Angel, I have to go out for a while," I said. "I'll get some breakfast sent up for you."

I wondered how she'd cope with Maisie's Manchester fry-up of chips, sausages, fried bread and black pudding. "But listen to me, Angel: do not leave this room. Do not go out dressed like you were last night, because if you do they'll mug you before you get out of the front door." And save me a hell of a lot of trouble, I thought.

"Where are you going, Tom?" she said in a small voice.

"I have to check in at my office. I'll be back in an hour or so," I said. Which was a complete lie. First I was going to buy a newspaper to find out whether or not I'd killed the guy I'd hit with the car: then I was off to the police station and turn everybody in. I'd had enough.

"If you need me, call my mobile phone," I said. I gave her the number and she took her I-phone 27 Super-S Deluxe or whatever it was and keyed it in. I stood looking at her sitting demurely on the unmade bed and the thoughts going through my head could have had me arrested. Angel sat there pretending she didn't know exactly what I was thinking. Then she looked up at me and smiled. I stood in an agony of indecision and it was the thought of what I had to do next that kept me from saying *the hell with it all,* locking the door behind me and throwing myself back into the bed. Instead I took a deep breath, shook my head and went reluctantly down the stairs. It was the moment I had been dreading over all others. I think on balance I'd have been happier joining in a gunfight with Hamilton Liu. I fed a coin into the telephone box on the wall and dialled Mary's number. A sluggish, sleepy voice said, "Hello."

As brightly as I could I said, "Hello Mary, it's Tom."

I held the phone away from my ear then, for a couple of minutes and made a note that I hadn't previously realized how rich, powerful and varied was Mary's control of the English vernacular.

I waited for the storm to die down, inserted another coin.

"Look Mary, I know that this sounds crazy but the reason I couldn't meet you yesterday was that I was kidnapped by a gang of Vietnamese gangsters and forced to take part in this gunfight and I only escaped by the skin of my teeth."

I have to admit that as an excuse, it didn't really sound awfully plausible. I was quickly made to realise that Mary's previous tirade had merely been a rehearsal, a kind of warming-up exercise for what was to come. The gist of it was the following:

Trying to decipher the few pitiful fragments of what remained of my brain, was a job utterly beyond all known methods of modern psychiatry.

To save everyone a lot of trouble, I should find a very tall structure and climb to the top.

There, I should fill my pockets with the rocks that were now cluttering up my head.

Then I should throw myself off.

Now I knew Mary read the newspapers and even though she slept late on a Sunday she must surely have seen the Saturday editions. I tried to explain that the person the police were looking for in connection with the murdered girl in The Ritz was in fact myself but I may as well have tried to stem Niagara Falls with a paper napkin.

Eventually I just put the phone down. I would have been prepared to bet a large sum of money that it would have been at least ten more minutes before she realized that she was speaking to the dialling tone rather than to me. At least, I reflected, that was one decision taken out of my hands. There was no chance of reconciliation after this. It was with something of a sense of relief that I turned out of the hallway and walked into the kitchen.

Maisie was waiting for me with a newspaper in her hand.

"Tom," she said, "there was a gun battle last night. There were five people killed. They were Chinese and Vietnamese. "Then you show up here covered in mud and blood, with a Chinese woman in tow?"

"Maisie," I said, "you're right and it does involve me, but not the way you think. Do me a favour Maisie and make sure she," I cocked an eye at the upstairs room, "doesn't leave here. Oh, and Maisie, I'll be back here in an hour and I'll have half the Manchester police force with me, so if you've got anyone staying here who'd rather not be around when that happens, you might like to tip them the wink.""

Maisie just looked at me and she said, "Tom, come into the parlour. Reckon you know where it is."

Dutifully I followed her. Of course I knew Maisie's parlour: where she'd patched me up, stopped my crying, comforted me, fed me and kept the monsters away from my door.

She sat down on an old, worn, red armchair, while I stood by the door, anxious to leave, and she said, "Tom, I want you to tell me what's happening."

"Maisie," I said, "in God's honest truth, I don't know myself. I only wish I did."

"Who's the girl then, Tom? She yours?"

"No, Maisie, she isn't mine. I'm not sure she's anyone's. She's just in a whole heap of trouble Maisie and I'm doing my best to sort it out."

"She's a very beautiful girl, Tom."

"Maisie, I'm a grown man. I have twenty-twenty vision, and I have to admit I've noticed that myself."

Maisie's old face cracked into a big smile. "I'm an old woman, Tom, and some of the things that happen nowadays, I don't understand. But there are some old, old truths, Tom, don't matter how old or how senile you are. One of them's this. The prettier the girl, the more trouble you're in."

"So how much trouble was your boyfriend in when he met you then, Maisie?" I said, smiling. I looked at the wall above the ancient dresser at the photograph of an impossibly young Maisie standing next to her man in his uniform – a man who looked more like a schoolboy than a soldier.

"You have time to sit down a minute, Tom?" she asked.

Even though I didn't I said, "Yes."

"It's a little too early for a drink isn't it?" she said. "No matter."

"Do you know how many kills you need to be an ace, Tom?"

"No Maisie," I said.

"You need five, Tom. You need to kill five of your fellow men in aerial combat, shoot down their planes and kill them and that makes you an ace."

"My fiancé was called Matthew. He was eighteen and I was seventeen. We decided we'd wait till after the war was over before we'd get married, raise our children. We were going to have four children, Tom, two girls and two boys and they were going to be the prettiest girls and the toughest boys you ever saw." She smiled. "I think they would have been too."

"But Matthew knew it was his duty to help to win the war so he decided to be an ace. After he was an ace they let him come home for three days, three whole days and he told me how those aces went into the sky every day and every day they knew they were going to die. How the siren sounded to call them to scramble because the next wave of Germans was coming across the Channel."

I looked helplessly at her, seeing the memories behind her old rheumy eyes.

"When the siren sounded there was some would pray and some would cry and some would sick up their rations against the hangar wall. Then they'd climb into their planes and take off to fight the Germans."

"So Matthew shot down five and then he was an ace. Unfortunately he didn't make six."

She was wiping her eyes now on her apron. I stood up

and walked over to her and put my arms around her. There was nothing to say.

"Tom, I never said that to a living soul," she said. "He was the only person I ever cared about, Tom. Except for you. I couldn't stand for you to be taken away from me as well. So please tell me, Tom, how much trouble are you in?"

"I don't know, Maisie. There's some guys trying to kill me, and there's some guys trying to kill Angel, and I don't have the slightest idea why. But when it's all over I'll come back and tell you."

"Promise?"

"I promise Maisie," I said.

"Take care, Tom," she said softly.

"You too, Maisie," I said. I took hold of her and gave her another big hug.

There's a wise old man out there somewhere and one of the things he says is: *Never make a promise that you aren't sure you can keep.*

I took the key to the big double gates and unfastened the padlock. The sun had started to shine through the clouds, but it didn't make much difference to the mood I was in.

I wondered then whether I should take my car, but decided it made no difference whether I was stopped or not. Either way I was headed straight to the nearest police station. I dragged open the doors to Maisie's yard. I walked around the back of the car to take a look in daylight, to see if there was any evidence to show I'd hit that guy outside Liu's place. There were no bloodstains but there was a decent-sized dent in the back. Right next to it was a nice neat bullet hole and I shivered in the sunlight thinking how

187

close I must have come to getting myself shot.

I jumped into my car, started her up, the engine sounding like a seventeenth century washing machine and drove away down the street but as I drove I wasn't thinking about Angel or Mary, Chinese gangsters or the Manchester police: I was thinking about an old woman and a young man who, a long time ago, had been an ace.

I drove on autopilot for a while until I remembered what I was supposed to be doing. I was supposed to go to the police to give myself up for a murder I hadn't committed and one I probably had. It was then that I remembered I'd told Angel to call my mobile phone. Now there are two kinds of people in this world. The first kind knows that they are not equipped to battle three murderous Chinese gangs and their stunning, treacherous women: that they are actually far better at tracking down lost dogs, loose women and stray husbands. This kind of guy goes straight to the police and sings like Luciano Pavarotti.

The second kind of guy decides that he's definitely going to the cops but the intelligent thing to do first is to stop by the office and pick up his mobile phone.

You can take a guess at which kind is represented by Tom Collins: not-very-famous private eye and world-class idiot.

Chapter Nineteen

Jake ran over what he'd picked up the day before. Karl said nothing, just nodding and smoking and drinking coffee and thinking.

Karl said, "So where does this Irene Drabowsky fit in? You think she's Eleanor Mann's illegitimate little sister from her mother's fling with the ball player. So who cares?"

"Irene Drabowsky's a pretty clumsy sort of name Karl. I reckon if you were an actress, it's not the kind of name you'd really want to see in neon lights on Broadway." Jake's blue eyes stared across the table. "This particular actress is twenty-five years old and her stage name's Melissa Francis." He handed over the handbill for the musical. "That's her," he said.

Karl put his cup of coffee slowly down onto his saucer and whistled. "If I didn't know different I'd say that was Eleanor Mann ten years ago," he said. Then he grinned that big open grin of his. "I told you, told you there'd be a dame at the bottom of this," he said.

Jake raised an eyebrow. "And I'm supposed to be surprised?" he said. "Anyhow all of this still don't tell me why Eleanor Mann hired me. You think she suspected Frankie was stepping out with her illegitimate little sister, wanted me to find out?"

Karl had always been the thinker of the two, the guy with the ideas, whereas Jake was more inclined to shoot first and find out why afterwards.

"You know what I think, Jake: I think this. Mrs Mann knew

189

when she married Frankie that she'd have to turn a blind eye to his outside activities. But she was ten years old when her mom went into hospital, eight-and-a-half months pregnant. Suppose she knew she had a little sister tucked away somewhere, and suppose one day she picks up the paper and there right in front of her is a picture of Frankie and his latest playmate."

Jake lit up a cigarette; blew smoke across the table. "So Frankie's got the ultimate come-on," he said. "He's got exactly the same woman he married, except suddenly she's ten years younger. No wonder Eleanor Mann's upset. Other women she can handle but not this. This is the one she can't take."

"So let's think what she'd do," continued Karl slowly. "I think she'd go to Frankie and demand he stop seeing her younger and prettier little sister."

"At which point," Jake continued, "knowing Frankie Mann, he'd find it the biggest joke for years and he'd laugh in her face."

"Exactly," said Karl. "So you know what we got here Jake? We got a woman scorned and you know what they say about that."

Jake crushed his cigarette in the ashtray. "Yeah; hell hath no fury like it. So why, exactly, is she hiring me?"

"Because," said Karl, "she knows Frankie's involved in the biggest scheme of his life but she doesn't know what it is. That's what she wants you to find out."

"Yeah," said Jake, "and the minute she knows what he's up to she's gonna give him an ultimatum. Either he stops this thing with her sister or she'll blow the whistle and bring the whole thing crashing down around his ears."

Karl nodded. He ordered more coffee, stirred in sugar, watching the coffee swirl around and around in the cup. Then he said, thoughtfully, "Jake, do you think she's got any idea what kind of danger she's in? After all, Frankie's already got rid of one inconvenient wife."

190

"Oh Jesus," said Jake, "maybe that business on the east side wasn't the only reason why he was talking with Scarletti." He jumped to his feet and headed to the door.

"Jake," said Karl. Jake turned, the door half open behind him and the cold wind blowing in the room. "Be careful, Jake," Karl said.

Jake drove his Chevy out to Frankie's big mansion in the exclusive northern suburbs with his foot flat to the floor and the whitewall tyres screaming but of course when he got there Eleanor Mann was dead.

*

As I drove away from Maisie's the wind had stopped, the rain had stopped and there was actually sunshine glinting through the clouds. I wondered if I would be able to see the sky from whichever prison cell they threw me into.

It was a Sunday morning in Manchester. Anyone sensible was getting in a few hours quality time with a pillow and a duvet, or eating bacon sandwiches and checking out the newspaper headlines. Which would all be about oriental lunatics blowing each other away with shotguns.

There was virtually no traffic on the roads at this early hour. I drove very cautiously into the street where I had my office in case the police had staked it out, not that it seemed likely on a Sunday morning, but all looked serene and peaceful.

I parked the car in the usual spot and walked round the corner. I was going to pick up my phone, then buy a newspaper to find out whether the shit I was in reached the top of my head, or only up to my ears. Then I was going to the nearest police station and beg them to arrest me.

I felt a little foolish to be clutching the gun in my pocket, because this was a nice quiet Sunday morning in a nice quiet street. What trouble could you possibly get into?

I inserted my key into the lock on the outer door and walked up the stairs to my office. I fitted the second key: the door swung quietly open. The problem was that the door swung open before I turned the key. I pulled the gun from my pocket and stepped through the door ready to murder anything that moved. The office was pretty much as I had left it. My chair still lay where it had fallen when I had dived onto the floor as Gladys Green strolled in; the telephone was still off the hook and my cell phone was still sitting on my desk waiting for me to unplug it, call Bill, and throw myself on the mercy of the Law.

However, there were three things that hadn't been there the previous Friday. On my desk held down by my heavy black ashtray was a small stack of fifty-pound notes. I didn't count them because I knew that there would be ten of them. Five hundred pounds. On my office floor lay a short, thick length of steel reinforcing bar, covered in blood.

And crumpled on the carpet, in front of my desk, was the half-naked body of Candy.

So they'd killed two birds with one length of metal. I was quite sure that there would be any number of witnesses who would swear they'd seen me leave The Yin & Yang Club with Candy, two nights ago.

Angel had told me that Hamilton Liu had left the house the previous evening. I wondered whether this was where he had gone, and whether he'd enjoyed himself immensely

192

beating this poor girl to death: and whether he'd now got his face back.

I didn't look closely at Candy's body; I didn't want to see what they had done to her. I picked up my cell phone and stared at the money sitting innocently on my desk. That money had my fingerprints on it, Candy's too. I stuffed the notes into my back pocket and stood there like a man in a trance. I was thinking, *what kind of a sadistic bastard would do something like that to anybody, anything, let alone a scared, skinny little girl?*

It was then that I heard the sirens and realized that whoever set me up like this would call the police the minute I arrived at the office. Which meant that there was someone out there watching me. I ran out of my office with my gun in my hand, but there was no-one around, not a soul visible on this quiet, sunny Manchester morning. I ran to my car. I didn't really know what to do now, only that I had to get away and think. As I raced past the newsagents I saw the headlines on the boards outside:

Five Chinese Dead in Gunbattle
Police Search for Mystery White Man

Well, I thought bitterly, I can't really get into any more trouble than this can I? Which only goes to show how hope springs eternal in the breast of the average idiot P.I.

I could hear the sirens sounding loudly as I opened my car door and slid into the seat. I pulled my phone out of my pocket, and saw I had several missed calls and two text messages from Mary. There was also one number I didn't recognize, but I knew who it was: Candy. I began to punch Bill's number into my phone: I had to talk to someone.

193

Then I heard something behind me. I whirled around to see a Chinese guy standing at the open rear door of my car, with a gun in his hand. I was still staring at him when the front passenger door opened. Another Chinese looked mockingly down at me. "As you weren't at your home this morning, Mr Collins, we thought that you might be in your office, even on a Sunday," he said politely. "A commendable work ethic."

He was about thirty years old, wearing an expensive, charcoal grey suit, a white shirt and a dark red tie. He looked as if he was on his way to a board meeting.

He reached across, took my phone away from me and dropped it into his pocket.

"I think that it would be better to go in our car, don't you, Mr Collins?" he said, politely. "I rather think the police might be looking for yours." By way of encouragement the guy at the back was waving his gun at me

Slowly and reluctantly I got out of my car. We walked to a dark blue BMW with tinted windows. A guy with a uniform and a peaked cap opened the door for me. I climbed in, followed by the gunman. The smartly-dressed guy climbed into the front. At least I was moving swiftly upwards in the kidnapping stakes. Yesterday I'd had to drive my own car. Today I got a chauffeur-driven BMW. Maybe next time they could kidnap me in a cherry red Chevy convertible.

I sat in the back of the car in a confused mixture of terror and anger. "Why did you have to kill the girl?" I asked, bitterly.

The man in the front seat stared at me. "We didn't kill Jenny Nguyen, Mr Collins. We're fairly certain that was Hamilton Liu's men."

194

"And the one in my office, I suppose you didn't kill her either," I snapped.

"I'm sorry, Mr Collins but I don't know what you are referring to."

"There's a dead girl in my office," I replied through my teeth. "She is – she was – a dancer, working at The Yin & Yang Club."

He turned to the man in the back seat who was lounging in the corner with his gun trained on my chest.

"Mr Chan," he said, "have you killed anyone in the past one or two days?"

Mr. Chan's squat, yellow face broke into a wide, un-pleasant grin showing rows of yellowing teeth capped with gold. "No boss," he said, sitting there pointing his gun at me and rocking with laughter.

"You see, Mr Collins. Not guilty," said the younger man, but even as he spoke I realized that it made no sense for these two to set me up for a murder and then kidnap me. But if these weren't Hamilton Liu's men, then who the hell were they?

"So who is this girl then and why should anyone want to kill her?" asked the urbane man.

I was trying to think who they could be and what they could want.

"I think she might have had some information," I said, "and Hamilton Liu had her killed before she could tell me."

"Information concerning what, Mr Collins?"

"I was looking for a woman called Angel Wong," I replied. "Candy, the dead girl, I think she may have known something."

"Looking for Angel Wong, Mr Collins. Aren't we all? I

don't suppose you happen to know where she is?"

I shook my head.

"A pity," he said. "It would have saved us and you an awful lot of trouble."

"I don't suppose you'd like to tell me who you are and what this is about?" I asked.

"Have you heard of someone by the name of Goodbye Johnny?"

I nodded.

"Well, we're taking you to see him. He'd like a word with you."

"But I thought Goodbye Johnny was in Chicago?"

"I do hope not, Mr Collins. It would be an awfully long drive."

All was silent except for the wailing of police sirens and the squeal of brakes as squad cars screamed to a stop outside my office. The driver carefully piloted the car in the opposite direction while the sun shone through the clouds, and the birds sat on the roofs of the old buildings lining the streets, no doubt thinking it was about time to head somewhere nice and warm for the winter. That reminded me that I could have been sitting on a plane with Angel Wong, headed off to some exotic tropical hideaway and I have to admit that right then that sounded a whole let better than a friendly chat with Goodbye Johnny, probably followed by a relaxing swim in the Manchester Ship Canal. I decided that if by some unlikely chance I ever came out of this alive, then I would call Mary, marry her and take a job filling up the shelves at the Ukrainian supermarket.

I should be so lucky.

As the BMW cruised along the Mancunian Way, the phone was ringing in the office of Superintendent Ted

McClusky.

"We've found Collins' car, sir."

"And Collins?"

"No, sir."

"Well in that case Pike, you imbecile, I suggest you arrest Collins' fucking car. Can you please tell me what fucking use, what use at all, is Collins' fucking car, if we don't fucking well have Collins," he screamed. He paused for breath. "So where's the car?"

"Outside his office, sir."

"Well, far be it from me to suggest anything to you bright young things, but has it occurred to you to check his office?"

"I was just coming to that, sir. We did. And there's a girl in there. A Chinese girl. She's dead, sir. Murdered. The murder weapon's on the office floor, but there's no sign of Collins."

McClusky took a deep, deep breath. His blood pressure had always been on the high side. He felt as if he was about to explode. "Any I.D.?" he asked.

"No, sir."

"I'm on my way. Don't touch anything till I get there," he shouted. He jammed the phone back on its hook, then snatched up the receiver again and began to hit the buttons.

"Hemshall," said a voice down the line.

Chief Constable Hemshall was legendary for his ability to remain calm and detached. He was invariably polite and quietly spoken, never used bad language and hardly ever raised his voice.

However, those that knew him well knew that there was a certain tone of voice, a certain slowing down of the pace of his speech, a certain very icy coolness, that was far more menacing than all the shouting and swearing of any of his senior officers.

"McClusky sir," said the Superintendent miserably. "We've found Collins' car, but not Collins. We've searched his office and there's a dead woman in there. Chinese. Apparently been murdered."

"Angel Wong?" asked Hemshall.

"We don't know yet, sir. I'm just on my way over there to check it out, but well, it seems likely, sir."

"If you could please let me know as soon as you get there?" The glacial tones almost froze the line to McClusky's ear.

"Yes, sir, of course, sir," he muttered and hung up.

"When I get my hands on you, Collins," muttered McClusky, "I'm going to rip out your liver and make you eat it."

Chief Constable Hemshall sat in his study where he had been reading the lurid headlines of the Sunday press. Another murder he didn't need.

He wondered whether the Chicago police had wanted Angel Wong dead or alive. Either way it wasn't going to do any good whatever for his career prospects. He had never had reason to meet Tom Collins during his brief career in the force. Had only met him once, the morning when he had spoken to him about the body they'd found in the Ship Canal. However, he wanted to meet him now. He wanted very deeply and desperately to meet Tom Collins, preferably in a sound-proof room, with a couple of large constables and a rubber hose.

He grabbed his coffee. It had gone cold. He resisted the temptation to hurl it against the wall.

Chapter Twenty

*J*ake sat in his office looking at the front page of The Gazette. *The headline read:*

ROBBERS MURDER SOCIETY HOSTESS

He heard a noise in the corridor, threw the newspaper on his desk, held Betsy down on the chair at his side. His door opened. Two guys stood there: one dark and skinny with mean, vicious eyes; the other built like the iceberg that hit The Titanic.

Jake put Betsy on the desk where his visitors couldn't help but notice. He lit up a Lucky. "I don't remember inviting you in," he said. "I don't allow pets in the office."

Lucky Mannino looked at Jake, puzzled.

"Weasels," grunted Jake. Willie's face went dark with anger. Lucky didn't get the joke.

"Ya better watch your mouth, Fist or I'll get Lucky to put his foot in it," snapped Willie the Weasel.

Jake lit up a Lucky Strike. "I'm busy. Whad' ya want?" he asked.

"You been workin' a case, Fist," said Willie the Weasel. He pulled up a chair. "Well the case is closed and you're off of it."

"Now just what case might that be, Willie?" said Jake. Anyone knew Jake, knew the soft, quiet sound of his voice knew that he was

199

awfully close to causing someone a terrible lot of grief.

"Frankie Mann's old lady, stoopid. She ain't in a position to retain you no longer, Fist. And if we find you snoopin' around there's going to be another unfortunate accident. Understand?"

"You've got two seconds to get out of my office and crawl back under your rock, Weasel. If you're still here when I count to two, I'm gonna pull you apart like a southern fried chicken and make that big punch-drunk stiff standin' next to you eat you, piece by piece."

"Hey, Jake, that ain't bein' very friendly," protested Lucky.

Jake said, "One."

Willie the Weasel jammed his hat on his head and rose to his feet. On his way out he turned and said, "You're gonna regret this wise guy."

*

We drove through the outskirts of Manchester and headed into rural Cheshire. Everyone south of Watford thinks that the industrial North is just endless acres of Coronation Streets with old pit workings in the background, but there's an enormous amount of rolling farmland, woodland, pretty rivers and picturesque little villages. In September with the last rays of the summer sun slanting down through the clouds and the trees starting to turn yellow and gold, it can be as pretty as anywhere in England.

Under normal circumstances on a quiet, sunny Sunday morning I would have enjoyed the drive. It was the kind of pleasant, nearly-but-not-quite-engaged type of thing I'd done with Mary. The difference being that normally there wouldn't have been a dapper, ruthless Chinese gangster in the passenger seat, nor a gun aimed at my chest by some gold-toothed thug. This may have been the reason that the scenery wasn't really making much of an impression on me.

Thinking about Mary reminded me of our earlier one-sided phone conversation. As if on cue my cellphone rang. The smartly-dressed guy took it out of his pocket, jabbed the 'yes' button and although I couldn't make out the words I certainly recognized the voice. Mr Smoothie sat there listening with a huge grin on his face, cocking a sardonic eye at me. When he'd had enough he shouted, "Wrong number," loudly into the phone and closed it down.

He turned to me. "Remarkable women the English, Mr Collins," he observed. "Very passionate. If I were you I'd tie the knot with that one. After all, it seems silly to take that amount of abuse unless you're actually married to her." He looked very happy with himself as he settled back into his seat.

I watched disconsolately through the window. For the first and only time in my life I was desperately anxious to hear the wailing of sirens, see a panda car glide in front of us and pull in with his STOP light flashing. I would even have welcomed a friendly chat with my old mate Ted McClusky. Unfortunately cops are like pubs and public toilets and exotic willing women desperate to take you to bed. There's never one around when you need one. There wasn't a cop car in sight during the whole of that journey.

I wondered if they realized I was armed but there was no way I could take out the gun and use it with Mr Chan sitting there with me firmly in his sights at a distance of two feet. I prayed that when we arrived at our destination, wherever that was, they'd take their eyes off me just long enough for me to use it.

Eventually we turned into one of the country lanes and drove past huge, secluded houses set back from the road, surrounded by old trees and well-tended gardens. We purred smoothly along till we arrived at a set of high, wide wrought-iron gates at the head of a long driveway approximately the width of the M6.

The gates opened automatically revealing a big grey stone house set in lush gardens. We cruised down the driveway, the gravel crunching under the wheels till the car stopped. The chauffeur opened the door and I climbed out to where another Chinese guy was waiting for me with a set of handcuffs.

Whatever faint hopes I had harboured vanished as they slapped me up against the wall of the house and searched me. They took away my gun, fastened my hands behind me then pushed me round the side of the house. I had a lump in my throat the size of a grapefruit.

I was being prodded past a garage big enough to house the London Transport Department when I stopped and stared in amazement. Among the assortment of BMW's and Range Rovers and Mercedes, there was a beautiful old Chevrolet. It had a split screen, thin whitewall tyres, and running boards built specifically so you could stand on them and keep your balance while holding a machine gun.

Even in my state of abject terror I couldn't help but gaze in admiration and envy. I knew that model. It was the sexiest of all the Chevys: a 1937 Master 85, 2 door coupe, with a V8 flattop engine and an idle speed that was so slow you could actually see the fan blades rotate.

For a second I forgot about Candy and Angel Wong and Goodbye Johnny. Then the guy called Chan saw me looking and said, "I don't know why he keeps that one either. Must be a hundred years old." With that they led me round the side of the house.

There were French windows opening onto a big lawn with fancy clipped hedges and about eighty or a hundred yards away was a little orchard, a small forest of apple and pear trees and other types I didn't recognise, the fruit hanging heavy and ripe in the late summer sunshine. We entered through a side door, walked past a huge farmhouse-style kitchen, and I was taken into what was obviously a man's study with book-cases, a desk, a cocktail cabinet, a sofa and two deep armchairs. There was an uncomfortable-looking straight-backed wooden chair placed by the side of the window. I guessed which seat I was bound for and I guessed right.

Chan made himself comfortable while pointedly clicking the safety catch on the gun he was aiming at me. The sun shone through the windows and lit up the old country prints on the walls while I sat stiffly on my chair waiting for Goodbye Johnny. I was wondering what he'd look like - old or young, tough, mean, but when the door finally opened I just sat there in complete amazement.

I'd been imagining some short, ugly Chinese thug, or a cold emotionless killer in a designer suit but I certainly hadn't been expecting twenty-something years old, five feet six, long wavy blonde hair and a figure that would have had Pamela Anderson thrown out of Baywatch for being too flat-chested.

She wore a long white dress slit high on the thighs and cut so low down the front you could almost see her kneecaps. She stood there smoking a cigarette, looking as cool as a polar bear on an ice floe. "Hi," she said brightly,

203

"you must be the detective. I'm Brandy." She sat down on the sofa, looking at me as if I were an old shirt she couldn't decide whether to keep or throw away.

"Johnny's out on business but he'll be back soon," she said casually. "Have you heard of him?"

"Yes," I admitted, "but I didn't realise he lived in Wilmslow."

"Oh this is just temporary," she waved a disdainful hand at her surroundings, "till Johnny gets what he wants. And you know what?" she said. "Johnny always gets what he wants."

She stubbed out her cigarette, took another from a pack of Marlboro on the coffee table and lit up, blowing a stream of smoke at the ceiling.

"So why does a big boy like you want to get mixed up in all this," she said, in a voice that owed a whole lot to too many late nights, too much booze and too many cigarettes.

"It wasn't my choice," I muttered. "I was just doing my job. I didn't ask to get beaten up and framed and kidnapped."

She looked at me coolly. "And it's going to get worse," she said, casually, "unless you co-operate." She stood and walked over to the cocktail cabinet, took a bottle of Jack Daniels and poured. She added a little Coke, a little ice, took a sip, added a touch more Coke and sat down again.

There was a glass-fronted cupboard on the wall above the cocktail cabinet with wine and whisky glasses and a small rack on which there must have been a dozen sets of car keys all neatly labelled. Goodbye Johnny and I shared the same hobby, I thought: collecting cars. Except his were real.

Anyway, we sat there and it could have been a scene

from any upper-class week-end. Me on a chair in this expensively-furnished country house, the blonde lounging on the sofa showing long tanned legs and way too much cleavage, smoking a cigarette and fluttering her eyelashes. Of course you'd have had to remove my handcuffs and the tattooed Chinese with a gun in his hand, but otherwise it was just chintzy.

This Brandy was some piece of software. She looked like a scaled down version of Marilyn Monroe. I couldn't decide whether she had more ice in her drink or on her fingers. A couple of impressive diamonds reflected back the light coming through the window and her nails were a nice deep red, presumably so that when she scratched someone's eyes out the blood wouldn't show.

She took a slow sip of her drink, licked her lips and said, "Why don't you just tell me what Johnny wants to know? Then you can go home and arrange flowers or whatever it is you do."

"It would help," I said, "if you'd tell me what it is that Johnny wants."

"Where's Angel?" she asked.

I shook my head. "I don't know," I said. "I've been trying to find her."

"Yes, we know you have. So either you're a lousy detective or you're a lousy liar, so which is it?"

"I guess I must be a lousy detective," I said.

She laughed showing perfect white teeth. "Tom Collins, you are lying to me. Me, I'm pretty relaxed about it, but if you keep lying to Johnny he'll just get mad and you won't like that at all. The last guy who made Johnny mad, Johnny took a blowtorch to him." She said it as matter-of-factly as if she'd been telling me what she had for lunch.

205

"Cigarette?" she asked, languidly.

The first cigarette I'd ever smoked had been the day my mother died. I'd tried again a year later, at the age of fifteen. I'd spent six days trying to look tough in the bike sheds then turning green and running for the school toilets. I'd smoked for a couple of years after that but I'd never been a really committed cigarette freak and I'd stoppd when I was nineteen.

"No thanks, I don't," I said.

She giggled. "Afraid it'll damage your health?" she asked.

I shrugged my shoulders as well as I could with my hands behind my back. She had a point.

"Why not?" I said.

She pushed a Marlboro between my lips and clicked her lighter, then turned and walked over to the cocktail cabinet. "You might as well have a drink as well," she said, "seeing as how it'll probably be your last."

She turned her back on me, took a glass and the bottle of Jack Daniels, added some ice and brought it over. She bent down slowly and carefully so she could show me her breasts, removed the cigarette from my lips and I swallowed it in one.

"More?" she asked, mockingly.

It was still well before lunchtime, early in the day even for Jake Fist to be drinking Jack Daniels, let alone me. However this didn't seem the time to get picky. "Yes please," I replied. I wasn't sure whether she meant more whisky or more cleavage but in the event I got more of both. It seemed an odd interrogation technique. Another half-hour like this and I'd be too drunk to speak.

"Is it too much to ask you why a Chicago mobster is

206

sitting in a country house in England, and why everyone's so desperate to get their hands on Angel Wong?" I asked.

She sat languidly on the sofa, puffing smoke into the air.

"Last night there was gun battle at a place owned by a rat called Hamilton Liu," she said.

"Yes, I heard about that," I said carefully.

I saw her eyebrows arch upwards as she gave me a big sardonic stare. "Hamilton Liu runs every major racket in Manchester," she continued. "Now Johnny's decided he'd like to expand his business, maybe open up here in England. So he's discussing things with Hamilton." She grinned wolfishly at me. "Mainly at gunpoint," she said and giggled. "We thought maybe the Tigers had saved us the trouble, but we hear Hamilton wasn't at home when they called."

She stubbed out her cigarette. "Now you see, Tom, I've told you what you want to know and I think it's only right if you tell me what I want to know don't you?"

"You still haven't told me why everyone seems to be looking for Angel Wong."

She sighed, shaking her head and inhaling through clenched teeth in a big disapproving breath that did interesting things to her chest area.

"Let's just say that Angel has something that Johnny wants. I did mention, didn't I, that Johnny always gets what he wants, do you remember?"

"So what happens to Angel if Johnny finds her?" I asked.

"Tom, we're not animals you know. She just has something Johnny wants and as soon as Johnny has it he'll let her go. We're not going to hurt her Tom, so it's pointless you holding out on us. Now why don't you just tell us where you're hiding her, so we can all sit down and have a nice little drinkie and then you can go home and watch the TV."

I thought of poor Candy beaten to death with an iron bar and Janet Wu tortured and murdered and I knew that this blonde bombshell was lying in her perfect white teeth.

"I'd tell you if I knew," I said, "but I don't."

She threw down the rest of her drink and wandered over to the cocktail cabinet to build another one.

I sat there wondering what the hell I was supposed to do. I knew that Angel wasn't even remotely as innocent as she made out. But I also knew that if I told Brandy where Angel was hiding, I wouldn't be allowed to go off and arrange flowers, have a little drinkie, watch TV or do anything else, ever again. They'd made no attempt to hide from me where I was going; to cover their faces, to disguise who they were. Which meant that they were completely confident that I wouldn't be running to the police the minute they let me go. As soon as I told them where Angel was, I was a dead man.

"Tom, we can do this nicely or we can let Johnny play with you. Now I'm asking you again: where's Angel Wong?"

"I don't know. If I did I'd tell you," I said.

She sighed and shook her head. "Tom, between kidnapping Chinese women and shooting guns all over the place, do you ever look at the newspapers?"

"I planned to this morning," I replied as calmly as I could, "only on the way to the newsagents I found a dead girl in my office. Then I got kidnapped, handcuffed, forced into a car and driven over here at gunpoint and somehow I must have forgotten."

She gave me a big amused smile and I have to admit that she was as cool and as sexy as any woman I'd ever seen. I couldn't detect a single flaw between that beautiful face, those luscious breasts, that sexy waist and her long, suntanned legs. She was perfect. You can take my word for it. I'm a detective. We're trained to notice this stuff.

"Tom, it's on the front page of all the papers," she said. "During last night's gunbattle there was a white man, six feet, thirtyish, escaped from the scene in a car. Every policeman in England is looking for him."

"Yes," I sighed, "OK I admit it, that was me. The Tigers kidnapped me and made me drive over to the Liu's place, but that's all I know. As soon as the shooting started I got the hell out of there."

"Taking Angel with you," she said.

"Angel?" I acted as dumb as I could. "Why would Angel be there? I told you, as soon as I'd dropped those guys there I just got away as fast as I could."

"Wrong answer again, Tom." She stood. "You seem to have a terrible problem telling me the truth but don't worry you'll tell Johnny soon enough. Johnny grew up on the streets of Chicago. They're mean streets, Tom and they make mean people. And Johnny's as mean as a rattlesnake."

I stared up at that sardonic blonde twisting her drink in her hands and for a heady few moments I forgot about my problems, the deep trouble I was in, the probability that I was about to be tortured with a blowtorch and dumped in the Manchester Ship Canal. I repeated her words to myself, savoured them: "Johnny grew up on the streets of Chicago. They're mean streets, Tom and they make mean people. And Johnny's as mean as a rattlesnake." The words went

209

round and round in my head before I was dragged back to reality by Brandy saying, "If I were sitting where you are I don't think I'd be looking quite so happy. You're pretty cool aren't you, you English? Well you won't be looking quite so cool shortly, I can guarantee you that."

The reality of my situation started to bite then. I tried to think what Jake Fist would do in a situation like this, whether I could strike a deal but my mind just didn't seem to be working properly. I could keep up the pretence that I didn't know where Angel Wong was but they'd just bring out the hosepipes and beat the truth out of me. Then they were going to kill me. Or I could co-operate and tell them. Then they'd kill me anyway. I had a burning desire to be back in Stretford, searching the streets for missing poodles.

Two days ago I'd had a run-in with two gun-toting gangsters in my office: the night before I'd been attacked by rottweilers in the middle of a pitched gun battle, but I hadn't either of those times had the feeling that was going through me now: the feeling that I was going to die.

I heard the sound of a car engine. Brandy smiled sweetly at me. "Looks like Johnny's back," she said. "Well, good-bye Mr Collins, I did enjoy our little chat. Johnny's going to take you somewhere quiet. We can't do it here. I absolutely hate the sound of people screaming." I was pulled to my feet. My legs felt like rubber and my head was spinning. I know I'm no drinker but I didn't think I'd had all that much. Brandy walked towards me. She took the pack of Marlboro and put them into my shirt pocket. "You're going to need them," she said and blew smoke in my face. She smiled sweetly at me. "Have a nice day Mr Collins."

I was taken again past the garage. I was trying to get a last look at that beautiful Chevy but my eyes refused to focus. In the driveway were two identical dark blue BMW's, both with their engines running; both with chauffeurs sitting in the front as if they were waiting to pick up someone rich and famous rather than someone who would very soon be a short paragraph in the obituary columns of *The Manchester Gazette*.

Standing on the driveway with his hands in his pockets, staring at me was a guy who looked as though he'd just stepped off the set of *The Godfather* (Chinese version). He was shortish and broad-shouldered, wearing a trench coat and a dark hat, but not the peaked type that shows you're some kind of menial. He had a dark blue shirt and a cream tie and he looked tough and mean and very sure of himself. He looked at me with the kind of cold, dead eyes that would have looked scary on a shark. "Know who I am?" he asked.

His words seemed to come from a great distance and I struggled to reply. "I can guess," I said.

"Where's Angel?" His flat, dead eyes bored into me. I knew it was very important but I couldn't remember. I cast a long, wistful look at the lovely old car sitting in Johnny's garage.

"Last time," snapped Good-bye Johnny. "Where's Angel. Tell me now and you get to live. The minute we throw you in there," he jerked his head at the BMW, "you're dead."

I decided I had to tell him.

"1937 Chevrolet Master 85 coupe," I said. "Sexiest of 'em all. Blue Flame V8 flattop engine, side valves, 6 in-line cylinders, splash oiler. Bearings too soft; tend to break."

He looked at me with puzzled eyes and it was then I realized that that blonde bimbo had slipped something into my bourbon. I tried then to explain to Johnny how I wanted to kill him and all his men and his lovely, treacherous blonde and set fire to his country house and steal his car but instead I started to giggle.

"Get him in the car," murmured Goodbye Johnny.

Then I tried to explain to him that I didn't want to die and I think I was crying but I can't be sure because everything disappeared into a deep, black pit.

Chapter Twenty-one

Jake watched the door slam behind Lucky Mannino and Willie the Weasel. He picked up the Chicago Gazette. *There was a nice picture of Eleanor Mann in diamonds and an expensive, tastefully-cut dress, looking like she spent her time looking after orphans and sick animals. The kind of gracious, classy dame who wouldn't even dream about being married to a crooked, cheating, murdering, real estate developer like Frankie Mann.*

Seemed like thieves had broken into Frankie's mansion, bent on stealing his antique jewellery and his art collection. When Mrs Mann had come down to see what the noise was all about they'd shot her four times and left her lying on the staircase.

Frankie was distraught.

The cops were taking it real serious this time. They'd put the matter in the personal hands of someone high up and committed and responsible: the Deputy Chief of police, Lew Kraski. He was expecting an arrest real soon.

Jake threw the newspaper into the trash and called Bart Stanton. They arranged to meet at six in a bar that Bart used. They ate in a burger joint and got philosophical over a few of Mr J. Daniels contributions to civilized American society. Around ten Jake called it a night.

He drove home, parked his car and put his key into his

apartment door. He opened the bedroom door quietly so as not to disturb Tanya. When he crept in the bed was full of blood and bullet holes and Tanya was sleeping the sleep where there aren't any dreams and from which you never awake.

The cops came later after a phone call from a concerned citizen. He told them his kids couldn't sleep because of some guy in the next block who was howling like a wolf at the moon

*

Terry and me were so excited. When Uncle Ted pulled up in his car outside our house we climbed over it in a frenzy, inspecting every part of it, the wheels, the wipers, the strange controls inside. He wasn't really our uncle. Just some friend of my Dad's that he went drinking and fishing with but we called him Uncle Ted. You could see how proud he was of his new car even though it was quite an old car, really.

He let me sit on his lap and turn the steering wheel and hoot the horn so loudly that all the chickens ran around the yard, clucking and squawking. Ma was wearing her Sunday dress, and the hat she only ever wore to weddings and to church.

We sat in the back seat with ma while my dad and Uncle Ted sat in the front. My dad was wearing a waistcoat and a white shirt with the sleeves rolled up and his shiny black shoes that he didn't usually wear because he said they hurt his feet. It was a beautiful day, fresh and clean with a gentle wind blowing in off the sea. We sat with our noses pressed hard up against the windows watching the green Irish countryside rolling slowly past. We'd never been to Dublin in our lives.

When we got to Dublin Uncle Ted stopped the car. Terry and me stared around in total amazement because even though we'd seen pictures, we'd never thought anywhere could be as big and as wide and as high and busy as this. We went into a room full of wooden tables with white cloths and men wearing suits and neckties. They were all wearing shiny black shoes. I wondered if all their feet hurt too and in that case why they didn't wear big brown boots like all the men in our village.

One of the men patted me on the head and said I was a fine young man and he reached into his pocket and gave me a bright shiny new penny.

We had sausages and mashed potatoes and gravy and there was a little silver dish on the table with sugar inside for us to put in our tea.

Ma took us walking through the streets. We stared in awe at the huge buildings that reached up almost to the sky. I hadn't thought there were so many people in the whole world. My dad and Uncle Ted went into a pub, while we stared in the shop windows and counted all the cars going by in the streets. My dad gave us threepence each to buy sweets. Eventually we drove back home and we all sang songs in the car until it started to go dark and Uncle Ted switched on the lights.

The fine summer day broke. Lightning split the skies with flashes of brilliance while the thunder rolled and boomed and echoed and the rain beat down on the roof of the car.

"Don't you be frightened now," Uncle Ted said. "This car's got rubber tyres. The lightning can't get through."

I fell asleep in the car and when I woke up my dad was carrying me upstairs to the bedroom. I lay awake in my bed

215

for a while wondering why life couldn't always be like that and why my dad couldn't always be so good to me.

Terry said in the darkness, "You asleep then, Tom?"

"No," I said.

"It's some kind of a place then, that Dublin isn't it?" Terry said. I nodded my head and said,

"Would you like to live there then, Terry?"

"No," Terry said, "I like it here better."

Then I fell asleep.

*

The old man was sometimes in a bad mood and he'd shout and swear and say, "Go on, away with yer, go away," glaring ferociously at me. Then I'd walk away with my hands in my pockets, down through the fields towards the sea.

I liked it walking alone on the small empty beach with the seagulls crying overhead and the wind whipping the salt spray into my face but I liked watching the old man better. I always approached him warily, but this was one of his good days and he smiled at me and said, "Come on son, come and sit down." He knew that I really loved to watch him plastering the paint on the canvas and the seemingly random brushstrokes magically materializing into rocks and trees and clouds.

Sometimes he faced the other way, painting the soft, low purple hills in the distance and the village nestling in the valley, but mostly he painted the rocks and the sea. He'd let me sit down on the grass or on a boulder, sometimes ask me to watch his painting for him and I'd get to sit on the small folding chair while he strode away into the fields or down towards the beach. He looked like a madman, an old fiery-eyed tramp, with his long grey beard and his battered hat and a brown coat that looked as though he'd taken it from a scarecrow in a field.

He used to sip from a flat silver flask. One day he gave it to me, invited me to take a drink. The raw spirit made me cough and gasp and my eyes water and he laughed delightedly as he threw paint onto his canvas. It was a beautiful spring day with a soft, warm breeze, the sun shining down through the clouds onto the water.

The old man tried to explain to me the theory of painting, the structure of the paint, how to read the light and the shadows, the mysteries of depth and perspective. When the light began to fade we just sat there watching the sky turn pink and the sun dip into the water.

He always said the same thing as the afternoon slipped away, sitting there, drinking from his bottle. "Jaysus, son, I wouldn't be dead for quids."

He lived on his own in a small cottage, a shack really, that must once have been some kind of outbuilding for one of the farms. I helped him carry his things back up the hill before he turned down the path to where he lived and gave me a smile and a wave of his hand and said, "See you next week then?" I nodded happily, but what I didn't know was that I wouldn't see him next week or ever again.

When I got home my father was sitting in his chair with a fire going even though it was a warm day, the thick peat smoke drifting away through the chimney and the smell filling the house. "Been wasting yer time with that old lunatic again?" he said sourly, sipping Guinness from a stone tankard he always used. "Painting his stupid pictures. Well you can say good-bye to him, Tom, because we're leaving in the morning."

"Leaving?" I said, puzzled.

"Aye, leaving, going away, buggering off, what do you think leaving means?" he said.

"But leaving what? Where are we going?" I said in a rising panic. Then Terry walked in and said quietly, "We're leaving Ireland, Tom. We're going to Manchester in the morning."

"But why, why?" I gasped, trying to hold back my tears.

"Because I bloody said so, now you'd better go and pack your things. And I don't want you taking any rubbish with you like comic books and such. We've enough to carry as it is."

Early the next morning Uncle Ted took us to the railway station in his car. He was grim-faced and he never said a word to my dad, just helped us put the suitcases on the train and shook my hand and Terry's and said, "Good-bye."

I sat on the train, almost choking on the lump in my throat, watching everything I'd ever known vanish before my tear-streaked eyes.

We caught a boat to Liverpool on a balmy spring day, with the sea flat and calm. My mother was sea-sick almost as soon as we walked down the gangplank. The whole way over my father was muttering on about her weak stomach, and how it was lucky Terry had got his genes and not hers and it was a bloody pity about me. In Liverpool we caught a train, staggering along the platforms with our heavy suitcases. When we arrived in Manchester it was raining.

We stayed in a tiny terraced house on a dirty street with some of my dad's relations. After a while we moved into our own place. It was small and dark and I spent many evenings alone in the room I shared with Terry, while he was out somewhere, playing football or fighting and just cried, wept for Ireland and the fields and the sea and the old man painting and the sun going down, turning the clouds pink and gold in the afternoon.

*

The two dark blue BMW's drove steadily through the countryside being careful to stay strictly within the speed limits, then left the motorway, drove through the Manchester suburbs and turned east, starting to climb the hills. Goodbye Johnny sat silent, his flat eyes staring through the tinted windows while in the car behind Tom Collins lay unconscious, dreaming his dreams.

*

It was my birthday. I was nine years old. My ma and my dad had given me a toy gun and some boxing gloves. I went to Maisie's for lemonade and cream cakes She wished me happy birthday and I felt far more at home sitting in Maisie's than I ever did with my real parents. I slipped off the chair and said thank you to Maisie. I was about to leave when she produced a parcel wrapped in gold paper. I opened it. Inside was a plain cardboard box. I looked at Maisie, wanting to prolong the excitement and she said, "Go on, Tom, open it." Inside was the most beautiful old car I had ever seen. I didn't know then but it was a 1938 Lagonda drop-head coupe, dark green, with doors and a bonnet that opened and a spare wheel strapped to the back. Where she got it from I don't know and Maisie never told me.

I put it back in the box and Maisie looked at me very oddly and gave me a tissue to wipe the tears from my eyes. I walked home hugging the car under my arm in total terror lest anyone should see me and steal my treasure away from me.

*

I stood sweating, looking over my gloves at my opponent. He was bigger and tougher and a lot better boxer than I was. I knew it was just a matter of how long I could back-pedal and dodge before he clobbered me. He moved well for a big boy and he was fast on his feet and with his fists.

He hit me twice with left jabs in the mouth; at the last second I managed to jerk my head aside as the right cross grazed my chin.

"For God's sake, Tom, hit him you bloody useless girl," shouted my father. Flailing out desperately I caught him right on the Adam's apple and he fell to the canvas retching and holding his throat and turning purple.

"Oh Jaysus, Jaysus," I said, falling to my knees beside him, "I've bloody kilt him," while the man who was supposed to be teaching us how to box jumped into the ring and started giving him the kiss of life.

I hadn't killed him of course, he was fine after a couple of days but I refused point blank to step into a boxing ring ever again.

"I don't know why the good lord ever gave you a cock," my father said. "It's of no bloody use to you."

He came home drunk virtually every night. Sometimes he'd start to hit me round the head calling me a wimp and a girl and a bloody disgrace and then my ma would step between us and tell him to leave me alone. Sometimes he'd start hitting her as well and me and Terry and my ma would all be holding onto his arms and trying to make him stop.

It was a few days later that I was walking in the street, kicking an empty cigarette packet and scoring imaginary goals through the lampposts on my way home from school when I saw a boy coming towards me. It was the boy I'd hit in the boxing ring. I clenched my fists in my pockets, looking for somewhere to run to. He walked up, stood in front of me looking easy and self-assured and said, "Hello there Irish, how's tricks?"

"Fine," I muttered guardedly, waiting for the inevitable blow.

"You nearly killed me back there," he said.

"Sorry," I mumbled.

He laughed and held out his hand. "No hard feelings, Irish," he said. We shook hands and from that day on we were best friends. His name was Bill.

*

Maisie was a Londoner. She'd come to Manchester many years ago. She never did tell me why but I guessed it had something to do with the war and the picture of the awkward young couple hanging on the wall.

Despite her years in Manchester she still had that Cockney twang and I wondered if that's why she had felt sorry for me, why she'd picked me up from the pavement: because she recognized another foreigner like herself.

Shyly I introduced Bill to her. I was immensely proud of

221

myself that I actually had another friend, not just an old lady and they got on fine. Sometimes it was both of us sitting in Maisie's parlour with a cake and a drink but this didn't happen so often now because now I was ten years old and I'd found something else to do. I'd discovered books.

After school and at week-ends I'd haunt the public library, losing myself in the far away worlds of those heroes who didn't know the meaning of fear and never ever lost a fight. Biggles and Treasure Island, Ryder Haggard and James Buchan.

Then I graduated to those guys who weren't just heroic; they had beautiful women throwing themselves at their feet and begging them to take them to bed. James Bond and The Saint. Philip Marlowe and Mike Hammer.

While my father swore at me and struck me and asked me when I was going to do something proper instead of acting like a nancy boy.

*

The two BMW's turned into a side road curving up the hillside. After a while they stopped. The driver of the first car stepped down and unlocked a padlock securing two large, rusted metal gates. He dragged them open, got back into his car and both cars drove through the gates. The driver didn't bother to close the gates behind them.

*

I sat in the pub talking to Bill. Mary was there too, staring around in icy disdain. It was very dark. Outside we could hear thunder sounding incessantly, lightning etching across the sky, the light bursting though the windows. I looked around and everywhere there were gangsters with guns peeping out of their pockets. They were pointing slyly at me and Bill and Mary, muttering amongst themselves and laughing. Jake Fist pointed a huge gun at them and told them to be quiet, but he hadn't seen the three guys on the pool table wearing big coats and hats. They weren't using pool cues; they were using machine guns. Gradually they formed a circle around us. "Bet you don't know where Suzie is," they said, laughing. They were all Chinese. I kept trying to explain to Bill, to tell him that we had to get out or we would be dead but he and Jake Fist just kept drinking beer and laughing as they pressed in all around us.

"Bill," I gasped, frozen with fear, "Bill, we have to go." Jake Fist pointed his gun at me and said, "You always were a bloody useless little Irish coward." He leaned across the table and slapped me hard across the face.

"Jake, Jake, why are you hitting me?" I gasped. Then I opened my eyes feeling the real pain of an open hand slapping my cheek. A flat, cruel Chinese face was looking down at me.

I couldn't understand what was happening, where I was, only that my head was aching abominably. I tried to put my hands to my head but I couldn't do it: they were fastened behind my back. The realization came flooding back to me.

They dragged me out of the car. I could see the hills rising steeply, looking peaceful and serene in the sunshine as I stumbled towards an old building of grey stone and rusty metal sheets, with half of the windows broken.

"Pleasant dreams, Mr Collins?" jeered Goodbye Johnny.

Tom Collins, non-violent, peace-loving, pacifist private

223

eye sent up a prayer to the gods, asking them to release my bonds and put a baseball bat in my hands so that I could pound and beat and bludgeon and smash his leering face into a bloody pulp. The panic rose in my throat as they pushed me through a pair of high, wide doors into an old semi-derelict warehouse. The clouds had almost vanished now, the sun low in the autumn sky.

They turned me around and as I caught a glimpse of the hills through the closing doors, the thought flashed through my mind that I would never see them again.

"I do hope you had a pleasant sleep, Mr Collins," said Goodbye Johnny, standing with his hands in his pockets as they slammed me against the wall. "Because it's not going to be very pleasant for you now."

Suddenly and painfully my head was filled with memories of the hills of Ireland, the bright cloudy skies, the sun sparkling on the sea. I looked into Goodbye Johnny's mocking black eyes and I heard again the voice of an old Irish painter, pulling on his silver hip flask, saying, "Jaysus, son, I wouldn't be dead for quids."

Chapter Twenty-two

*I*t had been two-and-a-half years; two-and-a-half years of a deep, festering hatred which Jake couldn't drown in whisky and couldn't lose in the arms of cheap women no matter how much he tried. And he'd tried real hard.

Bart had gone public with Kraski's plans for the station, which had killed any chance of Frankie Mann getting his dirty little hands on it. He'd also printed a front page and leaders asking why the police couldn't find any clues as to the killers of Eleanor Mann. Not that it made any difference.

Lew Kraski had retired with a gold watch, a police pension and the plaudits of a grateful public ringing in his ears. Chicago central police station was still there at South State and Sixteenth.

Jake sat on the barstool in Joe's remembering. He had thought it was all over, all gone until two people had walked into his life and started off the whole damn thing all over again.

The first had been Willie the Weasel, tip-toeing away from some poor defenceless schoolgirl covered in bruises and needle marks. Willie had unwisely thought that in this place, and at this time of the morning he didn't need his goons to protect him, but the Gods had looked at their chess board, had placed a beat-up sixteen year-old in one corner, Willie the Weasel on the second row and Jake at the *bottom of the stairs.*

The second had been a gorgeous twenty-something blonde who'd walked into his office and said, "I think my husband's trying to kill me."

Suzie: that goddamned Suzie. Who'd woken something in Jake he thought had been long dead: murdered by a half dozen .33 calibre bullets fired into his bed two-and-a-half years before. They'd sat and talked a little over at great-aunt Pauline's and she'd told him her sad story, how she'd married the guy she thought she loved and how soon it was she'd realized her mistake.

"I liked him because he was tough," she said, "and I'm a woman and I like tough. But I don't like tough and cruel. Why can't a man be tough and good?"

Jake had told her, "Get real sister. Wise up. The kind of guy you're lookin' for doesn't exist, except in some book by some sixty-year-old woman who wouldn't know a real man from a chimpanzee. I'll keep you safe and I'll take out your ever-lovin' husband too, but I ain't no agony aunt and I ain't no shoulder for cryin' on neither." He'd seen her look at him with sad, hurt eyes and he'd walked away, trying not to feel like he felt and gone straight to Joe's.

Jake bought one for the road and left a decent tip for Joe. He sank his drink, climbed down off his barstool and went to the gents.

*

They dragged me in, slammed me up against one of the rough, crudely concreted walls, undid the handcuffs and looped the chain over a rusting, galvanized iron pipe running around the warehouse. Then they locked them again, leaving me standing on tiptoe with my arms above my head. I felt sick and dizzy with a great roaring in my head and even the dim light that made its way into the warehouse hurt my eyes.

Motes of dust drifted down in beams of sunlight shining down from tiny windows set high up in the walls. Boxes and cartons were stacked on the rough concrete floor. I looked around in a daze, my thoughts woolly and confused, my mind playing tricks.

The five Chinese inspected me like I was a side of beef. The collar of my jacket was now somewhere over the top of my head, my shirt had parted company from my trousers and my exposed midriff must have been a very tempting target because that's where Chan, the guy with the gold teeth, hit me first.

Instinctively my knees jerked upwards, my feet came off the floor and an explosion of pain went through my wrists as I hung there for a moment from the handcuffs. It must have looked like jolly good fun because the Chinese who'd been driving Johnny's car walked over and hit me as well. He wasn't, I observed distantly, as good as Chan. Probably hadn't had as much practice, but he was still pretty good at it.

They took turns in hitting me while Goodbye Johnny and the well-dressed guy, the one who'd sat in the front seat of my car, carried on a conversation about some shipment or other. They weren't even looking in my direction and for some reason I thought of a story I'd once heard about some actress. They were shooting a scene where she'd been lying naked in a bath, while a technician was sitting up a ladder right above her not taking a blind bit of notice and doing The Times crossword. She didn't know whether to be grateful or furious. It struck me as funny and I started to laugh. The two men stopped. Goodbye Johnny walked up to me.

"Glad to see that you're enjoying yourself," he said. He muttered something in Chinese and Chan drew back his fist and hit me under the jaw. My head jerked back into the concrete wall and I almost passed out.

After a while your mind tries to turn you away from the pain, to deflect your thoughts from the fists smashing into you; to distract you from the fact that you can't breathe and you can't scream because there's no air in your lungs and in any case there's no-one to hear you. There was a dark haze in my head and in front of my eyes, shot through with bright blue bolts of pain. My thoughts turned to Mary. At least she'd have to believe I'd had a good reason for standing her up when I turned up dead somewhere. In my mind I said goodbye to her and goodbye to my brother Terry too. In a lucid moment, while every muscle in my body was stretched taut, tensed to bursting point, waiting for the next blow, I realized that was why they called him Goodbye Johnny.

The beating stopped, and I struggled to get some air into my tortured lungs. Through the mist of pain I saw Johnny standing in front of me. "Where's Angel Wong?" he asked.

There seemed no reason why I shouldn't tell him. Either way I was a dead man. I wondered whether they'd kill me first or leave me there, go check out whether I was telling the truth and then kill me later. As if it made any difference. Whatever happened it was hopeless for me. I didn't have a partner to come to my rescue and I didn't think I'd see Wally Holden charging in with guns blazing to save me.

Goodbye Johnny shrugged his shoulders and said something to Chan, who picked up a length of metal pipe from the floor. His cruel eyes glittered and I saw the flash of his gold-toothed grin as he belted me in the chest with it. I almost passed out again with the pain. My eyes were filled with tears so that when I caught a movement at the back of the warehouse I couldn't make out who it was, standing there in the shadows. He was big and wide, standing confident and easy, a cigarette hanging from his mouth, his hands in his pockets and a sardonic smile on his face.

He took the cigarette out of his mouth: blew smoke into the still air. *"Don't say a thing, kid,"* said Jake Fist. *"The minute you tell them where she is they'll kill you."*

I stared at Jake, gasping and crying, tears diluting the blood running down my face and dripping onto the warehouse floor.

Johnny said, "We can keep this up all day, Mr Collins. Now I'm asking you again, where's Angel Wong?"

"Don't tell him Tom," said Jake, *"You can handle this. Stall for time. While you're alive you still have a chance."*

"No, Jake," I gasped. "You're wrong. I'm just a small boy from Ireland, a no-good detective scared to death and afraid of dying."

Goodbye Johnny was trying to work out what I was saying but I wasn't talking to him. "I'm sorry Jake, I can't take any more," I said and I knew that what everyone had always said had been correct. My father had been right when he'd jeered at me as I pored over my books; so had the Manchester yobs who'd routinely beaten me up outside The Ship calling me a soft, gutless little Irish bastard. So had the panel who'd told me I didn't have what it took to stay in the police. All that time in the gym, the skipping around the punchbag; all those hard-bitten tough-guy stories: it was all just so much bullshit.

I looked into Goodbye Johnny's black, expressionless eyes and then, quite clearly in the silence of that warehouse I heard a voice. It was a husky, quiet voice, sad lips murmuring low in my ear and for a moment I thought it was Janet Wu except that Janet Wu was dead. Then I knew who it was.

"Tom," whispered Suzie, *"I'm a woman and I like tough. But I don't like tough and cruel. Why can't a man be tough and good? Be tough now, Tom. Be tough for me."*

"It's no use, Suzie," I said, through my tears, "I'm not the man you think I am." I stared at Johnny and I saw Suzie's sad face looking at me from the shadows of the warehouse as I said, "Angel Wong's at Maisie's place; the Belvedere Apartments in Shawcross Road in Manchester. She's in a room on the first floor. You can have her and do anything you like to her, but please don't kill me."

At least, that's what I intended to say, but somehow it came out as; "Fuck you, you little yellow bastard," and I spat my blood into his face.

Jake Fist grinned at me and nodded his head, his arm around Suzie. I smiled back at them as Goodbye Johnny's face went dark with anger. He pulled a packet of tissues from his pocket and slowly and methodically wiped the blood and spittle from his face. He had a chilling self-control that was more frightening then any violent display of anger would have been. He threw the used tissues onto the warehouse floor. "Very well, Mr Collins," he said. "Now we're really going to hurt you."

He said something in Chinese and they took off my shoes and my socks. I hung there, beaten, bloody, terrified and I nearly fainted when I saw the smartly dressed guy

230

walking across the warehouse holding a big set of industrial bolt cutters.

As I stared in terror at those bolt-cutters I remembered with a remote strange clarity sitting in my office talking to Bill on the phone and hearing Bill saying to me, "They beat the shit out of him and for good measure they chopped off three of his fingers."

"It was you wasn't it?" I said.

Johnny held up a hand. "What do you mean?" he asked.

"Cheesewire Charlie," I gasped. "You killed him. You set up Hamilton Liu so that the Tigers would start a war with him and leave the coast clear for you."

"My goodness, Mr Collins, how very clever of you," he sneered. "I was beginning to think you weren't a detective at all. It was so simple. We just called him at The Yin and Yang Club. Told him the cops were on his tail, which they were of course, and told him to use the emergency exit. There would be a car waiting for him. Which there was," he said with a chilling, cold indifference.

I knew then that whatever happened I was going to die. He would never have admitted that and let me live. He looked at Mr Chan, still holding the metal pipe.

"Now which toe would you like to lose first, Mr Collins?" said Goodbye Johnny.

Chan smashed the little toe on my right foot and this time I did pass out.

I came to from someone hitting me across the face – it was the second time that day but I still hadn't quite got used to it. I stared at the bolt cutters and this time I knew I didn't have anything left inside me. This I couldn't take, now I had to tell them. I looked for Jake but I couldn't see him. In the silence, broken only by my laboured breathing,

231

a telephone rang.

Goodbye Johnny reached into his pocket, spoke briefly and rapped out instructions to his men.

He said to me, "Don't think it's over for you yet, Mr Collins. It hasn't even begun."

He turned on his heels and he, Chan, his driver and the smartly-dressed guy walked swiftly away, leaving the driver of the car that had brought me sitting on an upturned crate, grinning up at me.

I think I passed out again. I don't know how long I hung there from my wrists but afterwards I realized that it could only have been a few moments.

The driver was watching me with a bored look on his face, picking his teeth with a splinter of wood. There was pain flooding through me from my head and my stomach, my chest and my toe. Then I saw Jake again, standing there in the shadows, touching a flame to the tip of his Lucky Strike.

"Tom," he said to me, *"there's only two things that count in this life. There's money and there's sex."* He chuckled. *"In your case I'd give him the money."*

"What do you mean, Jake?" I gasped, and saw my Chinese guard grinning up at me.

"For God's sake, Tom," whispered Suzie, *"you have money. You have five hundred pounds. Use it, Tom."*

"The old one-two Tom, remember?" said Jake Fist and then I realized what he meant.

"I'll pay you," I gasped desperately. "Let me down and I'll pay you anything you like."

The guard just laughed at me.

"Look," I said, "I have money, I have five hundred pounds right here in my pocket. Let me down and it's yours."

His little eyes narrowed even further, then he stood up, walked over and put his hand into the rear pocket of my jeans where I'd stuffed the money that had been left on my office desk.

I had one chance. It wasn't much of a chance but it was the only one I had. If I didn't at least try and take it I would die in agony. I looked down at him as he ferreted in my pocket for the money.

"*Now, Tom, now!*" snarled Jake in my ear. I put all my weight onto the chains around my wrists and with every ounce of strength I could muster I jerked my right knee full into his jaw. I distinctly heard the crack as something broke. I heard Jake Fist laughing. "*The old one-two,*" he said. Then Suzie whispered urgently in my ear. "*You've got two minutes till he comes round, Tom. Get moving!*"

A few yards away from me was a pile of boxes. I worked crab-like along the wall on tiptoe until I could climb onto one of them. I almost sobbed from relief as the weight was taken off my tortured wrists. I looked up at the water pipe from which I had been hung, clenched my teeth and jerked down with all the force that ten years of going to the gym and three days of blind terror can bring to you. There was a cracking noise. I saw rusty brown water leaking out where the pipe was joined to another a few yards to my left.

The guy on the floor started to groan. I kicked aside two of the boxes and climbed a little higher. I had stopped believing in God, indeed in gods of any kind the day that I had come home from school to see my father slumped wearily on the sofa, drinking from a pint bottle of beer and he had told me my mother was dead. So I didn't pray to

233

God. Instead I said, "Please help me now, Jake."

"*Go, Tom, go,*" screamed Jake Fist and I closed my eyes, held my knees under my chin and jumped.

There was a loud bang and I landed in a dazed heap on the warehouse floor with water pouring over me. I scrambled to my feet, limped to where the pipe had broken and pulled away the chain. As fast as I could I shuffled back to where the driver lay on the floor moaning, trying to sit up. I smashed him as hard as I could in the face with my manacled hands, hit him again and the moaning stopped.

I searched through his pockets until I found a bunch of keys. You can try this sometime in the comfort of your own home. Get your girlfriend to handcuff you, give you the key and try to unlock yourself. It'll take you hours. Given the panic I was in I dropped the key twice then forced myself to be calm. Using my teeth I inserted the key into the cuffs and turned it anti-clockwise. There was a click and I was free.

Almost sobbing with relief, I grabbed the guard's car keys, his gun and his phone. I pulled on my shoes, blessing Maisie briefly. She'd bought them two sizes too big or I'd never have got them onto my swollen foot. I hobbled across the warehouse, trying to ignore the excruciating agony radiating from my foot, almost gibbering with the fear that Goodbye Johnny and his men would return before I had the chance to get away. I could feel the pain shooting through my chest with every breath I took and I knew I had at least one broken rib.

I limped outside, the light like an explosion in my head. It was deserted. I saw the dark blue BMW parked in the shade by the warehouse doors, climbed in, started the engine. The driver had left his peaked cap on the dash, his jacket neatly folded on the front seat. He wouldn't be needing them again, I thought. I looked in the rear view mirror and there was Jake standing hand-in-hand with Suzie in the doors of the warehouse. I waved good-bye and saw the grin on Jake's face, the nod of approval as he tipped the brim of his hat and suddenly I realized that Jake Fist was proud of me – me, Tom Collins.

I sat there in the driver's seat for a few seconds watching Jake Fist smiling, feeling, despite all the pain shooting through my body a strange, pleasant contentment. Then another voice in my head said, *"Tom, for Christ's sake, get out of here."*

I rammed the selector into *Drive* and screeched away out of the car park, through a couple of ancient, rotting iron gates and into a winding road. I knew pretty much where I was. I was in the foothills of the Pennines where there were plenty of abandoned warehouses and mills from the old cotton days. I also knew that there was only one reason Goodbye Johnny would have left me alive. That phone call he'd received was to tell him that they'd tracked down Angel Wong. He was going to check it out. If it was correct he intended to come back and kill me. If not he'd have me tortured some more till I told them what they wanted to know. Then he'd kill me. If they really had found Angel then right now Goodbye Johnny and his men were heading for The Belvedere. I had to warn Maisie to get herself and Angel a long way away before they came calling.

Every time I hit the accelerator, pain exploded through my foot, but I tried to ignore it as I fished the guard's mobile phone from my pocket. I cursed the modern phone system. In the old days I knew everyone's phone number by heart, including Maisie's, but now it was just a single digit shortcut on my phone. My mind was still reeling with the pain and whatever drugs that blonde bitch Brandy had filled me with and try as I might I couldn't remember it. I hit the buttons for directory enquiries.

After an age a voice said, "Which number do you require?"

As I gave Maisie's name, I heard that beep on the phone that means the battery is running low. I held the phone to my head almost screaming in frustration, jerking the car one-handed around the bends in the road, skating down the hill, until the voice gave me a number that I remembered now from the old days. I stabbed at the buttons and dialled The Belvedere. All I could hear was the constant pipping of the engaged signal. I hit the buttons again. Maisie's number was still engaged and I had a cold feeling going through me now which had nothing whatever to do with the wind whistling through the open window.

I still knew Bill's number and I called him, driving one-handed like a madman, heading back into Manchester. "Bill," I shouted, "get to Maisie's, warn her….." The phone beeped and the line went dead.

With a great scream of rage, I hurled the phone across the car. The pack of cigarettes that Brandy had thoughtfully stuck into my shirt pocket had somehow survived the beating I'd been given. Next time I get hung from a pipe and beaten half to death I'll get Marlboro to sponsor me. I fished one out, lit it with the lighter from the dash and concentrated on my driving. I could feel the drugs that Brandy had given me draining away, my clarity and consciousness slowly returning and even as I recklessly jumped three sets of red lights, roaring through the empty Sunday streets into the familiar neighbourhood where I had spent my childhood, I knew that I was too late.

I swerved around the corner. At the far end of the street I could see a blue BMW disappearing through the traffic lights. It was hardly likely to belong to anyone living in this dismal dump: most of them couldn't afford a bicycle. I stamped on the brake, trying to ignore the pain exploding through my foot, threw myself out of the car and raced into the hotel but I knew already what I would find.

Maisie was lying in a crumpled heap at the foot of the stairs.

"Maisie, Maisie," I groaned, trying to lift her, but she was dead, shot through the side of her old wrinkled head. The phone was dangling uselessly from its cord, revolving slowly and I could hear the constant pips of the engaged signal in the stone cold Sunday silence.

I held her in my arms. In death she still had the same half smile she had worn when she rescued me, took me into her parlour, cleaned me and fed me and kept my nightmares away. For a few moments I was numb, bewildered, praying that this wasn't real, that I'd wake up in my bed to find it was just a passing dream. I stared down at her, dead in my arms and I remembered the promise I'd made to her a few short hours before. I carried her past the kitchen, through to her bedroom and laid her on the bed. As I looked at her, lying there so old, so small, so fragile I realized that I would never see her again, that someone had quite casually ended the life of this courageous, honest lady, my oldest friend. I turned away, walked to the door and the fear, the terror, the lead weight in the pit of my stomach that had been my constant companion for the last three days had vanished.

In its place was a dense black rage.

Somewhere, over the roaring of the blood in my head I heard the sirens of police cars. It would be Bill racing to The Belvedere, but it was too late now, everything was too late. As I opened the door of the BMW I heard it again: a low, sad, sexy voice.

"Why can't men be tough and good?" whispered Suzie. *"Be tough now, Jake. Be tough for me."*

I fished out another Marlborough, stuck it in my teeth, lit it up, knocked the selector into Drive and floored the accelerator. The pain in my head, my chest, my foot, was forgotten. I had a gun in my hand and hatred in my heart as I went after Angel Wong and the men who'd killed Maisie.

Chapter Twenty-three

*H*e'd had a short career as a heavyweight boxer until he'd been banned for life by the Boxing Commission for taking a dive without tipping them off about it first.

Then he'd been sent down for three years for breaking some guy's jaw in a bar. Inside he'd found religion briefly, courtesy of a skinny ex-priest named Moses. When he'd turned down Moses' amorous advances Moses had knifed him in the ribs. Meantime his wife had run away with a Brazilian samba dancer on a cultural tour of Brooklyn. Her name was Maria. The dancer that is, not his wife.

After they let him out he got himself hired as top enforcer with the guy who'd paid for him to take the dive in the first place: Bruno the Bear Scarletti. Maybe that's why they called him Lucky.

Lucky Mannino was not the brightest fairy light on the Christmas tree. In fact you could have fit all of his brains into an egg and still have had room for the chicken. Still, he was as straight a guy as you could find anywhere in the rackets.

If somebody needed to be killed, Lucky Mannino would kill him: if he just needed a simple broken leg or a tap on the head with an iron bar, Lucky would do it efficiently, cheerfully and with absolutely no malice whatsoever. Lucky had a simple sunny disposition, a wide sweet smile, an undying devotion to Bruno Scarletti and more muscles than a Pan-Am stewardess.

"How's it goin' then Jake," he asked anxiously.

239

Jake Fist squinted through the pain in his head. "Great Lucky, just great."

"Jeez Jake, I was worried I might of killed you," said Lucky. "The boss woulda been furious."

"Yeah, guess he would," said Jake.

He looked slowly around, slowly because his head was throbbing so badly that if he moved it quickly he was afraid it would come loose from his shoulders. He was cold, saw his breath rising like smoke in the air. Sides of beef hung from hooks on the railings like the corpses of dead men.

The last thing Jake remembered he'd been zipping himself up in the gent's in Joe's. Out of the corner of his eye he'd seen Lucky emerging from one of the closets but he'd been just that half a second too slow.

He'd figured that he'd be safe in Joe's, that not even Scarletti would make a try for him in a crowded bar. But when a guy the size of Lucky Mannino walks out of the restroom with someone thrown over his shoulder the average schmuck, whose concerns are mostly drinking too much and lying to the wife about it, well he just reaches for his dry martini and carries right on drinking. From his barstool Jake couldn't see people coming into the bar, but Joe must have seen.

Jake hung by his wrists from the rail in the cold and the darkness and the silence. He was going to get hurt now, hurt real bad but nothing could hurt as bad as knowing that Joe had sold him out.

Not that it mattered now. Now nothing mattered.

*

I drove like a maniac along the quiet Sunday streets and out onto the M62, my foot flat to the floor, the pain from my smashed toe a constant reminder. Every time I breathed was like a knife stabbing me in the ribs, my head

240

was banging like an Indian war drum and there was blood on the steering wheel from where the handcuffs had cut into my wrists but it was all an irrelevance, as if it was happening to someone else.

It seemed like only seconds when I saw the BMW cruising sedately in the middle lane in front of me. I picked up the chauffeur's cap from the dashboard and pulled the peak way down, low over my face. They would see me behind them of course; they would recognize the car. But they had no way of knowing who was driving.

Unlike my Escort, the BMW had all mod cons including windows that worked at the push of a button. I let down the window on the passenger's side and moved into the outside lane until I was alongside. I could see the driver, Chan, and Angel Wong, but no sign of the well-dressed guy or of Goodbye Johnny.

The driver looked across at me and waved his hand. The last time I had seen him he had been sitting, laughing as they prepared to take my toes off with a bolt-cutter. He looked again and I saw his jaw drop as he realized that it was me. It was the last thing he ever saw. I put two bullets straight through the window and into his wide-eyed face.

The car careered across the motorway, spun round several times and came to rest on the hard shoulder, nose up against the crash barrier. I slammed on my brakes, pulled the car over, and hopping and hobbling like a crippled rabbit, I raced back. Everywhere I could hear the sound of screaming brakes and tires as the other users of the motorway swerved to avoid the pile-up. Blasting horns destroyed the calm of the Sunday morning, enraged motorists shook their fists, but none of it meant a thing to me.

241

Chan jumped out, trying to take cover behind the passenger door. I shot him twice, once through the window, watching the glass explode, and once through the door, seeing a neat little hole appear in the metal. He fell sideways onto the tarmac. He was in a bad way, bleeding from the mouth. I grabbed him by the coat, slammed him into the side of the car and screamed, "Where's Johnny?" He looked at me uncomprehendingly, pain etched in his face. I beat him around the head with the gun savagely, until a voice in my ear said, "Tom, stop, stop!"

I hit him one more time, stood up and stared at Angel Wong.

"Johnny's at the house," she said quietly.

I didn't say anything, just picked up the gun lying on the floor; pushed it into my pocket; grabbed Angel Wong by the arm and marched her down the motorway. "Maisie, what happened to Maisie?" I shouted at her.

Whatever you say about Angel Wong, she was as calm and composed as a nun going to say her prayers. "You're hurting me, Tom," she said, pulling my hand away from her arm.

I pushed her into the car and said to her again: "What happened to Maisie?"

"She tried to stop them. She stood at the bottom of the stairs and said that they couldn't take me away. Then she picked up the phone and started to call. Chan, the small one, he told her to put the phone down. Maisie ignored him and then she must have got through to someone, because she started to speak. Chan just walked up to her and shot her."

I slammed the car into Drive and screeched away. One of the passing drivers must surely have called for help. I wanted to get away before the police arrived. I had things to do.

I saw Angel staring at me. I must have looked like something from a horror movie, filthy, soaking wet, my face and shirt covered in blood, but she said nothing, just stared through the windscreen.

I pulled off at the first exit, down to a roundabout, turned into a country lane and skidded to a halt at a pretty country bus stop with nice green trees waving their branches overhead and pretty little flowers peeping out from the hedgerows. The homicidal rage that had come over me had cooled down a little – not a lot but a little – but I still had a lot of unfinished business to attend to. I turned to Angel Wong.

"You tell me the truth, the whole truth and you do it now," I said, speaking slowly and deliberately to her. It was only then that I realized I was still holding the gun in my hand.

"OK, Tom, please calm down," she said.

I stuck the barrel of my gun in her head. "You're one inch away from dying, you lousy lying bitch," I hissed.

There was a long silence while the birds chirped in the trees, the crickets made nice pleasant country noises and Angel, the ice-queen sat frozen in the seat.

"I've just spent a couple of unpleasant hours," I said, conversationally, "firstly with a blonde bimbo called Brandy and then with Good-bye Johnny. Remember him? The one who's supposed to be in Chicago? Well he's just been trying to take my toes off with a bolt cutter. You told me that you'd run out on him a few days ago, but it appears that he's actually been living here in deepest, darkest Manchester."

I was feeling the rage rise up again inside me. "I've been knocked out, kidnapped, drugged, tortured; my client murdered in the Ritz; there's a poor broken little girl lying beaten to death on the floor of my office and Maisie's dead. And it's all because of you!"

I was shouting now and for the first time since I'd met her, I could see fear in Angel's lovely dark eyes. I don't think she'd understood that I could be as angry as this. Frankly, neither did I. I was still holding the gun to her head and she swallowed nervously.

"Hamilton Liu runs all the major Chinese rackets in Manchester," she said. "Drugs, arms, protection, book-making, illegal immigrants, girls. You name it."

"Goodbye Johnny's got big ambitions. He's the big boss now in Chicago. He's got deals worked out with the triads in L.A. and New York and Vancouver. But him and Hamilton go back a long way, back to the old days in Hong Kong. Hamilton Liu's uncle was responsible for Johnny's father's death. Johnny's made his money now, he can leave his Chicago business with his leightenants. What he wants to do now is to break Hamilton Liu, ruin his business, destroy his gang, wreck his life."

"So how long has he been here?"

"About two months. He's bought a big house in Wilmslow and I think he's already involved in some of the rackets.

"So what's all this from you about not going to the police?"

She smiled mirthlessly. "The police? In Chicago half the police work for Johnny. I don't know about here but I can't take that risk."

That didn't sound right to me either. Another lie but I

244

let it pass. It wasn't important.

"So now we come to the million dollar question Angel, and believe me if I think you're lying to me again, I'll shoot you. Why the hell is everyone looking for you?" I asked.

"I stole something from Goodbye Johnny," she said quietly.

I pulled the gun away from her head. "So what did you steal?" I asked.

"Some information."

"Angel," I said, and I was rapidly losing control, "I'm not a mind-reader and I'm not psychic. Some information about what?"

"The records of all his customers."

With a mighty effort I kept my hands from her throat.

"What customers?" I grated. "The people who bought his houses? The guys he bribed to do his real estate deals?"

She replied to me like she was speaking to a particularly obtuse three-year-old. "The customers for all his drug deals of course."

I tried hard to get hold of myself. "So you've stolen the records of the drug deals done by the biggest mobster in Chicago?" I said as matter-of-factly as I could.

She nodded her head with her dark hair falling over her face, like I'd asked her whether she preferred her eggs poached, or fried.

"How did you steal it?"

"He thought I didn't know the code to his computer but I did. So I downloaded everything onto a flash drive."

"So what were you doing with Meredith Liu and her husband," I asked, breathing deeply and carefully.

She stared at me as if I was Ronnie the Retard. "I was trying to sell them the information."

I put my head in my hands and groaned.

"And where is this flash drive now?"

"It's in a bank safety deposit," she said calmly, "and only I know where it is."

I sat there, thinking through my next move when Angel said. "Tom, I want you to drive me to Johnny's place.

"Are you crazy?" I asked. "He'll kill us both."

"Look, Tom, there's only one way to end this. I have to give Johnny the flash drive."

"But the minute you walk in there he'll shoot you," I said.

"Not without the drive, he won't," she said calmly.

"OK, OK, so he'll beat the truth out of you first and then he'll shoot you," I said in exasperation.

"No he won't, Tom. He won't kill me."

"And what makes you so sure of that, all of a sudden," I snapped. "You think you give him back this flash drive that you stole, that about ten people have died over and he just gives you a big hug and a thank you note and a ride home?"

She was looking at me now and again I could see a hint of something in her eyes. "Johnny won't kill me, Tom," she said again and she looked as if she was expecting me to slap her pretty face.

"Give me one good reason why not," I said.

"Because Goodbye Johnny's my husband."

I didn't know whether to laugh, cry, or throw myself into the nearest river. I sat there remembering how I'd spoken to another oriental beauty on a morning that seemed a lifetime ago, when she'd walked into my office and asked me to find Angel Wong.

"Her husband," she'd said, "his name's Johnny," and

me so preoccupied with wondering what she looked like under that slinky black dress I hadn't really taken any notice of what she'd said. If I'd put two and two together then maybe all of this could have been different. And maybe Maisie would still be alive. I felt the blackness welling up inside me again.

"So in that case, who's the blonde bombshell?" I asked.

"Chinese men have always had more than one wife, Tom. In the old days they were called concubines and you could have as many as you could afford. In Hong Kong and Singapore, any Chinese man could have four wives up until the nineteen sixties. It's just the same today. Any rich Chinese thinks he can have as many mistresses as he likes. I've put up with all the others, but this Brandy, she's a poison bitch. She wants him and all his money to herself and she doesn't care who gets hurt in the process. I told Johnny that he either got rid of Brandy or I would walk away. Of course he didn't believe me. Chinese men are so damned arrogant. While I was in Chicago and he was in Manchester he told me he wasn't with Brandy but I knew he was lying. That's why I came here. And that's why I ran out on him. OK, right now he's as mad as hell but he won't kill me. He'll send me away but he won't shoot me – as long as I give him the memory stick."

I thought about Karl Zieger saying to Jake Fist, 'There's a dame at the bottom of this somewhere or I'll eat my desk.' Jake asking why Eleanor Mann would bother about one more woman, and Karl saying, 'Other women she can handle but not this. This is the one she can't take.'

Tough, gorgeous, blonde Brandy had been the last straw: the one she couldn't take. So Angel had planned to take exactly the same revenge on her cheating husband as

247

Eleanor Mann on hers: bring the whole business crashing down around his ears.

I thought over what she'd told me. No wonder the Vietnamese had been trying so hard to find her: the estranged wife of their major rival with enough evidence to send him down for a hundred years. It explained the police too. The Chicago cops must have been desperate to get their hands on that stick and in these days of polite co-operation between the forces someone from the very top must have been leaning very hard on the Chief Constable.

"So where's Johnny now? He was in the car when they left the warehouse."

"They took him back to the house before they came for me. Johnny wouldn't come looking for me himself. He wants me dragged in to him while he sits there. He's the big boss and he has to play the part."

Which was why they'd taken so long to get to Maisie's.

I sat there deep in thought. I knew that Angel was still lying to me about one thing. It had been in the back of my mind all the time she was talking and I knew that I was right. I was also far from convinced by what she'd said. I thought Johnny would almost certainly kill her whether she was his wife or not. But it fitted in with what I wanted to do. Goodbye Johnny always got what he wanted. He wanted Angel. He wanted the stick. And I wanted Goodbye Johnny. Once again Collins' Law kicked in. "OK," I said. "Let's go."

"Tom," Angel was looking at me with an expression which a disinterested observer could have mistaken for tenderness, "you're in a terrible mess. Let me clean you up a bit."

She was still holding that same Louis Vuitton bag and

she reached inside and pulled out a pack of disposable hankies soaked with the kind of perfume that would make the owner of a Turkish brothel wince.

For the next five minutes Angel cleaned the blood from my face and arms. I sat there, eyes half-closed and for a few seconds thought of sunning myself on that tropical beach with a large drink in my hand. It didn't work: not with the memory of Maisie lying by the stairs. I opened my eyes, stared at Angel dabbing away at my forehead and then I did the damnedest thing. I grabbed her hair at the back of her head and kissed her fiercely on the mouth, encountering no resistance whatever.

I've mentioned before my complete belief in the future of the human race and here, if required, is further evidence. The whole of the Manchester police were looking for me; so were three gangs of oriental thugs. I was beaten half to death; nursing a couple of broken bones; had three, maybe four dead men behind me and was contemplating the murders of two more. Yet I just couldn't resist the lure of a pretty face.

As I held Angel's black hair in my hand, her soft lips against mine I had the feeling that someone was watching me. I turned to look but it was just a blackbird sitting in the trees. The blackbird had his coat collar turned up and a hat shading his face. He stroked a cigarette lighter, touched fire to the tip of a Lucky in his beak and winked at me.

I kissed Angel again, just to remember what it felt like. Then I stuck another Marlboro in my mouth, lit it from the fancy dashboard lighter, turned the car around and headed for Wilmslow.

Chapter Twenty-four

Jake tried to ignore the pain in his wrists as he hung from the rail in the meat warehouse waiting for Bruno Scarletti. He knew that wouldn't even start to count as pain when Bruno went about his business.

When he'd come home to find Tanya stretched out dead on his bed he'd wanted to take a machine gun and a few hand grenades and go start World War Three but Scarletti was just too well protected. So, after a while, he'd retreated into waking in the morning with a hangover and spending his evenings in Joe's fashioning another one.

He'd spent two-and-a-half years trying not to think of himself as a bad P.I. and a worse drunk. He'd just taken those cases where some poor, married sap had fallen for a sweet little hooker and Jake got a percentage of the six figures he paid his wife to forget about it.

He'd been doing what he did best, checking out a quiet, respectable businessman with a blonde, all-American wife, two lovely girls and a regular spot at the church twice every Sunday. However, on his business trips he and his eighteen-year-old secretary were somehow always forced to share a sleazy hotel room just like the one Jake was looking at now.

Jake had seen Willie the Weasel twice since Tanya, both times at long range and both times surrounded by tooled-up heavies. Willie's sex life consisted of feeding the coke or crack or heroin habits of young girls; the younger the better, in return for allowing Willie to do what he liked with them. This usually included smacking them around with his fists and sometimes sticking his gun up their crotch and offering to blow them away. He never actually pulled the trigger: it was just for laughs. He was a fun guy was Willie.

Jake was buying answers with US currency from the bored guy behind the hotel desk, a guy he knew from too many other late nights and lying spouses. The last person Jake expected to see padding down the stairs at three in the morning was Willie the Weasel.

Willie grabbed for his gun but he was way too slow. Jake had him up against the wall, holding his throat in his left hand and sticking his gun so far into Willie's ribs that it felt like it might come out the other side.

"Use your head Fist. Bruno'll kill you by inches if anything happens to me," said Willie.

Jake grinned a big, hollow, mirthless grin. "Willie, I'm going to give you exactly the same chance you gave to Tanya, is that OK with you then Willie?" gripping him by his Adam's apple with Willie's eyes bulging out of his head. Jake shot him three times in the guts, dropped him on the floor like an empty sack and left him leaking his life out on the bare wooden boards.

As Jake turned the guy behind the desk knew he was looking death right between the eyes and he said, "Me, I never saw a goddamned thing. I went for a leak and when I came back," he shrugged his shoulders.

Jake said, "For your own sake Clancy, you'd better believe what you just said."

He drove his Chevy carefully back to his empty apartment and knew that he had only a matter of hours before Bruno Scarletti would come looking for him. The very next day Suzie had walked into his office, shone those clear blue eyes at Jake and said, "I think my husband's trying to kill me."

But now all of that was worthless, gone, as cold and as dead as a

251

body on a slab.

Now Bruno was going to get Lucky Mannino to beat Suzie's whereabouts out of him, and Jake was gonna let him do it, just long enough so that he could tell Bruno a convincing lie. It was just a question of how many times Jake could lie to Bruno before Bruno lost patience and killed him.

He was a dead man anyway, whether he told Bruno the truth or not but he'd made a promise to Suzie: a promise that she'd be safe. That was all there was to it. He didn't owe her a thing; hell, he didn't even like the woman. It was just that he'd made a promise and Jake Fist didn't break his promises.

He heard a sound. Scarletti was standing there, his breath leaking like smoke in the frozen air. He had a big crooked grin on his face and another guy with him, a hood called Bellini with a reputation for being real, real nasty.

*

McClusky sat in his chair in his office while Matthews sat uncomfortably in front of him, wondering if there were any vacancies in some quieter and less risky occupation. Like the SAS.

McClusky was in the mood to murder the first person who opened his mouth. He'd spent his Saturday night at Hamilton Liu's place watching the bodies being dragged out and taken away; his Sunday morning in Tom Collins' office with a poor Chinese girl dead on the floor and the forensic guys dusting and photographing and bagging and tagging. The words of the Chief Constable were still ringing in his ears.

"So how many bodies is that now, McClusky? Six? Seven? Eight? And how much do we know? Nothing,

McClusky: nothing at all. Who's the dead girl in Collins' office? We don't know. All we know is who she isn't; and she isn't Angel Wong. So where is Angel Wong? We don't know. But we think that the person who does know is Tom Collins. And where's he? We don't know that either. So, McClusky, it seems that there's an awful lot we don't know and precious little that we do know and in the meantime Manchester's being turned into a passable impersonation of the Wild West."

There was a pause. "You've got twenty-four hours to start finding some answers, McClusky, after which you'll be pedalling a bicycle and helping old ladies across the street. Do you hear me?"

"Yes sir, I hear you," grated McClusky.

He sat in his chair, his hangover raging. "Listen," he said to DC Matthews, "I'm going to The Bell for a beer. Anybody asks you, I'm in the toilet. Anything breaks, you give me a call." He glared at Matthews waiting for him to say something, anything he didn't like.

He waddled away from his desk, took the lift down three floors and walked the few yards to The Bell; the pub that the Manchester Police Force had been using since the day it opened and without whom the place would have gone bust years ago. It was a quiet Sunday lunchtime, just a few old folks nursing their halves of bitter and their bottles of Guinness. McClusky pushed open the door and glared around the room. He walked to the bar.

"Pint of Boddington's," he growled, "and a bloody large whisky.

*

253

As I drove I was thinking. After a while I stopped the car and jumped out.

"Tom," shouted Angel in a panic, "where are you going?"

I opened the passenger door, took out the chauffeur's jacket that was resting on the seat.

"OK Angel," I said, "this is what we do. They're expecting a blue chauffeur-driven BMW with you in the back seat, so that's what we give them."

"But what about you Tom, what will you do?"

"They won't take any notice of me," I said, "in one of their cars and wearing a chauffeur's outfit."

I pulled on the jacket. It was about ten sizes too small, the sleeves coming down to just above my elbows. The only way to fasten the buttons would have been to slit it up the back, but it covered my blood-stained shirt and at a cursory glance no-one would notice anything wrong.

"I'll drop you off and then turn round and drive out of the gates," I said. "I'll wait for you outside but I'm telling you now Angel, the minute I see anything I don't like I'm away as fast as this thing can carry me. Understand?"

She nodded and I thought how nice it was for me to be lying to her for a change. Then I thought about Johnny's hoods; gold-toothed Chan and the driver.

"What about the other two?" I asked. "Won't he wonder where they are?"

"Tom, they're hired hands. They're not going to sit in on my private discussions with my husband. Johnny won't even realise they're not here."

"I hope you're right," I said.

The sun had gone now, dark black clouds piling up on the horizon, matching the mood I was in. A few spots of

254

rain spattered against the windscreen. The wipers smeared Manchester grime all across the windows but that was fine by me. The windows were tinted, probably darker than was legal and I figured that there was no chance that anyone would take the trouble to peer through the darkened windscreen and the grime to check out who was under the chauffeur's cap.

I turned into the same country road into which I'd been driven by Goodbye Johnny's kidnap crew about four hours and a lifetime ago and I pulled up at the fancy wrought-iron gates. I said into the microphone, "Parcel for Mr Johnny."

The gates swung wide and I drove slowly down the driveway, keeping my head down and my hat pulled over my eyes until I drew up outside the imposing front doors of the country house.

"Good luck," I said as she opened the car door. She picked up her shoulder bag and gave me a wan smile that almost had me pull her back into the car and drive the hell out of there. Then two heavies were grabbing her by the arms and pulling her away.

I read a novel once; a good novel about China, where the main theme was that no one ever takes any notice of the rickshaw puller. I sat there in some amusement as two Chinese guards stood cover at the front doors watching the drive, and the roadway, and the trees and ignored me completely as I parked the car on the gravel outside the country mansion.

I checked both of my guns, climbed out of the car and worked my way around the side of the house, easing my way past Johnny's garage and his collection of Mercs and BMW's and off-road 4 x 4's. I pulled off the chauffeur jacket and left it by the wall.

The French windows were open into the garden: there were windblown apples and pears lying on the lawn, the trees shivering as the wind picked up, starting to blow as the sun retreated behind the building storm clouds. There was a small topiary garden too. I never could understand why anyone in their right mind would spend hours trimming their privet hedges till they looked like ducks, or dinosaurs, especially when the whole thing was half hidden at the back of the lawn. Behind the shaped, statuesque bushes was a high wooden fence. I noted wires running along the top, no doubt connected to some sophisticated alarm system.

I flattened myself against the brickwork and peered cautiously through the French windows but none of the five people inside were looking at the view. They were looking at Angel, on her knees before her Lord and Master.

*

In the Bell, McClusky knocked back his whisky in one gulp and sat guzzling his beer. The phone in his pocket began to ring and he slapped his glass back onto the bar.

"Jesus friggin' Christ," he muttered angrily, holding the phone to his ear.

"It's Matthews, sir."

"Who the hell do you think I thought it was," he shouted. "What is it?"

"You're not going to like this, sir," said Matthews.

McClusky's face was turning purple. "Can you just get on with it, Matthews, you prick," he shouted.

"There's been a car crash and a shooting on the M62

sir. Two men in a BMW. Both Chinese; both dead. There was a Caucasian seen leaving the scene with a Chinese woman in another BMW. We don't have the number."

"And I don't suppose we have a description of this Caucasian," hissed McClusky through gritted teeth.

"Yes we do, sir," sighed Matthews unhappily. "Sounds exactly like Tom Collins, sir."

"Get a squad car. I'm on my way back," grated McClusky. He switched off the phone, took the remains of his beer in his hand and poured it down his throat in a rage.

"You have no idea how much I'm looking forward to getting my hands on you," he muttered as he climbed off his bar stool. He stopped, shocked, his eyes wide open, bulging out of his face like a frog. He gasped for air, staggered a few steps forward then fell, face down on the pub carpet.

"Oh Christ," whimpered the girl behind the bar. She raced over to McClusky's prone form.

"For God's sake help me," she shouted. Two of the guys drinking at the bar ran over and turned McClusky onto his back.

"Call an ambulance," shouted one, urgently.

The girl was pounding on his chest. "Shouldn't you give him mouth-to-mouth or something?" she said, panic-stricken.

There was a trickle of beer running from the side of McClusky's mouth onto the old, stained carpet. The older of the two men looked at his companion.

"Not bloody likely," he said.

*

I squatted on my haunches on the tarmac path that ran in front of the lawn, peering cautiously into the drawing room. Carefully I pulled the gun out of my pocket and slipped off the safety catch.

Goodbye Johnny was lounging on the sofa like an Emperor on his throne, Brandy standing with a huge, sardonic, triumphant smile on her face, a cigarette in one hand and a glistening crystal glass in the other. She was wearing thin, diaphanous harem pants and a white blouse tied loosely at the bottom showing off her breasts and her tiny, tanned waist. She looked as if she had just stepped out of a sultan's boudoir, assuming that in the days when sultans had boudoirs they had blondes in them. I'm not a historian. I don't know this stuff.

The guy, the smooth guy who'd been chatting to Johnny while they were beating the crap out of me was sitting comfortably on a pink and white chintz arm chair, a perfect dimple in the perfect knot holding his discreet red tie to the collar of his Brookes Brother shirt, looking disinterestedly at Angel kneeling on the carpet. Her arms were held behind her back by two of Mr damned Johnny's acolytes and my hands were shaking on the trigger of the gun.

"Welcome back Angel, I do hope you enjoyed your trip," said Brandy, her voice dripping with saccharin. Goodbye Johnny looked at her, said, "Shut your mouth," and she went silent.

"Where's the flash drive?" he said.

"It's in a safe deposit, Johnny," Angel replied quietly.

Goodbye Johnny stood up, walked over to her and slapped her forehand and backhand across the face.

258

"Where is the bank, where is the key?" he said in a monotone. He hit her again and I had to physically bite my swollen lip to restrain myself from walking in and blowing the bastard's head off.

I heard Angel speaking in a tiny voice. "I'll tell you Johnny as long as you promise to let me go. I'll give you the drive, and disappear. You'll never hear from me again, that I promise."

"Let you go?" said Johnny, mildly. "Let you go, Angel?"

"How well do you know, my little Angel, the history of China?" he asked quietly. "Do you know the story of Zhen Fei, the favoured concubine of the Emperor Guang Xu?"

I heard Angel catch her breath and she said, "Yes, Johnny, of course I know that story."

"She was wrapped in a carpet and dropped head first into a well in the grounds of the Forbidden City," he continued. "It was considered a merciful death for a courtesan who had betrayed the Emperor."

"You are not an Emperor, Johnny and I am not your courtesan; I am your wife. You talk of betrayal when you betray me every day with your hussies and your harlots. In any case Zhen Fei was thrown in the well by the Empress, not by the Emperor."

There was a cruel smile on Johnny's face.

"I'm sure Brandy would be only too happy to play the part of the Empress," he said.

Brandy stood staring down at Angel, kneeling on the floor and I could see a doubtful look on her face that showed that not even this frozen-hearted bitch was too happy at the thought of a cold-blooded murder.

"Johnny, I came to you today to try to end this war; to stop the killing; a way for both of us to leave with honour,"

259

said Angel.

Johnny continued as if she had not spoken.

"I'm not sure if you are aware of it Angel, but in the grounds of this house there is an old well. It was sealed by a metal cover, presumably for safety reasons. Two of my men have removed that seal. The most that you can hope is that I am merciful to you and let you die honourably instead of screaming your life out which is what you deserve. Now where is the flash drive?"

I stood by the French windows, hearing the wind rustling the leaves on the apple trees in that quiet English country garden and I knew that Goodbye Johnny was at least partially crazy.

"Please Johnny, don't do this," whispered Angel. "There's been too much killing. Why do we need more?"

Goodbye Johnny's air of unnatural calm was replaced by a shriek of fury. "You're giving instructions to me, me?" he shouted. He took her hair in his left hand raised his right fist and the rain was starting to fall again, pattering against the windows and spotting the tarmac pathway as I walked into his beautiful drawing room with its Chagall and Miro reproductions and its polished French furniture.

"Hi Johnny, how's things?" I said.

There was a total silence in the room. On the wall behind the sofa hung an antique French mirror, the glass a little crazed; the silvery backing missing a few parts: something like me.

I looked in the mirror and I saw a bruised, desperate face that I hardly recognised, a face that could only have looked like me in a distorted, drunk nightmare; my shirt crusted with dark dried blood. I grinned at the assembled company as they sat or stood, in a frozen tableau in that pleasant, comfortable English drawing room, pointed my gun at Johnny and said, "I understand Johnny that we in the west are total barbarians, unlike you civilized eastern types but we generally take exception to hitting women, especially when they're being held down by someone else."

I walked forward and cracked him across the face with the hand holding the gun. He fell backwards, sprawled against his plush upholstered sofa with blood leaking onto his Wilton carpet. I had my gun pointed at him thinking about Maisie and about what he'd planned to do to Angel, but even as my finger tightened on the trigger I realized that I couldn't do it. Jake Fist would have blown him away in a heartbeat but not me. I couldn't just shoot him, sitting there, staring at me even after what he had done.

"Come on Angel," I said. "Let's get out of here. Did you honestly think in your wildest dreams that this piece of excrescence would let you walk away after what you did to make him lose his precious face?"

She looked up at me; her face stained with tears and blood from where Johnny had hit her and dragged herself to her feet.

Johnny sat back on the sofa, holding his jaw and I have to give him his due: or maybe it's just a natural Chinese thing to be really cool when everything's falling apart around you.

"Congratulations, Mr Collins," he said. "How did you manage to get away?"

I saw a movement from one of Johnny's guards and pointed my gun at him. He froze.

"Jake Fist saved me, Johnny," I said. "Jake and Suzie. They came all the way from Chicago and they saved me. Jake and Suzie and five hundred pounds of blood money;

thirty pieces of silver, Johnny; the price of betrayal."

He had no idea what I was talking about and I had to stop myself, steel myself, because I thought for a moment that maybe I was losing it, maybe going a little insane and this was no time and no place to lose control.

"By the way, they're all dead, Johnny," I said. "All of them. Mr Chan with the gold teeth, the guy who was supposed to watch over me, your driver." I was trembling with rage but I still couldn't bring myself to kill him.

"And talking of luck, Johnny," I continued, "when you're spending your next thirty years in the can you can tell yourself that today was your lucky day. You see unfortunately I have a real problem killing people in cold blood, even worthless trash like you. So just put your hand in your pocket, bring out your gun and drop it on the floor. And please, please make one sudden or suspicious move so that it'll give me an excuse to shoot you dead."

"I don't carry a gun, Mr Collins. I hire people for that," he said.

I looked at Angel and she nodded.

I covered Johnny's bodyguards. "Take out your guns, drop them on the floor," I said. "Anyone wants to be a hero, I shoot you first and then I shoot your boss."

They eyed each other nervously. Two guns fell to the floor.

"Kick them over here," I said. I took out both magazines, dropped them in my pocket and threw the guns into a corner of the drawing room.

"Now you," I said to the Brookes Brothers suit.

"I don't carry a gun," said Mr Smoothie, smoothly.

Well, I'd seen the outline of his shoulder holster quite clearly while he was talking to Johnny in the warehouse:

262

while I was swinging by my wrists from the water-pipe like Tarzan on a bad day. It just gave me an excuse to do what I'd been aching to do for hours. I walked over to him and smashed him right-handed across the face, knocking him off his chair and knocking the smirk off his conceited face at the same time. He yelped. I liked it. It felt good.

I reached down, pulled him back onto the chair, stuck my gun in his face, reached into the front of his suit and brought out a small and highly efficient-looking silver-plated .38 calibre handgun. I didn't know what make it was. Gucci probably.

"Never wear a designer suit and a shoulder holster at the same time," I said.

I thought about that for a moment. It would make quite a decent line for insertion into *Detecting for Dummies*.

I ejected the bullets and threw the gun in the corner with the others. I felt easier now. They were all unarmed, their guns sitting empty in the corner of Goodbye Johnny's tastefully decorated reception room, the ammunition in my pocket. I didn't realise then that I was condemning all of them to death. Personally I never look at my horoscope in the papers and I'm not a clairvoyant. If I were, I'd never have been a detective in the first place.

"What about me, Tom?" simpered Brandy. "I don't think there's anywhere I could hide a gun in this outfit but you're quite welcome to search me."

I stared at her loosely-tied top, her diaphanous pants and reluctantly I shook my head. She was a great piece of work was Brandy.

"What you're hiding in there is more dangerous than a nuclear missile Brandy," I said. I walked crabwise across the room trying to keep everyone in my field of vision and

263

motioned Angel behind me as I cradled the phone on my shoulder, starting to dial 999.

"Tom!" screamed Angel, but I had already seen one of Johnny's goons sizing me up. As he leapt at me I stepped aside and shot him in the shoulder. He slumped to the floor, whimpering.

The phone was ringing in my ear and I stood with my back against the wall waiting for Johnny's guards to burst into the room. They must have heard the shot. A voice down the line said, "Which service do you require?" and at the same moment there came the screech of car tyres and a distant smash as if someone had driven at high speed through a pair of wrought iron gates.

Sirens screamed shrill through the air; the alarm system went into overdrive, and I heard the staccato, crackling chatter of automatic weapons fire.

I dropped the phone, grabbed Angel by the hand and raced out of the French windows into the garden in the pouring rain.

Chapter Twenty-five

*L*ucky Mannino had the grace to look mournful as he took back *his huge right fist a couple of inches and Jake felt like someone had driven a truck into him.*

"Sorry Jake. Just business. Nothin' personal."

Lucky got into his old routine then, combinations and dancing footwork and Jake would have admired seeing a professional at work if he could have seen anything at all.

Lucky paused, breathing heavy and Bruno Scarletti said: "Come on Jake, be sensible. You tell me where Suzie is, we all go home."

Jake stared at him out of the eye which wasn't closed. Blood dripped from his mouth onto the floor of the warehouse.

He ignored Scarletti and spoke to Lucky. "Jesus, Lucky," he croaked, "is that all you got? I had worse beatings from the cleaning lady."

Bellini joined in then, helping Lucky out. Jake grunted and groaned, pretending he was hurt worse than he was until after a while he sagged against his wrists.

Scarletti said, "Jake, I'm asking you again."

Jake was hurting and the voices in his head were saying, Jake, You don't owe this dame nothin'. Tell the guy what he wants to know. *Then Scarletti would shoot him and it would all be done: all the remembering and the fighting; the drinking and the whores.*

Jake looked at Scarletti and said, "Bruno, man can't even control

265

his own wife don't deserve no respect from me and no answers neither."

Scarletti's face tightened. He nodded at Bellini and a grin came over Bellini's face as he picked up the small blue can, pumped the button on the handle, took the gold cigarette lighter from Scarletti's hand. There was a hiss, the smell of petrol, and Bellini adjusted the flame so that even in the darkness of the warehouse it was almost invisible. Jake heard the subdued roaring noise of it and stared into space, every muscle in his body tight as a wire as he felt the heat on the exposed skin where his shirt had pulled away from his pants. He could smell the burning of his own flesh and through the agony, somewhere in the blackness, Jake heard someone scream.

"Where's Suzie, Jake?" asked Scarletti.

Jake could feel the sweat pouring down his face as he gasped, "Aw what the hell's the use. It's a small hotel over by the Loop, Bruno. It's called the Belvedere Apartments. She's in room 5 on the first floor."

"I hope for your sake that's the truth, Jake," said Scarletti. "You wait here and watch him, Lucky," he said, "and don't kill him till we get back. This I want to see." Scarletti and Bellini walked out into the night.

Jake hung in the darkness, his body a throbbing, aching, burning mass of pain. He figured he had about an hour before they came back and lit the blowtorch for real.

*

I threw Angel unceremoniously in a heap into the ornamental garden with its little trees clipped in the shape of ostriches and rabbits. I squatted down behind two old apple trees, the windfalls crunching beneath my feet and a few lazy wasps trying to decide whether to wing it through the rain or to burrow into the apples and hide. I knew how

266

they felt.

A car screeched between the garage and the house, tyres screaming and churning up the lawn and rocked to a standstill. It was the same black Toyota that had brought Lucky Luk and Hamilton Liu to my office. Johnny and his men were all frantically throwing themselves across the room trying to get to the corner where I'd thrown their guns, but they never stood a chance. Four gunmen fell out of the car, armed with machine pistols, and Goodbye Johnny's French windows disappeared in a hail of bullets.

I saw one of Johnny's guards throw his arms in the air and fall to the carpet; Johnny stagger back and collapse onto the sofa with his face contorted in agony, a hand held to his chest. Three of Hamilton Liu's men were raking the room with automatic fire and the quiet Sunday afternoon was full of the sound of gunfire and screaming; alarm bells wailing like banshees across the rain-soaked Manchester countryside.

I took careful aim through the rain, squeezed the trigger and saw one of the gunmen fall onto the green manicured lawn. They had no idea where the shot had come from; I doubt if they even heard it over the sustained cacophony of noise. They just kept pouring fire into the country house drawing room. I watched helplessly as the antique French mirror disintegrated, the old prints dissolved, the furniture collapsed under the sustained hail of bullets, until a white hand was raised in the air from behind the sofa.

A calm voice shouted, "Stop!" A small thin man emerged from the Toyota, a gun in his hand and a triumphant grin on his face. It was Hamilton Liu.

At the same moment the alarm bells went quiet. Suddenly there was a total, eerie silence. No birds singing;

267

no crickets chattering; only the steady hiss of the rain and a faint moaning which might have been coming from Goodbye Johnny or from Mr Smoothie who didn't look quite so dapper now, spread-eagled over the back of his armchair, covered in blood.

Brandy emerged from behind the sofa with her hands in the air and stood staring at Hamilton Liu. Behind her tan she looked as white as a ghost.

Hamilton Liu walked forward until he was standing just inside the wrecked remains of the drawing room. The rain beat down, plastering my hair to my scalp, and my clothes to my body. The wounded gunman, the one I had shot was crawling towards the car, the rain beating and hammering down on him. Angel stared at me from her makeshift hideout. I just looked at her and shook my head.

Hamilton Liu began to speak, and I could hear him with crystal clarity, his words falling like small stones dropped into a pool: or a well. "Sit up Johnny," he said, mockingly, "so that we can see you."

Goodbye Johnny straightened slightly, his hands clasped across his chest trying to stem the blood leaking onto the sofa. His face was working, trying to speak but nothing came out.

"Get on your feet," said Liu softly. With a great effort Goodbye Johnny staggered to his feet, a haunted look on his face. He looked wildly around him but there was nowhere to run.

Slowly and with great deliberation Hamilton Liu pulled a cigar case from his inside pocket. He stuck a cigar in his mouth, replaced the case and brought out an expensive-looking lighter. Goodbye Johnny was swaying on his feet, trying to stand upright with Brandy staring at Liu, the rain pattering on the lawn and the wind sighing through the branches of the apple trees.

Hamilton Liu lit his cigar, dropped his lighter back into his pocket and casually shot Johnny in the knee.

Johnny collapsed onto the floor, groaning. Brandy dropped her hands and started to move towards him. Hamilton Liu said sharply, "Stay where you are or you'll get the same." He took a step forward and put his foot on Goodbye Johnny's stomach.

"So how's it feel then, tough guy?" he said. "Thought you'd just be able to move in and muscle me out did you?"

He put his weight on his foot. Goodbye Johnny groaned again, blood running from his mouth.

Liu stepped back, raised the gun. Two shots rang out and Johnny's body jerked, twitched on the floor then lay still.

I sighted along the barrel of the gun, my hands trembling in the rain.

Brandy was trying hard to maintain a semblance of composure. She pulled a package of cigarettes from the waist-band of her pants.

Hamilton Liu stood there, gloating. "Miss Alexander, I believe?" he said. She nodded.

"I'm going to have an awful lot of fun with you, Miss Alexander," he said, his calm clear voice filled with a terrible menace. "Though I doubt if you will enjoy it quite as much as I will." He crooked a finger. "Come here," he said.

She was trying very hard to maintain her cool demeanour but the cigarette was shaking in her hand as she walked slowly towards Hamilton Liu.

He pulled out his lighter and held it courteously to the

end of Brandy's cigarette then reached out and tore at the knot holding Brandy's blouse together. The top fell apart. Liu stuck his cigar in his mouth, reached out a hand and casually fondled Brandy's magnificent breasts. "Oh yes," he breathed, "I'm going to have a lot of fun with you."

Brandy just stood there, smoking her cigarette, staring at him with utter contempt in her eyes.

I thought of Janet Wu lying on the bed with the burns to her breasts, poor Candy crumpled on my office floor and Goodbye Johnny groaning in agony his kneecap destroyed. I knew with complete certainty that what Bill had told me had been correct. Hamilton Liu was a guy who enjoyed his work. I wondered what he had in mind for Brandy. She was one cold-blooded bitch but nobody deserved whatever it was that Hamilton Liu was going to do to her. I had my gun cradled in the fork of the tree branch, squinting through the rain.

In the police I'd been a lousy marksman. I had no enthusiasm for shooting at targets, whether of men or just the little round ones. I had no enthusiasm for the force either and my results had had my instructor shaking his head. Apparently I put too much weight on one hip or something, causing me to constantly miss left. That had been indoors, in good light. Now I was looking at the back of Hamilton Liu's head in rapidly failing light; in pouring rain with a wind blowing across the lawn and through the trees and the butt of the gun was slippery in my hands.

Much as I hated Goodbye Johnny I hadn't been able to shoot him as he lay sprawled across the sofa looking at me and even though I despised the murderous piece of human garbage I was looking at now I hesitated, my hand trembling on the trigger. I was also acutely aware that if I missed I had a very good chance of hitting Brandy. I centred the sights on Hamilton Liu's head but I just couldn't do it. Then I saw him standing in the trees, the smoke of his cigarette mixing with the rain.

"You saw what he did to Janet Wu and to Candy," said Jake Fist. "You gonna let him to do the same to Brandy? Now take a breath a real deep breath, long and slow."

I did as I was told.

"Don't hold the gun so tight. Relax your hands. Now breathe out, real slow and tighten your fist. Don't pull the trigger, just squeeze real slow and easy."

I heard the explosion as if it were from a great distance away and felt absolutely no emotion or remorse as Hamilton Liu slumped face forward onto the floor of the lounge.

"Nice shooting, Tom Collins," said Jake and he vanished into the rain.

The three gunmen hurled themselves aside and began firing randomly into the garden. Leaves and twigs rained down on me but they still had no idea where I was, hidden behind the trees in the rain. They loosed off a few more shots before they began dragging Liu's body to the car. They threw him in the back together with the wounded gunman. The car fishtailed across the lawn tearing its smooth surface into mud and roared away back towards the driveway. Hamilton Liu's gunmen were hanging out of the windows firing a few parting shots into the house and the gardens.

I peered though the sodden tree branches looking for Brandy but she was nowhere to be seen. Then I heard the sound of a car engine starting. I realized that she was trying to make a getaway in the BMW which I'd driven to

271

Johnny's place – and in two seconds she'd be right in the gun-sights of Hamilton Liu's thugs.

"Brandy," I screamed uselessly. I heard the BMW's engine, the tyres screaming, the chatter of automatic weapons and a tremendous crash. I forgot completely about Angel as I raced clumsily across the soaking, muddy lawn, past the garage and round to the front of the house.

The black Toyota was turning into the main road through the wrecked and twisted gates leaving the BMW piled up against one of the trees lining the driveway, black smoke pouring from the engine. Hamilton Liu's men had shot out the windows, the lights, the tyres, everything. I could smell the pungent, acrid smell of petrol in the still air and it was then that I remembered Brandy's hand trembling as Hamilton Liu lit her cigarette.

"Brandy," I yelled, "Brandy," hobbling as fast as I could along the rain-sodden driveway toward the shattered car, the stench of spilled fuel strong in my nostrils. In those fevered moments I thought for an instant that I was back in the dream: the dream where I was running in slow motion towards my mother; where however hard I tried I couldn't get any closer and I knew that nothing I could do would save her.

I was running frantically, slipping on the rain-slicked gravel, the pain shooting through my foot, screaming, "Brandy, Brandy, get out of the car!" Then I saw a tiny light, a small tongue of flame rising lazily from the car engine. I stopped running and shouting then, because there was nothing that I could do, just shield my face with my arms as a huge explosion shattered the air, an eye-aching flash of light lit up the Manchester skies and the car and the tree it had hit went up in a great sheet of flame

272

Chapter Twenty-six

*L*uck Mannino sat on a sack, the gun looking like a toy in his huge hairy fist.

"Why you protectin' this broad for, Jake?" he asked. "Jeez Jake, the woman belongs to Bruno. He wants her back; it don't have nuthin' to do with you."

"You're a big dumb peasant, Mannino," said Jake. "You don't have the brains God gave to a centipede. You're ugly and you're stupid and you can't box and you can't hit. Go on; hit me with your best shot. I've had worse from my grandmother."

Jake knew he was wasting his time. Lucky was far too placid to rise to this kind of bait but he kept on anyway, trying to needle him because he knew that being beaten to death by Lucky Mannino was infinitely better than what was going to happen when Scarletti found out there was no such place as The Belvedere Apartments.

"Come on Jake, we were always friends," said Lucky Mannino placidly. "There ain't no call to talk that way," and he sat clicking the safety catch of his gun on and off, gazing at the beef carcasses hanging from the rails and whistling a song. Jake didn't know the title but he recognized the words well enough. He'd heard that song sung by any number of sulky-eyed, cigarette-husky broads in dim dark dives, and dangerous gin-joints.

'You gotta, accentuate the positive....eliminate the

273

negative.... latch on to the affirmative...' *If it had been Willie the Weasel whistling he'd have known he was just taking a rise but Lucky wasn't bright enough. He was probably trying to cheer Jake up.*

Jake hung there, the pain beginning to bite now. He heard a noise at the rear of the warehouse and he steeled himself. He'd thought Bruno would take longer than this to find out that Jake had sold him a pup. He wondered how long he could hold out against Bellini and the little blue flame.

Lucky looked up at Jake. "Guess Bruno's back," he said happily and a voice in the darkness said, "Don't do anything stupid, Mannino. Just keep your back to me, hold out your gun real slow and drop it on the floor."

Lucky whirled around shooting blind and Jake heard the soft double cough of a silenced handgun. Lucky Mannino crumbled slowly to the floor clutching his chest and stared at Jake with pained, uncomprehending eyes.

"Jake?" he said pitifully, "Jake?" because Jake was his friend and maybe he could make sense out of this for him. Jake just hung from the rail staring bleakly at him until Lucky's head settled on the cold concrete floor and the light went out of his eyes.

Lucky Mannino: whose luck had finally run out.

Jake stared down at Lucky's body. It was just like Lucky's boxing career, he thought. He never knew what hit him. He looked into the shadows at the back of the warehouse.

"Jake Fist, the messes you get yourself into," said a soft, quiet voice. Karl Zieger was standing there with a gun in his hand and Suzie by his side.

*

274

I stood there staring at the blazing bonfire that was the remains of a blue car, a tall tree and a beautiful woman, feeling the heat on my face with a sick empty feeling in the pit of my stomach. There was nothing I could do now, nothing anyone could do. I turned around and walked back through the open front door of Johnny's desirable country residence.

One of the two guards Johnny had left at the front entrance lay sprawled half in and half out of the doorway. There was blood running in little red rivers down the driveway mixing with the rain. The other guard was lying face down in the hallway on a blue and white oriental rug, his blood slowly obliterating the grinning face of the Chinese dragon. I stepped over his body clutching the gun tight in my fist but I knew I wouldn't need it now: that it was all over.

Goodbye Johnny was lying on the floor. I bent down and checked his pulse even though I knew he was dead, his empty eyes staring glassily at the ceiling. He was gone, gone to a place where he couldn't hurt anyone anymore, couldn't poison those around him with his mean, miserable shallow hatred, his twisted definition of love and loyalty and betrayal.

I reached down and closed his eyelids.

"Goodbye, Johnny," I said.

There was another body spilling blood onto another carpet, a bullet-riddled corpse lying among the shattered remains of the French windows. The smartly-dressed guy was lying over the back of the sofa and I was gratified to note that the red stain covering his white shirt was an exact match for his Pierre Cardin tie. Colour co-ordinated all the way to the grave.

Angel was sitting on the floor next to Johnny looking shell-shocked; soaking wet, her dress sticking to her like a second skin. She was covered in mud and old leaves and bits of shrubbery and there was blood on her face and her dress and on her hands.

"Are you OK?" I asked.

She looked at me dumbly and nodded. Her face was streaked with rain, maybe tears.

Hamilton Liu had gone, thrown into the car by his men but I didn't need any confirmation that he was dead too. I'd seen the blood spatter over Brandy before she made a run for it – no wonder she wasn't thinking too clearly and I could see the blood and the splinters of bone on the carpet.

I started then to feel sick and dizzy, my wounds hurting and the bodies all around me. I took a few shallow breaths feeling the deep, searing pain in my chest, staring through the ruined French windows into the garden in the shattering Sunday afternoon silence. Then for some reason I thought of an old Irish painter standing in the fading afternoon of a summer's day, the sun sinking into the sea, pulling on his silver hip-flask, looking at me and saying, "Jaysus son, I wouldn't be dead for quids."

I stared into the rain. Even though I was destined for a prison cell I knew now that I would see again the sun rise over the low purple hills. I was close to weeping. I closed my eyes tight for a few long seconds. When I opened them again Angel was looking at me, scared, my finger tight on the trigger of the gun.

I walked through the carnage to the table in the corner, picked up the phone and dialled 999.

"What's the address here?" I asked her.

"I don't know," she whispered.

I could hear the voice on the line saying, "Which service do you require?"

We had a wrecked house; a torched car; half a dozen bodies, and Tom Collins, famous private eye didn't even know where we were. "Police, fire and ambulance. Better make that two ambulances," I said. I described the location of the house. "You'd better get here fast," I said. Then I hung up.

"Come on," I said to Angel. "We're out of here." I had no intention of waiting for Liu's mob to come back with reinforcements. This time I really was going to the police. I grabbed Angel by the hand. She picked up her Louis Vuitton bag and followed me, unresisting.

I went into the study, the place where I'd had my chat with Brandy, opened the cabinet door and helped myself to a set of car keys. I also helped myself to two other things: one was Brandy's bottle of Jack Daniels. It seemed a shame to waste it and she wouldn't be needing it where she'd gone. The other belonged to me and was responsible for an awful lot of the violence of that quiet suburban Sunday.

In the garage I stared at all the cars Good-bye Johnny wouldn't sit in the back of any more. I stood there for a few moments before I opened the door, stuck the keys in the ignition and sat there listening to the noise of the engine. I pulled onto the driveway, squeezed the car past the burning remains of the BMW and two minutes later we were driving down the country road with the whole damn mess behind us. For the third time that day I heard the wailing of sirens. Two fire engines and a police car raced by followed by two ambulances and more police. It wasn't difficult to spot the house. There was a huge pillar of

277

smoke standing straight in the still damp air like the remains of a nuclear explosion.

There was a gentle wind blowing the dark clouds across the trees and fields and the rain was starting to come down real heavy now, bouncing off the streets, flattening the flower beds and the hedgerows and drumming on the roofs of the quiet, placid country houses. By the time the fire engines reached the wreckage of the BMW they probably wouldn't be needed

But they'd be too late for Brandy.

I could hear the swish of the wet road beneath the wheels and feel the car moving on the corners as the water got under the tyres. The clutch was tough but it was my right foot that was hurting like hell, not my left, so I grinned and took it like a man and only nearly passed out when I had to hit the accelerator.

There was a portable radio sitting on the top of the dashboard. I hit the button and saw Angel looking at me with amazement as I started to sing along, happy as you like, me and Elvis belting out Jailhouse Rock in the rain. I guess she thought that I'd finally lost it; gone a little crazy. She was probably right.

I took the bottle of Jack Daniels, unscrewed the top with my teeth and took a long mouthful before passing it over to Angel. Right now drink-driving was the least of my problems. They didn't have cars where I was going. They couldn't get them through the cell doors.

I wound down the window to let in some air, saw Angel's face grimace as the raw spirit hit her, then I took the bottle away from her and I said, "OK Angel, lying time's over. Now where's the flash drive?"

Her dress was soaked and stained. She looked like a

small frightened child half curled up on the passenger seat, shaking with cold and the reaction that sets in when you've just seen half a dozen people shot to death. Not to mention seeing your husband dying in agony just after outlining how he's planning to kill you and his latest mistress an unwilling participant in her own cremation.

She stared at me with blood on her forehead and the wind blowing her hair across her tear-streaked face. The rain was coming in through the window and Angel shivering with cold so I closed it and sat there, driving the car, holding the bottle and waiting to hear another of Angel's fairy tales. I tried to ignore the fact that she was without any doubt whatever, the most beautiful woman I'd ever seen, any time, anywhere.

I said to her, "Angel, you've lied your pretty little head off to me since the first time I saw you. The last lie you told me was about that drive being in a bank safety deposit and I'd appreciate, just for once, if you'd tell me the truth."

"How did you know?" she asked.

"Because you can't just walk into a bank and order a safe deposit like it was a McDonald's or something. You have to have an account with them and even then they want i.d., proof of where you live and lots of other stuff. Between running out on your wonderful husband and going to hide with the lovely Lius I don't think you would have had the time to set it up. I kept wondering why you were so attached to your Louis Vuitton bag that you'd stop to save it even when there was a gang of murderous Vietnamese trying to shoot everyone they could find. Since then you've never let it out of your sight. There's something very important to you in that bag, isn't there? So why don't you just stop the bullshit and give me the stick."

279

"Tom, do you think I would be so stupid as to have the drive with me where anyone who searched me could find it?"

"Angel," I said, "the one thing I've never thought about you is that you're stupid. I think you were clever enough to work out that no one would realize that you had the brass cheek to carry that stick with you. Now I intend to use it to strike a bargain with the cops which might just save my neck and yours too. So I'm giving you two choices. The first is that you're going to reach in that bag, pull out the stick and hand it over to me. The second is that I'm going to stop this car in the middle of the street and beat it out of you."

"So at last you show that you have some of the skills of a detective," she said. She turned to look at me with a wistful, little-girl smile on her face, her hair stuck in the tracks of the tears on her cheeks. The song on the radio had changed and now it was Frank Sinatra singing, '*Come fly, come fly away with me…*' I think that if, at that moment, there had been any possibility of flying away to a deserted island with this duplicitous, scheming, lying, gorgeous creature I would have been on the first plane out.

"You're partly right. I did have it with me," she said. "And you're right about the bag. It was sewn into the handle. I did it myself before I ran out on Johnny."

I'd guessed as much. It didn't make sense otherwise.

"So hand it over," I said.

"I can't," she replied. "You see I'd managed to convince the Lius and everyone else that it was in a safety deposit. You're right that they never thought I'd be so stupid as to have it with me. But today I couldn't take the risk that Johnny would search me and find it. That drive was my bargaining chip, my ticket out, or so I thought."

I could see her starting to think again about Johnny and the plans he'd had for her. I didn't say anything to her about her being so confident that Johnny wouldn't kill her just because of the minor fact that he'd once stuck a ring on her finger. OK, so he'd promised to love her and so on till death did them part. I don't remember anything in the marriage vows where you have to swear you won't be responsible for the parting.

"So where's the drive then, Angel?" I asked

She gave me a wistful smile. "I hid it," she said.

"Where?" I asked.

She took the bottle from me, unscrewed the cap. "Take a drink, Tom, I think you'll need it,"

I reflected that just three days ago I would have been horrified at the thought of sitting at the wheel of a moving car, drinking neat spirits from the bottle. I took a mighty swig and handed it to her. She took a drink herself.

She showed me then her Louis Vuitton bag, one of the handles detached from the body. "I hid it in the BMW," she said. "I pushed it down the back of the passenger seat as you drove to Johnny's place. I thought that was the last place anyone would ever think to look."

I took the bottle from her and then I started to laugh, forgetting about Chan and the metal pipe he'd hit me with until I was reminded by a feeling like an electric shock ripping through me. I gasped and took another long swig against the pain of the broken rib in my chest, stabbing me through.

So what this whole thing had been about was gone; a useless scrap of melted plastic in the burnt-out wreckage of that car.

I kept on laughing, ignoring the pain as I put my arm around Angel. Then, just because the whole thing seemed so utterly and completely absurd and wasted I kissed her and not for the first time that day I saw tears in her eyes as I let Angel go, moved the gear shift from second to third and watched the wet streets of Manchester roll by.

Where are you now, Jake Fist? I thought. Come on, come and take a look at what you've done. Tom Collins, the famous private eye, riding along with a beautiful blood-streaked woman; an open bottle of bourbon; Frank on the radio; a houseful of bodies behind me; a smoking gun in my pocket and I was driving a white '37 Master 85 Chevrolet coupe with white leather seats, twelve inch running boards, a split screen and white-wall tyres on wire wheels.

The song changed again on the radio. I didn't know the words but I hummed along anyway to a deep, husky female voice singing *'you gotta, accentuate the positive…eliminate the negative… latch on to the affirmative..'*

My head ached, my ribs hurt like hell, my foot was agony and I was looking at about six hundred years in the pokey. I don't think I ever felt happier since the day I left Ireland.

I thought I saw a movement in the rear-view mirror and I turned, startled. Jake Fist was sitting in the back seat, his hat tipped back on his head, smoking a cigarette. He grinned at me, blew smoke in the air. "Happy birthday Tom Collins," he said.

In all the chaos of that manic Sunday I'd completely forgotten. Today was my birthday.

"Why thank you, Mr Fist," I replied, tipped the bottle to him in a mock salute and took another slug.

Angel looked at me, puzzled and said, "Who are you talking to?"

"No-one," I replied. "No-one Angel. Just the voices in my head."

I looked in the mirror but Jake had gone.

I held onto the wheel, watching the wipers play their slow dance, leaving their trails across the windscreen in the pouring rain and I wished I could drive that Chevy for ever.

Chapter Twenty-seven

*J*ake looked at Karl and Suzie standing in the shadows. "What took you so long?" he said.

Karl Zieger grinned. He checked through Lucky Mannino's pockets and came out with a key in his hands. He stood looking up at Jake, with that big easy grin on his face.

"Something you'd like to say?" he enquired.

"Yeah, get me down will yah, I'm freezing to death here," Jake replied.

"No, that ain't it," said Karl.

"Jeez. What does a guy have to do to get help around here? OK Karl, thanks," said Jake.

"There you see, that didn't hurt did it?" Karl reached up and unlocked the handcuffs. Jake took two uncertain, dizzy steps and sat down on the cartons where Lucky had been sitting, whistling his song just a few moments ago.

"Come on Jake, time to go," said Karl, leaning down and picking Jake up by the arm.

"No Karl," said Jake. "You go. There's something I have to do."

"Jake, you're in no shape to take on Scarletti now. It's three in the morning and you're beaten half to death. Let it go, Jake. There'll be another time."

"No Karl. I can't let it go. This has to be finished and it has to be finished tonight."

Karl picked up Lucky's gun. "OK Jake. You hit that side of beef over there and I'll let you stay," said Karl, knowing Jake could hardly see, let alone fire a gun.

A shot rang out. The side of beef jerked and swayed slowly in the darkness.

Jake grinned a crooked grin through his split lips. "Not bad for an old guy," he murmured.

Karl shook his head in admiration. "OK Jake," he said. "Only if you're staying, so am I.

"No Karl. No. This is for me to do and I got to do it on my own. It's the only way I can look at myself in the mirror in the morning."

"If you ever see the morning, Jake."

"Yeah, well, I think the sun will probably still rise anyway, don't you, Karl?" He lit up a Lucky, drew smoke into his tortured lungs.

"Karl."

"Yeah Jake."

"After the last time you said that if I got myself in a mess you wouldn't be around to help me out."

"Aw hell Jake, what are friends for?"

"You were right, Karl. You were right and I was wrong and I owe you. Not just this but a lot more besides."

The two men looked at each other in the gloom, Suzie watching them and wishing someone would look at her that way.

Jake said, "Could you help me move this guy out of sight?"

Together Karl and Jake dragged Lucky Mannino into the corner and threw a couple of old sacks over him.

Jake pulled on his cigarette. "Take Suzie home, Karl. Look after her for me would yah?"

Karl gave Jake a strange sideways look. Why would Jake want him to look after Suzie? But he didn't ask Jake the question because he already knew the answer.

He nodded. "OK Jake," he said quietly.

Jake Fist settled down in the shadows by the door. It was cold as a graveyard. He checked his watch: the sun would be up shortly. He sat in the cold, patient and immobile as an Indian, waiting for Bruno Scarletti.

*

And that's pretty much the end of it. Well, not quite the end, because that conniving little temptress Angel had one last lie left over which I'll tell you about shortly.

When I arrived at the station there was no welcoming committee, no one waiting there for me. They were all out scouring the Manchester countryside, searching in ditches and hedgerows and drains for Big Bad Tom Collins and his gang of murderous oriental thugs.

I parked the Chevy in the spot reserved for the Deputy Commissioner and limped into the station with Angel in tow. When the duty officer saw us, wet, filthy, beaten up and covered in blood his jaw dropped so far, so fast that I was afraid he'd make a dent in the desk. When I casually dropped two guns in front of him and asked for McClusky, I thought he was going to faint.

Within seconds we were confronted by an armed team who could probably have invaded Iraq. Angel was hustled away still clutching her Louis Vuitton bag and within a very short time I was sitting in front of an impressive array of Manchester's finest.

The list of charges would have made Ned Kelly proud: taking and driving away; kidnapping; assault; battery; unlawful possession and use of firearms; withholding evidence; interfering with a crime scene; obstruction of the police; reckless driving; driving an unlicensed vehicle; (that damned Chevy), and of course; several murders.

I surveyed the list of crimes I had committed and made a mental note to insert another piece of good advice in *Detecting for Dummies*. This one reads: *when everything else fails, tell the truth* and would be what the computer geeks call a compulsory field for all beautiful women of oriental origins. Accordingly I went in minute and exhaustive detail through every single occurrence, starting with the moment Janet Wu had walked through my door and ending with my calling the cops from Johnny's place. I omitted a few details such as Janet Wu's non-monetary offer, and how Angel looked in her underwear – cops are timid creatures and get easily embarrassed.

When I then pointed out that I was about to faint from lack of food, loss of blood and generally having had a long hard day they rustled up a mug of tea and a plate of chips which I demolished well inside the existing world record.

They made me go through it all again while a stenographer laboriously typed it out and by the time they were satisfied it was two in the morning. They then sent me under armed escort to the hospital where they did makeshift repairs on the more obvious cuts and bruises. I buried my head gratefully in the pillow and collapsed into a long and dreamless sleep with a nervous police constable sitting at the end of the bed in case I woke in the night, took the drip out of my arm, stabbed him with it and hopped away on one foot.

The next morning they cleaned me up, bandaged my ribs and put my broken foot in a plaster cast. I was wheeled back into my room and climbed back into the hospital bed. While I was trying to work out which old-age home I should check into when they let me out of jail the door opened and in walked Dennis Hemshall, the Chief Constable of the entire Greater Manchester police force.

"Good morning, Mr Collins," he said. "I trust you are feeling better." Once again I had to repeat the whole thing, word for word, from beginning to end.

"That's quite a story, Mr Collins," murmured Hemshall, "If I hadn't seen it for myself I would think you'd invented it. You have caused me more trouble in the last five days than the entire criminal fraternity of Manchester in the last five years. There are quite a few senior officers in my patch who would quite cheerfully hang you from the ceiling and continue where Goodbye Johnny left off."

This was more or less what I'd been expecting. "Talking of which," I said, "where's my old mate, Ted McClusky?"

"He's not very far away actually Mr Collins. He's two floors up in the heart unit, attached to various drips and needles and bits of hi-tech machinery. They think he'll survive." There weren't many things which, at that moment, could have made me feel better, but this was one of them.

"What happened?" I asked, thinking that, at least, couldn't be put down to me.

"He had a minor stroke, Mr Collins," replied Hemshall. "Around about the news of your third or fourth murder, I can't quite remember which," and I swear there was a smile on his face.

So that's my fault too, I thought gloomily. Still, one more life sentence wouldn't make much difference. "So what happens to me now?" I asked him. "How many years am I going to get?"

I've mentioned that there weren't too many things that Hemshall could have said to make me feel better but what he said next almost had me leap out of bed, throw my arms around his neck and give him a big kiss. With a bedside manner like that the guy should have been a doctor. To my utter amazement, he leaned forward and said, "There are various factors involved, Mr Collins, none of which I'm at liberty to advise you of, which mean that we feel it may not be in the best public interest to prosecute you. However you will speak to no one, say nothing whatever about a single event of these past few days to anyone, unless it is myself or a judge in a court of law. And this especially means the press. Should we, for instance, see your face smiling at us from the front page of the *Manchester Gazette*, Mr Collins, then I'll personally make sure that you'll grow old and die rattling the doors of your cell and pleading for another crust of bread to dip into your water. Is that clear?"

I just lay there staring at him and he added, "You will also be available to us instantly and at a moment's notice for anything we might want you for, such as statements, i.d. parades, court appearances and anything else. Which means that long holidays in the Bahamas are not advisable. In fact, you will keep us advised of your every movement, even if it's only walking round to the corner shop for a packet of sweets. Do you understand?"

I nodded my head and he turned and walked away leaving me lying there, completely stunned.

"What about Angel?" I asked, as he opened the door to my room. "What happens to her?"

Hemshall turned and said, "Ms Wong has been helping us with our enquiries. We'll know more in due course." With that he closed the door and left.

I slept through most of the rest of that day. The next

289

morning, despite the doc's protests I checked myself out. I thought about going up to pay my respects to McClusky but decided against it. I didn't want him having another heart attack and me with another killing on what was left of my conscience. I refused the offer of a wheelchair and an ambulance, accepted a large plastic bag full of painkillers and called a cab. Three minutes later I limped out of the front door on a borrowed crutch and told the cabbie to take me home. He gave me some fairly odd looks, not surprising really considering the state I was in. Anyway he kept his eyes on the road and his mouth shut, for which I was grateful as I wasn't exactly feeling in the mood for small talk.

When I got back to my apartment I checked behind the door and under the sofa and so on for Chinese gunmen waiting to murder me. There was no one.

I stripped off as best I could and took a makeshift shower, not easy when about forty percent of you is covered in bandages. With some clean clothes and a cup of hot black coffee in front of me, I called Bill. He told me they'd already offered Angel a deal as long as she co-operated and that even though she'd been involved up to her gorgeous neck in the whole business there wasn't really anything major they could pin on her. I put the phone down.

There was something that I'd avoided doing ever since I'd walked out of Goodbye Johnny's place dragging Angel along behind me, but I couldn't delay it any longer. When I'd picked up the car keys and the bottle from the study I'd also picked up something else there which belonged to me. It was my mobile phone. That little invention had already caused me a lot of grief. Without it I wouldn't have gone in to my office on the Sunday morning that seemed now like a distant dream. I would also have kept Maisie's phone number in my head and maybe could have given her enough time to get out before Johnny's men had come around.

As soon as Johnny had received that phone call, while I was hanging in the warehouse, I'd known that call could have only been about one thing: that they'd found Angel Wong. And I'd known at the same time exactly how they'd found her.

Reluctantly I took my phone and stared down at it. There were two missed calls from Maisie's number. It didn't matter now who had called me; Maisie or Angel, or why. Goodbye Johnny's men had taken my phone off me and when it rang they would have seen the number come up on my phone. They just called back and heard Maisie, in that terrible telephone voice of hers that I used to constantly tease her about saying; "The Belvedere Apartments. Mrs Gibson speaking; how may I help you?"

From there to finding the address was child's play. Even Tom Collins, private detective could have done it. Then I got to wondering what would have happened if that call hadn't been made. I thought about gold-toothed Chan and his bolt cutters and knew that the result would have been the same anyway. I would have given them Maisie's address and now we'd probably both be dead.

I looked at my second missed call. Maisie calling me while Chan and the other thug were dragging Angel down the stairs. The last call she'd ever made.

There were still two text messages waiting for me from Mary. I opened the first one, read it carefully then deleted them both. I felt I should call her up, explain exactly what had happened but I wasn't sure whether this was because I felt I owed it to her or just to make me feel better. In any event I was under a vow of silence from Hemshall.

I sat around my apartment for a while but I couldn't spend the whole day staring into space, thinking about the last few days. My car was still in the police pound, not that it mattered. I wouldn't be driving anywhere until they took the plaster off my foot. In any case I wasn't really looking forward to getting back behind the wheel of my Escort after the last car I'd been in.

It occurred to me then that I could just have driven the Chevy to my place, left it outside, taken a cab to the station and no-one would have been any the wiser. I cursed myself for not being in possession of a proper criminal mind. No wonder I hadn't made it in the police force; but to be fair when I'd been sitting in the front of that Chevy I'd been expecting that the only thing I'd ever have been capable of driving again would have been a wheelchair.

I picked up the phone, called another cab and told him where to take me.

He looked at the bandages on my head, the plaster cast on my foot and in the twenty minutes it took him to drive to my office that cabbie told me about the time he'd broken his arm as a kid when he fell off a swing in the playground and how you'd never believe it but he'd broken the same arm again when he fell off a ladder painting his house and how his wife's arm had got stuck in the washing machine and his mother had slipped falling out of the bath and had to have a hip replacement and that National Health Service, well it's a disgrace isn't it, having to wait two years to get your piles operated on, if you're lucky, and the nurses are so underpaid aren't they, compared to bleedin' M.P.'s who don't do nothing except sit around swigging champagne all day at the taxpayer's expense and so on and so forth. By the time I arrived at my office I had a sore foot, a sore head, a sore chest and chronic earache.

I pushed open the door and checked to see if anything had been happening. It hadn't; I didn't care. There were no bodies lying on the floor: no blunt instruments. The forensic boys and the fingerprint guys had finished their work and gone. I thought about calling someone to fix the lock on the door but decided I couldn't be bothered. What was there to steal? I went to the Ukrainian supermarket.

The rainwater was making rivers down the gutters. Empty cans and used matches and cigarette butts hurried past on their way to the sewers. Some guy who obviously thought he was test-driving for the next Grand Prix drove down the street and sprayed dirty water all over me. I shrugged my shoulders. It was my own fault, being dumb enough to walk around the back streets of Manchester in the rain.

As I limped into the store I remembered how I'd promised myself that I'd marry Mary and spend my time filling up the supermarket shelves. I decided to think that one over.

I bought a bottle of Jack Daniels. The naked models in the empty shop window stared at me in stony disapproval as I took the bottle back to my office. I opened the metal drawer of the filing cabinet and filed it away under 'W' (For whisky).

Carefully, painfully, I put my feet on my desk. I wondered if what had happened to me had been real; if I would wake up and see another spoilt, middle-aged housewife with a fake fur and a lost poodle, another tight-faced, teary woman, long gone to seed, complaining that her husband was coming home too late from his office.

I looked at the ceiling. There was a hole there where they'd removed the bullet and I knew it wasn't a dream. I gazed at the letters on my window:

Tom Collins

Private Detective

For the first time in my life that's what I felt like.

Chapter Twenty-eight

*J*ake heard the footsteps outside in the night. Scarletti and Bellini walked through the warehouse door.

"What the devil," breathed Scarletti, looking at the place where Jake had been hanging. They looked wildly around, grabbing for their guns. Two shots rang out and Bellini fell, clutching his chest. Scarletti stood very still, staring down the barrel of Jake's gun with his hand still trying to pull his own piece.

"Drop it on the floor, Bruno, nice and easy," said Jake softly. Scarletti let his gun fall to the ground. "Where's Lucky?" he said.

"Lucky's gone to that great big meat warehouse in the sky Bruno. When you see him give him my respects. It won't be long."

"How did yah get away?" asked Scarletti.

"Friends, Bruno. Walked in and helped me out," replied Jake.

"So how the hell would they know where you was at?"

"Not all women are fools, Bruno. You just thought Suzie was like some painting on the wall or something, hanging around all day doin' nothing and lookin' pretty. She knows more about your rackets than you do Bruno. She guessed you'd bring me here."

"Jesus," sighed Scarletti, "dames. I shoulda known. You feed 'em, clothe 'em, marry 'em for Chrissakes and this is what you get."

"Yeah. It's an ungrateful world, Bruno."

"OK to smoke?"

"Go ahead."

Scarletti took a package of cigarettes, tapped one out and placed it in his lips. He flicked the wheel on his lighter, held the flame to the cigarette. He knew Jake was watching him and he knew Jake was thinking the same thing. That the last time he'd seen that lighter it had been at the tip of a steady, hissing blue flame.

"I suppose you're gonna kill me now then, Jake?"

"Correct," drawled Jake.

"Can't say as I blame yah really," said Scarletti, drawing on his cigarette. "Jeez, Jake, we'd have made a great team you and me but I suppose it's too late now?" he raised an eyebrow.

"It was too late a long time ago, Bruno."

Scarletti just nodded, smoking his cigarette in the darkness while the streets of Chicago slept.

*

My watch told me it was four in the afternoon. I limped over to my filing cabinet and looked under 'W'. I poured myself a generous shot, lit up a Marlboro and sat with my feet on the table. There wasn't one part of me that didn't hurt. I felt as if I'd gone ten rounds with a herd of buffalo but hell, I was tough now. Now I could take it.

I sat there drinking the whisky. There were a couple of questions I wanted to ask myself so I decided to take the easy ones first.

How was it that while I was being dragged away from Goodbye Johnny's place, drugged, handcuffed, terrified and on my way to a slow and painful demise, I'd still managed to stop and spend a few seconds gazing with admiration and envy at a beautiful old car?

And again why had I accepted a cigarette from

gorgeous, blonde Brandy? It certainly wasn't because I felt I needed one – the last few I'd smoked had made me throw up. The simple answer was that even while she was casually threatening me with Death by Blowtorch, my major pre-occupation had been to check out whether or not she was wearing a bra. Even when you are about to be beaten to a pulp and murdered these things are important. Ask any normal male.

(Oh and by the way she wasn't.)

I took another philosophical slug from the glass and asked myself another question.

If I'd been offered either ten minutes with the car or ten minutes with Brandy, which would I have gone for? It was what the Americans call a no-brainer. However much I loved that car and however much I hated that blonde it would still have been ten minutes with Brandy, blowtorch or not.

It all goes back to the comments I've made several times about my total faith in the survival of the human race. They say that man's first instinct is self-preservation: however, Collins' Second Law of Human Behaviour says that no matter how desperate the circumstances, however dire the straits, the average male can still be reduced to a slobbering wreck by the sight of a stunning pair of headlamps.

I sipped my whisky and thought about this for a while but there was one more question to which I needed the answer: why, exactly, had Hemshall let me off scot-free? That stuff about, "not being in the public interest to prosecute," just didn't ring true. It would have been OK if my only offence had been parking my car in the Deputy Commissioner's spot but the list of charges they'd read out to me should have had me on hard labour for the rest of my natural. Why should it be against the public interest to sling me in a dungeon for a few thousand years? I'd have thought the public would have been all in favour. There had to be more behind it and whatever it was I had to know.

I picked up the phone and called Bill. The phone rang a couple of times while I added a little to the level of my glass and then I heard Bill's voice saying, "…..Manchester police"

I said, "Bill, can you please tell me what the hell, exactly, is going on?"

"What do you mean?" asked Bill.

"Bill," I said, "they don't let people run around shooting off guns and causing fatal crashes and laying waste to half of Manchester and tell them not to worry because it'll all be OK in the morning. And they don't release multiple murderers with a pat on the head and tell them they're not too concerned about it as long as I don't mention it to anyone. There's something going on here, Bill, something I don't like, so make me feel nice and comfortable and happy here, Bill. What's the deal and who's made it?"

"Sorry Tom," said Bill, my best mate. "No idea what you're talking about," and the line went dead.

I had the nasty feeling that somewhere, somehow I was being set up but I just couldn't work out how it would make sense to pin anything else on me. Wasn't there enough already? I sat there, deep in thought, trying to work out an angle on all this but as usual Tom Collins, private detective was blundering around in the dark. The only positive conclusion I could come to was to have another whisky and I was unscrewing the top of the bottle when my phone rang.

"Yeah?" I said.

"Mr Collins?"

I said nothing, listening to the silence down the line.

The voice said, "Mr Collins, Chief Constable Hemshall would like a word with you if you don't mind. Fifteen minutes be OK?"

I put down the phone, shut up the office and went down the stairs. I looked carefully around the familiar streets. Even at this early hour it was almost dark and I walked nervously along the pavement staring into every doorway and every patch of shadow, wishing I had my gun in my pocket. There was nothing.

I walked to the corner and caught a passing cab. "Manchester Central Police Station," I said.

*

Hemshall stared at me over his desk. "You look even worse than the last time I saw you," he said, unsympathetically. "How's the injuries?"

I sat down carefully on one of the old, uncomfortable chairs in front of Hemshall's desk. "They're just fine," I replied. "What's all this about?"

"There's someone wants a word with you," he said. He pressed a button on his phone and spoke briefly. "Would you like a coffee?" he asked.

I shook my head.

"Something stronger?" he asked and a brief grin appeared on his face. "God knows you look as if you could do with something."

He reached into an old cupboard by his desk and pulled

299

out two heavy cut crystal glasses and a bottle of Glenmoranjie. He poured two small measures and handed one glass to me. "The privileges of high office," he said.

I didn't have a clue what this was all about and Hemshall must have seen the wary look on my face. "Don't worry, it's not poisoned," he said and as if to prove his point he took an appreciative sip of his whisky.

I heard the door open behind me and looked suspiciously over my shoulder. A huge red-faced, unfriendly-looking constable stood in the doorway. Beside him was Angel Wong. Warily I stood. She looked very small and very tired, and unutterably beautiful. She looked at me for a few seconds and walked towards me. "Hello Tom," she said quietly.

"Hello Angel. So how's things?" I asked, lamely.

She looked up at my beaten face, the bandages round my head. "My, oh my, you really are a mess," she said.

Then her arms were around me and her lips were on mine and the bruises and the broken rib didn't hurt any more.

"Ms Wong has requested a few minutes with you, Mr Collins," said Hemshall. "Quite forcefully, I might add." He stood and walked to the door. "You have five minutes," he said, closing the door behind him.

Angel looked up at me with a small, wan smile. "I never did thank you properly for saving my life," she whispered.

"Hey, it was nothing," I said as bravely as I could. She stood on tiptoe and kissed me again and I remembered the two previous times I'd kissed her. Once at the wheel of a white '37 Chevy and once in a stolen blue BMW when I'd thought the only thing I'd ever kiss again would be the inside of a lid on a pine box.

"It wasn't nothing, Tom," she said. "What you did was never 'nothing'. What you did was something, Tom, something brave and tough and wonderful."

I tried my best not to blush. It was nice to be appreciated for once but we'd already used up two of our five minutes and I wasn't any closer to getting any answers. I took her by the arm and I said, "Angel, please, what's all this about? What deal did you pull with the Chief Constable and how the hell did you manage it?"

She stood there with her eyes flashing and a big smile on her face. "The flash drive, Tom," she said. "Even though Johnny's dead that drive has all the information the Chicago police need to wrap up half a dozen drug gangs, importers, pushers, dealers, users. They're absolutely desperate to get their hands on it. That's why your British police were after me. It was some political deal made right at the very top. And that's why I was so desperate not to go to the police in the first place."

"But you told me it had gone up in smoke in the BMW," I said bitterly.

"It did, Tom, it did. I wouldn't lie to you," she said impishly. I gave her a look that would have blistered the paint on the door if there'd been any, to which she responded with a smile that almost melted the varnish on Hemshall's desk.

"What I told you was true, Tom. I really did hide it in the car and it really did go up in flames. But what I didn't tell you was this: the day I walked out on Johnny, before I went over to Meredith's place, I called at a computer supplies place. Then I walked into Starbucks."

"So?" I replied

"I made a copy Tom."

I wondered how they'd managed to put all that beauty and all those brains into such a small package. "And where did you hide it?" I asked.

She laughed. "I gave the guy in Starbucks twenty pounds to hold it for me and a promise of another twenty pounds when I came to collect it. I told the police they could have the drive as long as they let you go, Tom. And me of course, though I actually haven't broken any of your English laws. Anyway the drive was still there and I think your English police managed to rack up twenty pounds between them when they raided the place. I think your guys must have talked to some of the heavy hitters in Chicago about it and decided to trade. So I made a deal with them, Tom. It was you for the flash drive."

She picked up the glass of whisky, handed it to me, while the light sparkled back from her twinkling eyes. "Well are you proud of me?" she asked.

I looked at her, lost in admiration and longing. I picked up the glass, tilted it so that it sparkled in the light from the electric bulb hanging from the ceiling and looked down at her smiling face. To my weary eyes she looked like an Angel from heaven.

I lifted my glass to her and I couldn't help it. In my best Jake Fist voice I said, "Here's looking at you, kid."

Angel gave me a sad look. "It's not a movie, Tom," she said. "It's not a detective story and it's not a joke. It's real life Tom and mostly you only get one chance. Me, I got two chances thanks to you."

Gently I cradled her head in my hands, held her body close to mine, kissed her passionately on the lips and Hemshall's voice said, "Time's up, Mr Collins."

I looked at him standing there, no trace of a smile on

his face and I said, "Thank you, Mr Hemshall."

I stared at Angel Wong. I knew that we'd meet again, in court; at the station; going over the details of the last few days but I also knew that I'd kissed her for the last time.

"Good-bye Angel," I said and I walked away down the corridor, out of the police station into the cold wet Manchester evening.

I stood in the street oblivious to the rain beating down on my bandaged head and dripping down my neck. Eventually I made out a yellow sign shining through the gloom.

I sat in the back soaked to the skin. The rain was pouring down, hammering on the roof of the cab, bouncing off the city streets like bullets but all I could see was Angel's sad, beautiful face in front of me. I could still feel her lips on mine and I thought of the next twenty years sitting alone in my apartment staring at my Bogart movies and my vintage cars.

"Where to pal?" asked the cab driver.

"Anywhere," I said. "Anywhere you like."

Chapter Twenty-nine

*S*carletti stared at him. *"I never did have no problems with guys,"* he said. *"Guys is easy. It's just money or cars or women, or just that they gotta split open some guy's head; but with dames,"* he shrugged his shoulders, *"you never know where you're at with dames."*

Jake's gun was centred unwaveringly on the second button of Scarletti's coat; the place where normal guys have a heart.

"Sometimes women are like children, Bruno; sometimes they're like people; sometimes you just gotta treat 'em right," he said. *"Maybe it would help if you didn't keep trying to kill 'em."*

Scarletti grinned his crooked grin. "Old habits," he said. *"You know how it is, Jake. So do I get me a last cigarette?"*

"Sure." Jake fished out a Lucky, threw it over. Scarletti reached into his pocket real slow, watching Jake watching him as he pulled out his cigarette lighter, flipped the wheel and lit the cigarette.

He looked around the cold warehouse, the white frosted steel walls, the frozen carcasses hanging like rows of dead men.

"Funny," he said, *"you never think it'll end like this."* He took a deep draw, blew smoke into the frozen air then flicked the cigarette away.

"OK, Jake," he said, *"let's get it done."*

Then, "Oh, Jake, there's one thing: Tanya. The boys didn't know it was her. They thought it was you." He spread his hands. *"It's the way it goes."*

"Yeah that's the way it goes," said Jake.

Outside in the blackness of the alleyway Karl Zieger heard the muffled sound of a gunshot and pushed his gun back into the pocket of his coat. He turned to Suzie. "It's time for me to go," he said, "and time for you to stay."

Jake heard a sound, whirled around on the balls of his feet, the gun still smoking in his hand. Suzie was looking at him from the shadows.

She emerged slowly and Jake said, "Jesus, Suzie, you almost got yourself killed." Then he said. "Where's Karl?"

"You told me once, Jake that Karl was one of the good guys. He was watching out for you, Jake. He was always watching out for you." There was a look of pain in Jake's eyes that had nothing to do with the beating he'd taken. He nodded and stared into space looking at nothing.

Suzie just stood there staring at Jake's beaten face and Scarletti stretched out on the floor. There was a look in her eyes like a bottomless ocean of sadness and hurt. Very softly in her quiet, husky voice she said, "Is it over, Jake?"

There was a long silence. Then in slow, slow motion Jake Fist let the barrel of the gun drop until it pointed at the ground.

"It's over," he said.

*

I lay awake for a long time listening to the rain on the windows. I was trying not to think about the way I felt, about the way my chest hurt when I breathed, the way my foot throbbed under the blankets, the dull persistent headache behind my eyes. I tried not to think about Maisie, and Goodbye Johnny and the sound of gunfire and the bodies lying in that country house. And I tried not to think

305

about Angel Wong peeling off her tight little Versace dress and sliding into bed beside me.

It was late in the morning when I pulled myself out of bed. What the hell. I had nothing to do, nowhere to go. I spent a while awkwardly showering and dressing and went to check on my food and drink supplies. There weren't any. I limped downstairs trying to work out how to use a crutch on the staircase. I called a cab.

I lunched on fried bread, bacon, beans, two greasy eggs swimming in oil, tomatoes, mushrooms, toast and four cups of coffee. After this I felt a whole lot better. I went to my office.

I cautiously pushed open the door. I don't know what I expected to find in there – Chinese gangsters, dead bodies, gorgeous scantily-clad women desperate to throw themselves at what was left of my body. Anyhow the place was deserted.

I checked my mail. Nothing. I checked my answering machine. Nothing. Reluctantly I booted up my PC and opened my in-box.

I had an invitation to a virtual orgy, (I decided I was virtually unavailable); an offer of half-price visiting cards, (I didn't plan to visit anyone); a subscription form for a mail-order Russian bride, (she'd never fit though my letter-box); three virus warnings, two pre-approved credit cards and promises of nights of endless ethereal gratification from Mandy, Monique, Anastasia, Carmen and Pierre. (Pierre?)

There were also three messages from Mary. The first called me a swine in thirteen different ways - I know - I counted them. The second said that she'd read the newspapers, and what a pathetic excuse it was to pretend that the person involved in the Ritz murder case was me.

The third was an abject grovelling apology. She'd seen my description splashed all across the papers and realized that there was only one idiot in Manchester who could possibly have unintentionally caused all that mayhem. The idiot in question being, of course, Tom Collins, private detective.

She asked me to forgive her, promised that she'd never ever doubt me again and asked me to please, please, please, pretty please, give her a call.

I was totally perplexed. I was so sure it was all over that I hadn't given it a thought. I must have sat there for an hour thinking it over, thinking of the past and wondering whether I wanted to live through all that again in the future. The problem was that every time I thought of Mary I saw Angel Wong looking up at me.

There was only one thing made any sense. I walked over to my filing cabinet and took out the bottle. Whisky is a great drink. You sit there and you decide that it's totally irresponsible to make rational decisions when your mental processes may be affected by the consumption of alcohol. Therefore it's only adult, logical and responsible to postpone any critical decisions until you're sober in the morning. And then you have another whisky.

I was still looking at Mary's messages on my screen when my office door opened. It was Arthur Golightly, looking as if he'd been hit by a beer truck. "What the hell happened to you?" I gasped. He had two black eyes and a huge white bandage covering his head.

"You're not looking too good yerself," he replied.

I pointed at the bottle of Jack Daniels. "Drink?" I asked.

"Aye, 'appen I will," said Arthur, and I poured him a slug.

"So what happened?"

"Well, I went out and bought missus a nice rubber corset, just like in them pictures and one of them, what yer call 'em, crutchless panties, you know where you can see absolutely…., aye, well, anyway, and when she walks in I throws 'em at her and says, "Right, you can get them on for a start.""

"So she asks me if I've gone stark staring lunatic and I just shows her them photos and says, 'What's sauce for t'goose is sauce for t'gander and right now, I'm the bloody gander.'"

"Well she looks at me a bit queer and I says, 'I think we'll start off with a nice couple of positions I've picked out of that *Kama Sutra*.' Then she picks up her corset and looks at me and says, 'Well, well Arthur, I do like a masterful man.'"

"So what went wrong?" I asked, puzzled.

"Well unbeknownst to me, the wife's mother's been listening to all this from next room. She comes runnin' in, accuses me of being a filthy disgustin' pervert and smacks me round the 'ead with a bloody great video camera. Off I went to 'ospital and they said I 'ad a fractured skull! So I've spent last week in 'ospital an' now I 'ave to avoid excitement and such like for two months. So now I suppose wife'll be back to 'er bingo again."

"Well I think this is actually something for the police, Arthur, if you want to take it that far," I said.

"No, no you don't follow do you? You 'aven't got me drift."

"Well what do you want me to do then Arthur?"

"Do? Do? I'd 'ave thought that was obvious. I want you to take some more of them photographs just to keep me goin' until I get well." Arthur Golightly took a mighty swig of his bourbon. "Grand stuff that," he said. "Then I want you to murder me mother-in-law."

Tom Collins, private detective swallowed the remains of his Jack Daniels. "Arthur, do you think I could get back to you on that?" I said.

Arthur Golightly gingerly patted his bandaged head. "Aye, well, don't take too long thinkin' about it," he said, as he left.

I watched the door close behind him. "Welcome back to the real world, Tom," I said to myself.

I sat at my table, stared moodily at my empty glass, played with my cars a little. I thought about the Chevy, and the BMW and cool blonde Brandy. At least she'd given me something to remember her by. I stood, walked over to my desk, opened the drawer and took out my dog-eared manuscript.

I'd been writing my novel about Jake Fist for three years. Three years of agonizing over the plot, the style, the characters. Eventually it was done, all except for one thing: the title. I don't know how many I'd pencilled in and scratched out. Then, while sitting in that country house with my hands cuffed behind my back facing almost certain death Brandy had said, "Johnny grew up on the streets of Chicago. They're mean streets, Tom and they make mean people. And Johnny's as mean as a rattlesnake."

And just like that, there it was, my title.

On the blank title page I wrote:

The Mean Streets of Chicago.

I wondered if any publisher would ever look at a title like that and then I decided that I didn't really care. I'd had enough. It was all over. No more endless rewrites, no more sleepless nights wondering whether I ought to substitute a semi-colon for a full stop; agonizing over whether I'd be made to stand in a corner by the Literary Council of England because I'd split an infinitive or started a sentence with an 'And'.

Jake Fist was going out just as he was, beaten up and grubby and smelling of Jack Daniels and if the publishers didn't like it, well the hell with 'em. Me and Jake would go over and shoot 'em all.

I thought I deserved a drink. I walked back to my table and picked up the bottle. Arthur had left a copy of *The Manchester Gazette* lying there. I picked it up and idly looked at the front page. A huge headline screamed:

FIVE BODIES DISCOVERED IN GARDEN

Neighbour alerts police to gruesome serial killings

Underneath was a picture of an old lady wearing a black hat, black coat, black gloves and a huge lop-sided grin. It was Gladys Green

I poured myself another Jack Daniels. A very large one.

I threw Jake Fist back into the drawer promising him that I'd come and rescue him as soon as I'd bought a large envelope and as I did so I heard, quite clearly, a small sexy voice whispering close to my ear. I paused and stared at my manuscript and the open drawer. It was a voice I had heard before; once in a grim Manchester warehouse over the gasping of my tortured lungs, the wild hammering of my heart, while the blood mixed with the tears running down my face; and again with a black rage roaring inside me as I carried Maisie's small body through to her room for the last time.

Now I heard it again, a soft faraway whisper from another place: *Is it over, Jake?*

I looked around my office at the scarred desk; the old computer; the battered safe; the faded gold letters on the rain-streaked window. I finished my whisky in two long swallows, shut my desk drawer, turned to my PC and deleted all the messages from my in-box.

"Yes, Suzie, it's over," I said.

I tucked my crutch under my arm, turned off the lights, closed the office door and went back to my empty apartment in the rain.

EPILOGUE

Jake dropped the gun into his pocket and reached for a cigarette.

"Come on," he said. "Let's get out of here."

Suzie walked over to him, put her arm around his waist. "Jake," she said softly, "do you think you could ever love again?"

"Love what?" asked Jake. "A gun? A bottle? A dark stinking alley in a Chicago backstreet?"

He pushed open the warehouse door. The sun was struggling to rise through the smog. At the end of the alley, among the garbage cans the winos snored in a litter of broken bottles and broken dreams.

"No Jake, a woman. A woman like me."

He looked at the streaks of red in the sky in the dawn. Every touch of his shirt against his blistered skin was agony, his ribs hurt like hell and the sweet taste of blood was in his mouth.

"You know what a wise man once told me?" He blew smoke into the still air. "He told me, 'Jake, if you ever fall in love you better do it in the early morning.'"

"You gonna tell me why?"

"So if it don't work out by lunchtime, you ain't wasted the whole goddamn day."

The only sound was her high heels crunching through the garbage.

"I got the whole day, Jake," she said.

The sun was illuminating the tops of the buildings around them. Jake looked up at them. They looked better in the dark. He tossed his blood-stained cigarette away; watched the red sparks dying.

"Let's just see if we can make this thing through lunch," he said.

He couldn't stand like that, leaning down on Suzie with his ribs hurting so bad so he stood, took out another Lucky, stuck it in his mouth, lit it up.

In the early morning, hand in hand, Suzie and Jake Fist walked home through the mean streets of Chicago

12464163R00185

Printed in Great Britain
by Amazon